How to Become a
Talkative Person about Food

和老外
打開話匣子

談飲食

　　面對老外您是否常有『單字不足』、『句型不熟』、『文法不通』而難以啟齒的困擾？本書在手便可搞定一切！**因為它揚棄窠臼式的單向學習法，特別改採現學現用的雙向方法，讓您能輕鬆地與老外暢所欲言。**因此，本公司以最嚴謹的態度為社會進修人士編撰此書。內容共設計 20 類熱門主題、20 篇主題閱讀、20 篇閱讀隨堂考、20 項句型分析、40 篇文法重點、160 句對話實用句、20 篇情境對話、同場加映 20 篇隨堂小測驗，其目的就是要讓讀者能用英文輕鬆和老外溝通，能使用最道地的英文用句，並藉此加強自己的英語能力，在地球村裡交到更多來自世界各地的朋友。

本書特色

　　本書依據國人在日常生活會話的需求，針對熱門主題進行編撰。本書囊括了 20 個單元：『一杯您始料未及的美味咖啡』、『芒果好『毒』？』、『痛快暢飲啤酒節』、『全自動迴轉壽司吧』、『健康小『堅』兵』、『熱騰騰的火鍋趣』、『最甜蜜的保健良方』、『創意烹飪法』、『世人最愛巧克力』、『慢食享生活』、『沙拉碗中的危機』、『工業農牧：利與弊』、『週一無肉日　減碳救地球』、『無所不能，無所不賣的日本販賣機』、『辣得讓人哇哇叫的辣椒還能促進你的健康』、『城市綠洲：便利商店改變台灣』，『地中海飲食還你健康好身材』、『非浪漫傳奇──台灣夜市文化』、『泡麵達人駕到』、『一口珍珠，一口奶茶，口口透心涼』。

本書九大結構

 暖身練習

讓你對該主題有初步的認識。

 重點來了

針對文法重點進行解析，讓你掌握文法要點。

 主題閱讀

針對主題進行深入探討，讓你充分了解相關知識。

 對話實用句

整理該主題情境高頻例句，讓你輕鬆掌握正確說法。

 閱讀隨堂考

閱讀完馬上測驗，讓你學習有效果。

 打開話匣子

依主要情境發展對話，讓你熟悉該主題常見對話。

 單字片語解密

列出重要單字片語，讓你用字更精準。

 隨堂小測驗

同場加映該主題小測驗，讓你能立刻活學活用。

 句型分析

針對難句進行分析，讓你不再害怕難句。

Contents 目錄

Kopi Luwak
一杯您始料未及的美味咖啡

1. Are you a regular coffee drinker? How many cups a week do you drink?

2. Do you have a preference regarding the type of coffee you drink? If so, what kind do you prefer?

對於忙碌的上班族而言,早上來一杯咖啡可是日常所需,若能在假日悠閒地享受一杯香醇的好咖啡,那更可是奢侈的享受啊!對於愛好咖啡的人來說,能喝到牙買加的藍山咖啡已非特別,但若能喝到麝香貓咖啡,可說是死而無憾了。麝香貓咖啡有個別名,叫做『有屎以來最香的便便』,名字雖然不雅,但卻是事實。這種經過『特別處理』的咖啡豆收集不易,因為不是所有麝香貓的便便都能幸運地被找到。當地人若找到這樣的咖啡豆,就會小心地收集,再經過挑選、晾曬、除臭、烘培等數道工序,製作出全世界最稀有、也最昂貴的咖啡。

Topic Reading　主題閱讀　　　　　🔊 01-01

One man's trash is another man's treasure[1]. Nothing supports[2] this better than the world's most expensive coffee—kopi luwak. The word kopi is the Indonesian word for coffee, and luwak is the word for the Asian palm civet, which is a rare[3] cat-like animal that only feeds[4] at night. Have you figured out[5] the connection[6] yet? Basically, the luwak's droppings have become the most wanted treasure by coffee lovers everywhere.

What is so special about kopi luwak? The first part is because of the luwaks. They eat only the ripest[7] and tastiest coffee berries. After the berries enter their stomachs, the fruit flesh is digested[8]. The seeds, or coffee beans, are fermented[9] and then passed out of their bodies. The fermented beans are the second part. After being cleaned and lightly roasted[10], the beans create a smooth, chocolatey coffee that has no bitter taste. Since the luwak only lives in certain areas of Indonesia and the Philippines, limited quantities[11] of these coffee beans are collected[12]. So don't be shocked when you see the price tag for kopi luwak—up to US$300 per pound. Now that is some expensive trash!

 Reading Exercises　閱讀隨堂考

_____ 1. What would be a good name for this reading?
　　(A) Strange Indonesian Customs
　　(B) A Most Unusual Type of Coffee
　　(C) The Eating Habits of Civets
　　(D) Kopi Luwak Isn't Worth the Price

_____ 2. Which is true about the Asian palm civet?
　　(A) They enjoy drinking coffee as a treat.
　　(B) They make wonderful pets.
　　(C) They don't eat berries, only beans.
　　(D) They don't eat during the daytime.

1. **treasure** [ˈtrɛʒɚ] *n.* 寶藏，貴重物品

2. **support** [səˈpɔrt] *vt.* 證實

   例: The experiment results supported Johnny's theory.
   實驗的結果證實了強尼的論點。

3. **rare** [rɛr] *a.* 稀有的，罕見的

4. **feed** [fid] *vi.* 進食（三態為：feed, fed [fɛd], fed。）

   例: Infants need to feed every three to four hours.
   嬰兒每三到四個小時就要吃東西。

5. **figure out...** 了解……

   例: I really couldn't figure out what he said.
   我真的無法理解他的話。

6. **connection** [kəˈnɛkʃən] *n.* 關聯

   例: There is a connection between smoking and cancer.
   抽煙與癌症之間有關聯。

7. **ripe** [raɪp] *a.* 成熟的

8. **digest** [daɪˈdʒɛst] *vt.* 消化

9. **ferment** [fɚˈmɛnt] *vt.* 發酵

   例: Fruit juices ferment easily if they aren't kept in the fridge.
   果汁如果沒有保存在冰箱的話，很容易發酵。

10. **roast** [rost] *vt.* 烘培

11. **quantity** [ˈkwɑntətɪ] *n.* 量，數量（與不可數名詞並用）
    a large quantity of...
    = a great deal of...   大量的……

    例: We need a large quantity of money and manpower for this project.
    這個計劃我們需要大量的金錢和人力。

12. **collect** [kəˈlɛkt] *vt.* 收集，採集

    例: I am collecting as much information as possible for my thesis.
    我正在為論文大量蒐集資料。

 Bonus Vocabulary 補充單字

1. **Asian palm civet** *n.* 亞洲麝香貓
   civet [ˈsɪvɪt] *n.* 麝香貓

2. **droppings** [ˈdrɑpɪnz] *n.*（恆用複數，指動物的）糞便

3. **flesh** [flɛʃ] *n.* 果肉

4. **smooth** [smuð] *a.* 平滑的，滑順的

5. **chocolatey** [ˈtʃɑkələtɪ] *a.* 巧克力味的

6. **limited** [ˈlɪmɪtɪd] *a.* 有限的

Sentence Structure Analysis 句型分析

After being cleaned and lightly roasted , the beans create a smooth ,

① ②

chocolatey coffee that has no bitter taste .
③

① 介詞 After 引導的介詞片語,作副詞用,修飾 ② ;

② 為主要子句;

③ 為關係代名詞 that（= which）引導的形容詞子句,修飾之前的先行詞 coffee。

Grammar Points 重點來了

❯ One man's trash is another man's treasure. 若從字面上直接翻譯的話,本句譯成「某人的垃圾是另一人的寶物。」也就是諺語所說的:蘿蔔青菜,各有所愛。你也可以這麼說:One man's meat is another man's poison.

❯ One man's trash is another man's treasure.

其中:

one...another...　　一個……另一個……（非限定的兩者）

例: Hobbies vary with people. One may enjoy swimming, while another may love hiking.
嗜好因人而異。某甲可能喜歡游泳,某乙則可能喜歡健行。

比較:

one...the other...　　一個……另一個……（限定的兩者）

例: He has two sons. One is a teacher, and the other is a soldier.
他有兩個兒子。一個是老師,另一個則是軍人。

1. My father only drinks gourmet coffee.

   我爸爸只喝美味的咖啡。

2. If I drink coffee after 5 p.m., the caffeine will keep me up all night!

   如果我下午五點過後喝咖啡的話，咖啡因會讓我整夜睡不著！

3. Many drinks, including beer and yogurt, use fermented ingredients.

   許多飲料用發酵的成分，其中包括啤酒和優酪乳。

4. This particular region is prized for its rich soil which is perfect for growing coffee.

   這個特別的區域因肥沃的土壤而被重視，這種肥沃的土壤非常適合種植咖啡。

5. Coffee beans are thought to have been first discovered in Ethiopia.

   咖啡豆被認為最早是在衣索比亞被發現的。

6. Caffeine has a stimulating effect that for some people can be almost addictive.

   咖啡因有刺激作用，對某些人來說可能會上癮。

7. Traditionally Chinese people preferred tea; these days coffee is becoming increasingly popular in China.

   中國人習慣上較喜歡茶，如今咖啡在中國越來越受歡迎。

8. My mom needs a cup of coffee in the morning or she simply can't function!

   我媽早上需要來杯咖啡，不然她無法正常工作！

9. Don't drink too much coffee or you'll get a headache from ingesting too much caffeine!

   別喝太多咖啡，否則你會因攝取太多咖啡而感到頭痛。
   ＊ingest [ɪnˋdʒɛst] vt. 攝取

10. There's nothing better than the smell of freshly-ground coffee!

    沒有什麼比新鮮研磨咖啡的香味來得好了！

Situational Dialogue 打開話匣子　🔊 01-03

S = Steven; A = April

 S: Hey, April! How was your trip to Indonesia?

 A: It was amazing! The beaches were incredible[1].

 S: Sounds fabulous[2]! I think I'll try to plan a trip there soon.

 A: I also brought you back a little souvenir[3]. Some local coffee!

 S: Wonderful! You know how much I love coffee!

 A: I'm not sure if I should let you drink it first or tell you its secret first.

 S: Huh? Coffee with a secret?

 A: Okay, I'll tell you. This is called "kopi luwak" and the beans have actually been processed[4] through the digestive[5] system of an animal called a luwak.

 S: Wait a second...did you say "through" the digestive system?

 A: Yep.

 S: So these coffee beans have actually come out the backside[6] of an animal?

 A: Yeah...out of a luwak; it lives in trees and kind of looks like a cat.

S: Are you sure this is safe to drink?

 A: Not only is it safe, but[7] it's some of the most expensive coffee in the world. You see this bag right here? It cost me almost US$300!

 S: Whoa! Well, this is one of the weirdest[8] things I've ever heard of but let's give it a try!

 Vocabulary & Phrases 單字片語解密

1. **incredible** [ɪnˈkrɛdəbḷ] *a.* 難以置信的，驚人的

2. **fabulous** [ˈfæbjələs] *a.* 極好的，驚人的

3. **souvenir** [ˈsuvəˌnɪr] *n.* 紀念品
   例: Mom and Dad brought back several souvenirs from their trip to Paris.
   爸媽巴黎之行回來時帶了幾項紀念品。

4. **process** [ˈprɑsɛs] *vt.* 將……加工
   be in process　　正在進行中
   = be going on
   例: This plant processes crude oil into usable products.
   該工廠將原油加工成實用產品。

5. **digestive** [dəˈdʒɛstɪv] *a.* 消化的
   the digestive system　　消化系統
   the respiratory [ˈrɛsp(ə)rəˌtɔrɪ] system　　呼吸系統
   the circulatory [ˈsɝkjələˌtɔrɪ] system
   循環系統

6. **backside** [ˈbækˌsaɪd] *n.* 臀部

7. **Not only...but (also)...**
   不僅……而且……
   由於 not only 置於句首，視為否定副詞，第一個主要子句要倒裝。
   例: Not only can she sing, but she can (also) dance.
   她不僅會唱歌，而且還會跳舞。

8. **weird** [wɪrd] *a.* 奇特的

9

✎ **Review Exercises** 隨堂小測驗

Part A: Fill in the blanks with the correct answers.

_____ 1. I find a cup of coffee in the morning to be very _____.
   (A) grateful
   (B) stimulating
   (C) refreshed
   (D) happy

_____ 2. There was a large _____ of people at the restaurant.
   (A) amount
   (B) number
   (C) plenty
   (D) groups

_____ 3. I can't figure out _____ kind of coffee to buy.
   (A) what
   (B) that
   (C) where
   (D) this

_____ 4. Not only does she cook, _____ she makes great desserts as well.
   (A) and
   (B) how
   (C) but
   (D) than

_____ 5. _____, organic food is becoming more and more appreciated.
   (A) Recently
   (B) In the past
   (C) Later
   (D) These days

Review Exercises 隨堂小測驗

Part B: Put the words in the following sentences in order in the blanks below.

1. ever / This meal / I've / is / the tastiest / had

_____

2. the most / exercise / I think / that swimming / refreshing / is

_____

3. it is / delicious, / Not only / stimulating, too / is coffee / but

_____

4. coffee / Some people / really drink / a large quantity of

_____

5. was shocked / the expensive price / of the / Jim / coffee / by

_____

Rare Mango Poisoning[1]
芒果好『毒』?

Warm-up Exercise　暖身練習

1. What is your favorite fruit? What is your least favorite fruit?

2. Have you ever had a reaction, such as a rash, after eating food? If so, what was the cause?

芒果在六千年前是印度女性不可或缺的美容聖品，芒果的果肉對皮膚有深層滋潤的功效，也是防暈止吐的天然藥品，果核能消暑、治感冒，芒果葉的萃取物能抑制大腸桿菌。遺憾的是，不是每個人都能吃這種千年聖果，有過敏性、肺結核或腎臟病患者最好少吃，以免誘發過敏原。

　　芒果屬於漆樹科果實，容易造成過敏症狀，其中主要的過敏原為漆酚（urushiol）的成分。一些特殊體質的人，會對芒果的樹汁液、果皮等過敏，引起皮膚的濕疹樣反應，也就是所謂的芒果皮膚炎。但芒果營養價值很高，維生素A含量高達3.8%，維生素 C 的含量超過橘子、草莓。建議對芒果過敏的人避免接觸芒果的樹幹、莖葉，尤其要避免接觸到芒果樹的汁液，因為其中所含有的過敏原最強。如果要吃芒果時最好請他人代為削皮，以免接觸到果皮上的過敏原。

Topic Reading 主題閱讀

Summertime in Taiwan is mango season. This is when they are the freshest and taste the best. It is also the season when some people walking around in the forest or mountains get poison ivy on their arms or legs. What do these two facts have in common[2]? Occasionally[3], when someone eats a mango, they will end up with a rash[4] around their mouths. This happens because mangos are in the same family as poison ivy.

When people touch the skin of a mango, they come into contact with[5] a natural chemical substance called urushiol. This is what causes the rash. Someone who is allergic[6] to urushiol may get an itchy[7] redness on their hands or around their mouths. In serious cases[8], it can spread[9] to the rest of the body. However, experts say mango poisoning is rare and could be avoided by only touching or eating the inside part of the mango. Since mangos are rich in[10] vitamins A and C, people should still enjoy this delicious summer fruit when they can.

 Reading Exercises 閱讀隨堂考

_____ 1. What is the main point of the reading?
    (A) The benefits of eating mangos.
    (B) How to Cook Mangos.
    (C) Mangos can cause skin problems.
    (D) Eat more fruit and vegetables

_____ 2. What is urushiol?
    (A) A chemical.
    (B) A rare type of mango.
    (C) A medical condition.
    (D) A vitamin.

1. **poison** [ˋpɔɪzn] *n.* 毒藥，毒物
   poisonous [ˋpɔɪznəs] *a.* 有毒的

2. **have...in common**
   有……的共通點
   have something in common with sb
   與某人有某些共通點
   have nothing in common with sb
   與某人沒有共通點
   例: I have a lot in common with my
   best friend.
   我和我最要好的朋友之間有很多的
   共通點。

3. **occasionally** [əˋkeʒənḷɪ] *adv.*
   偶爾，偶然
   = on occasion
   = once in a while
   = from time to time
   = (every) now and then
   例: Cindy has to work on the
   weekends from time to time.
   辛蒂有時候週末得工作。

4. **rash** [ræʃ] *n.* 疹子
   break / come out in a rash
   突然長滿了疹子
   例: Tom came out in a rash after he
   ate seafood last night.
   湯姆昨晚吃了海鮮之後就全身長滿
   了疹子。

5. **come into contact with...**
   碰觸到……
   contact [ˋkɑntækt] *n.* 接觸
   例: Zoe screamed when she came
   into contact with the freezing
   lake water.
   柔依在碰到冰冷的湖水時尖叫了一
   聲。

6. **allergic** [əˋlɝdʒɪk] *a.* 過敏的（與介
   詞 to 並用）
   allergy [ˋælədʒɪ] *n.* 過敏反應，過敏
   症（與介詞 to 並用）
   例: I like dogs but unfortunately I'm
   allergic to them.
   = I like dogs but unfortunately I
   have an allergy to them.
   我喜歡狗，但不幸的是我對狗過敏。

7. **itchy** [ˋɪtʃɪ] *a.* 發癢的
   例: This sweater makes me itchy all
   over.
   這件毛衣使我渾身發癢。

8. **in some cases**　　在一些情況下
   in most cases　　在大部分情況下
   例: In some cases people have
   to wait quite a few days for an
   appointment.
   在某些情況下人們得等待好幾天才
   能看診。

9. **spread** [sprɛd] *vt.* & *vi.* 散播（三態
   同形）
   spread a disease / rumor
   散播疾病 / 謠言
   例: The disease is spread by
   mosquitoes.
   這個疾病是藉由蚊子傳播的。
   The disease spreads easily.
   這個疾病散播地很快。

10. **be rich in...**　　有豐富的……
    = be high in...
    be low in...　　……的含量低
    例: Spinach is rich in iron and
    calcium.
    菠菜中富含鐵及鈣質。

1. **poison ivy**　*n.* 毒葛，氣根毒藤

2. **family** [ˋfæməlɪ] *n.*（動植物等的）科

3. **substance** [ˋsʌbstəns] *n.* 物質

4. **urushiol** [uˋruʃɪl] *n.* 漆酚

5. **poisoning** [ˋpɔɪznɪŋ] *n.* 中毒

Sentence Structure Analysis 句型分析

Someone | who is allergic to urushiol | may get | an itchy redness on their
❶ ❷ ❸ ❹

hands or around their mouths .

❶ 為本句主詞；

❷ 為關係代名詞 who 引導的形容詞子句，修飾先行詞 someone；

❸ 為本句的及物動詞；

❹ 為 ❸ 的受詞。

 Grammar Points 重點來了

Occasionally, when someone eats a mango, they will end up with a rash around their mouths.

▶ end up / wind [waɪnd] up + 介詞片語 / 現在分詞　　最後 / 到頭來 / 結果……

注意:

"end / wind up..." 作不完全不及物片語動詞用時，表『最後 / 到頭來 / 結果……』，其後可接介詞片語（介詞 + 名詞）當補語，如本單元閱讀的句子即為此例；之後亦可接現在分詞當補語，但若此現在分詞為 being，則 being 可省略，直接接名詞或形容詞即可。

例: Al's parents ended up getting a divorce because they quarreled all the time.
艾爾的父母由於時常吵架，到頭來以離婚收場。

Although I graduated from law school, I wound up (being) a hair stylist.
我雖然是法學院畢業的，但最後我成了髮型設計師。

1. Have you ever had a rash after eating a mango?

   你曾經吃完芒果後長疹子嗎？

2. That's because mangos are in the same family as poison ivy.

   那是因為芒果和氣根毒藤屬同一植物科。

3. Some people get an itchy redness on their hands or around their mouths.

   有些人會在雙手或嘴巴周圍產生發紅發癢的反應。

4. Are you allergic to fruit? Do you have any allergies?

   你對水果過敏嗎？你對任何東西過敏嗎？

5. Mangos are rich in vitamins A and C.

   芒果富含維他命 A 和 C。

6. Experts say mango poisoning is rare.

   專家表示芒果中毒很罕見。

7. What other types of fruit do you enjoy eating?

   你還喜歡吃其他什麼種類的水果？

8. I'm partial to strawberries and cherries myself.

   我自己偏愛草莓和櫻桃。

   ＊be partial [ˋpɑrʃəl] to...　　偏好……

Situational Dialogue　打開話匣子　 02-03

E = Evelyn; M = Mike

 E: I can't believe I got a rash from eating a mango. Have you ever had a rash after eating a mango?

 M: No, actually I haven't. But I've heard about people getting rashes that way. My sister told me that's because mangos are in the same family as poison ivy.

 E: Really? I didn't know that. I guess that explains the rash. Maybe I should stop eating mangos.

 M: Mangos are rich in vitamins A and C, so they are good to eat. You can avoid getting a rash by only touching and eating the inside of the mango.

 E: That's a good idea. Are you allergic to fruit? Do you have any allergies?

 M: I don't have any food allergies. However, I'm allergic to chocolate.

 E: A chocolate allergy. How terrible!

 M: Yeah, tell me about it. What other types of fruit do you enjoy eating?

 E: I'm partial to strawberries and cherries myself.

 M: I like those, too, as well as Buddha's head.

Tell me about it.

我也是這麼覺得 / 還用你說嗎？ / 我早就知道了。

: A: I get so annoyed with Henry!

B: Tell me about it. He drives me nuts.

甲：我真的很氣亨利耶。

乙：我也是這麼覺得。他讓我要抓狂了。

Review Exercises 隨堂小測驗

Part A: Fill in the blanks with the correct answers.

____ 1. These are the freshest blueberries I _____.
  (A) ever taste
  (B) have ever tasted
  (C) ever have tasted
  (D) have been tasting ever

____ 2. _____, telling the truth is the best option.
  (A) In case
  (B) In most cases
  (C) In a case
  (D) In the case

____ 3. This rash is very _____.
  (A) itchy
  (B) itch
  (C) itched
  (D) itchiness

____ 4. My brother has to be careful because he has a peanut _____.
  (A) symptom
  (B) rash
  (C) allergic
  (D) allergy

____ 5. I only eat mangos once _____ while.
  (A) in a
  (B) of a
  (C) with the
  (D) on some

Part B: Fill in the blanks by choosing the correct words from the box below.

break out	cases	allergic	Occasionally
rich in	end up	spreads	partial

I seldom eat fruit, although I know I should eat it more. Fruit is (1) _____

vitamins that are good for the body. However, I am (2) _____ to one type

of fruit: apples. If I eat apples, I always (3) _____ in a rash around my

mouth. (4) _____, the rash (5) _____ to other parts of my body.

In most (6) _____, though, the rash isn't too bad. Even though I get a

rash when I eat them, I'm still (7) _____ to them. So I usually

(8) _____ getting a rash every now and then.

Oktoberfest
痛快暢飲啤酒節

Warm-up Exercise 暖身練習

1. What type of alcoholic beverages do you like to drink? How often do you drink alcohol?

2. What type of festivals do you like to go to?

德國慕尼黑啤酒節,於每年九月的第三個週末,一直舉行到十月的第一個週末,為期約兩個禮拜。啤酒節源自於一八一〇年的皇室婚禮,全國百姓為此飲酒作樂,盡情慶祝。此後,規模日益擴大,演變成眾所皆知的慕尼黑啤酒節。

啤酒節由繽紛熱鬧的遊行揭開序幕,大會依慣例在特蕾莎廣場上搭建數座巨型帳篷,參與的民眾於帳篷內盡情地暢飲啤酒。另外也提供傳統美食,如德國豬腳、香腸,讓大家盡情享用。在臨時搭建的舞台上,安排有現場樂團演奏,熱鬧的氣氛迅速散播開來,最後往往演變為一場萬人的派對。

慕尼黑每年在這個時候都會湧入數以百萬計的觀光客。根據當地觀光局統計,光在這兩星期的慶典期間,平均喝掉的啤酒總量竟然超過五百萬公升!你是啤酒的愛好者嗎?那麼你千萬別錯過慕尼黑的啤酒節。

With a 12-gun salute and the tapping of a keg by the mayor of Munich, Germany, Oktoberfest gets under way[1]. This 16-day festival takes place[2] in late September. It is one of the most important events in Germany and has become famous worldwide. More than six million Germans and tourists take part in[3] Oktoberfest each year to eat, drink, and celebrate[4]. Traditional German food, like sausages, potatoes, and cheese, is consumed[5] with many different kinds of beer.

At Oktoberfest, many people drink too much beer and then pass out[6]. These people are called "beer corpses" and are often brought to a medical tent to receive[7] help. But starting in 2005, special tents have been set up[8] for "quiet Oktoberfest." This is mainly for families who do not drink or

have young children. Altogether, Oktoberfest has 14 main tents with seating for 100,000 people on 103 acres of land. Women work in traditional clothing and can each deliver[9] up to eight mugs of beer at a time[10] to the guests. So whether you enjoy beer or simply want to experience[11] the biggest festival in Germany, visit in late September for Oktoberfest.

Reading Exercises　閱讀隨堂考

____ 1. What are "beer corpses"?
(A) People who have died from too much beer.
(B) Empty beer bottles on the tables.
(C) The waitresses who serve beer.
(D) Beer drinkers who have passed out.

____ 2. What type of food is NOT mentioned in the reading?
(A) Sausages.
(B) Desserts.
(C) Vegetables.
(D) Dairy products.

Vocabulary & Phrases 單字片語解密

1. **get under way**　　開始進行／發生
   例: The new construction has gotten under way.
   新的建造工程已經開始進行。

2. **take place**　　舉行；發生
   例: The costume party took place last night.
   那場化妝舞會於昨晚舉行。

3. **take part in...**　　參與……
   例: These performers will take part in the opening ceremony.
   這些表演者將會參與開幕儀式。

4. **celebrate** [ˋsɛləˌbret] *vt.* 慶祝
   例: How will you celebrate your birthday?
   你的生日將怎麼慶祝？

5. **consume** [kənˋsum] *vt.*
   攝取（食物）；消耗
   例: I consumed the whole pizza in 10 minutes.
   我在十分鐘之內就吃光了整塊比薩。
   Running consumes much of our energy.
   跑步會消耗我們很多體力。

6. **pass out**　　昏倒
   = faint [fent]
   例: Tom passed out after standing in the sun for hours.
   湯姆在太陽下站了幾個小時就昏倒了。

7. **receive** [rɪˋsiv] *vt.* 收到
   例: Sam received a package in the mail today.
   小三子今天在送來的信件中收到一份包裹。

8. **set...up / set up...**　　架設……，安裝……
   例: Can you help Sam set up the equipment?
   你能不能幫山姆安裝那些設備？

9. **deliver** [dɪˋlɪvɚ] *vt.* 運送；發表（演講）
   deliver / make a speech to...
   對……演講
   例: Postmen do not deliver mail on Sundays.
   星期天郵差不送信。
   I feel honored to deliver a speech to you.
   我很榮幸能對諸位演講。

10. **at a time**　　一次，每次
    例: You can't take more than two pills at a time.
    你一次不能服用超過兩粒藥丸。

11. **experience** [ɪkˋspɪrɪəns] *vt.* 體驗，經歷
    be experienced in...
    在……頗有經驗
    例: During the past five years, Taiwan has experienced many natural disasters, such as earthquakes and typhoons.
    過去五年中，台灣遭遇到很多像地震、颱風等天然災害。
    John is well experienced in writing.
    約翰在寫作方面頗有經驗。

Bonus Vocabulary 補充單字

1. **salute** [səˋlut] *n.* 鳴禮炮；敬禮

2. **tap** [tæp] *vt.* 為……裝上龍頭／閥門

3. **keg** [kɛg] *n.*（用來裝酒的）桶

4. **mayor** [ˋmeɚ] *n.* 市長，鎮長

5. **festival** [ˋfɛstəvl̩] *n.* 節慶，慶典

6. **worldwide** [ˋwɜld͵waɪd] *adv.*
   遍及全世界地

7. **corpse** [kɔrps] *n.* 屍體

8. **altogether** [͵ɔltəˋgɛðɚ] *adv.* 總之；
   全部

9. **seating** [ˋsitɪŋ] *n.*（某處的全部）
   座位

10. **acre** [ˋekɚ] *n.* 英畝

Sentence Structure Analysis　句型分析

But starting in 2005, special tents have been set up for... 可等於：
But since 2005, special tents have been set up for...

 since 表「自從」，可作介詞或副詞連接詞，所引導的片語或子句修飾主要子句時，該主要子句應採現在完成式或現在完成進行式，句型如下：

主詞 + have / has + 過去分詞 + since...　　自從……以來就一直……

或：主詞 + have / has been + 現在分詞 + since...

例: I have lived here since 2000.
自 2000 年起我就一直住在這裏。

I have been studying English since I went to college.
自我唸大學後，我就一直在學英語。

Grammar Points　重點來了

▶ 16-day 為『數字詞 + 名詞』的複合形容詞，其名詞部分恆為單數。

a five-year plan　　　　　　　　五年計畫
a zero-degree temperature　　　零度氣溫

So whether you enjoy beer or simply want to experience the biggest festival in Germany, visit in late September for Oktoberfest.

▶ 其中 whether...or... 表『不論……還是……』

例: Whether you like juice or coke, just help yourself.
不論你喜歡果汁還是可樂，請自便。

1. He's wanted to check out Oktoberfest for years.

   他多年以來一直很想去看看啤酒節。

2. She is a teetotaler, which means she doesn't drink.

   她是個禁酒主義者，也就是説她不喝酒。
   ＊teetotaler [tiˋtot!ɚ] *n.* 禁酒主義者

3. There are many slang terms for getting drunk, including being "hammered."

   關於喝醉酒有許多俚語，包括被『鎚昏』了。

4. That doesn't sound like my idea of a good time.

   那聽起來不像是我想的那麼好玩。

5. I'm very much looking forward to my upcoming trip to Munich.

   我非常期待我即將要去慕尼黑旅行。

6. Oktoberfest is a German cultural event that celebrates food and beer.

   啤酒節是德國慶祝啤酒與食物的文化活動。

7. Over six million people come to take part in this annual event.

   有六百多萬人會來參與此項年度活動。

8. Traditional German food includes sausages, potatoes and cheese.

   傳統的德國食物包括香腸、馬鈴薯、與起司。

Situational Dialogue 打開話匣子   🔊 03-03

M = Mark; A = Anna

M: I can't believe this is finally happening! I have my ticket and there's just one week to go!

A: Going on vacation?

M: Kind of...I'm going to Oktoberfest in Munich, Germany! I have wanted to check this out[1] for years!

A: I see. Oktoberfest is a beer festival, right?

M: Yes. But it's also the biggest festival in Germany! Over six million people come to take part in this annual[2] event that serves as[3] a kind of tribute[4] to German beer.

A: Well, I do like German food, especially sausages, but I guess Oktoberfest wouldn't be a place for me because I don't drink.

M: Actually, in 2005 they started setting up special tents for families and those who don't drink. You could still come and sample[5] some of the local food!

A: Um...I think I'll pass[6]. Six million drunk tourists doesn't sound like my idea of a good time. I imagine there are some people who get really hammered[7]!

M: Yeah! They're called "beer corpses," but there are medical tents where they take care of[8] super drunk people. On-site[9] nurses make sure no one becomes a real corpse.

A: Well, you have a great time, Mark! And don't forget to take some pictures.

1. **check out...** 看一看⋯⋯

= take a loot at...

例: Everybody says that that movie is very good, so I've decided to check it out sometime next week.

大家都說那部電影很棒，所以我決定下星期找一天自己去瞧瞧。

2. **annual** [ˈænjʊəl] *a.* 每年的，一年一次的

3. **serve as...** 擔任⋯⋯

例: The smoker's death should serve as a warning to other young people.

這個癮君子的過世應視為其他年輕人的借鏡。

4. **tribute** [ˈtrɪbjut] *n.* 稱頌

pay tribute to... 向⋯⋯致敬

例: People gathered in front of the actor's tomb to pay tribute to him.

人們聚集在這位演員墓前向他致敬。

5. **sample** [ˈsæmpl̩] *vt.* 品嚐；採樣

例: Jimmy sampled the delights of Italian cooking for the first time.

吉米第一次品嚐了好吃的義大利美食。

6. **pass** [ˈpæs] *vi.* 不參加

7. **hammer** [ˈhæmɚ] *vt. & vi.* 鎚擊

例: John heard someone hammering next door.

約翰聽到隔壁在敲東西。

8. **take care of...** 照顧⋯⋯

例: Would you take care of my baby while I'm away?

我不在的時候，可否請你照顧我的小寶寶？

9. **on-site** [ɑn ˈsaɪt] *a.* 現場的

Review Exercises 隨堂小測驗

Part A: Fill in the blanks with the correct answers.

____ 1. Every year, many Christmas parties _____.
(A) take place
(B) have taken place
(C) took place
(D) are taking place

____ 2. Whether you prefer beer _____ wine, you shouldn't drink too much.
(A) and
(B) or
(C) but
(D) nor

____ 3. Wendy hasn't worked here _____ 2010.
(A) for
(B) been
(C) since
(D) in

____ 4. John is _____ much looking forward to visiting Germany.
(A) very
(B) really
(C) quite
(D) always

____ 5. I have to take care _____ my little sister this afternoon.
(A) of
(B) with
(C) to
(D) for

Part B: Match the terms on the left with the definitions on the right by writing the correct letters in the blanks.

____ **1.** tribute   a. an honor

____ **2.** check out   b. yearly

____ **3.** teetotaler   c. eat or drink

____ **4.** consume   d. begin

____ **5.** get under way   e. a non-drinker

____ **6.** annual   f. investigate

____ **7.** corpse   g. a dead body

____ **8.** hammered   h. drunk

Automated Sushi Bar
全自動迴轉壽司吧

![Warm-up Exercise icon] **Warm-up Exercise**　暖身練習

1. Are you a fan of sushi? What ingredients do you like in sushi?

2. What do you think about robots making your food?

迴　轉壽司店在日本和台灣都算是相當普及。在日本除了可以平價吃到好吃的壽司外，許多迴轉壽司店還發明了多種噱頭來招攬顧客：除了現宰鮪魚秀外、還有結合遊戲的點菜方式。而發明迴轉壽司的是在大阪的「元祿壽司」創社者白石義明先生，他從朝日啤酒廠的啤酒瓶運輸帶得到靈感而將其引用到壽司店中。

I n thousands of sushi bars, delicious plates of food travel along conveyor belts to satisfy[1] hungry customers. Kura, a popular chain of sushi bars that is located throughout Japan is even more advanced[2] than this. Most of the work at these places is done by machines. Now, not only does a conveyor belt deliver[3] your food, but a computer system takes your order[4] and records how much you have eaten.

Other parts of Kura's operations[5] have also been automated. First, all of the sushi rice balls are made by robots. Second, on the bottom of each plate is an IC chip which keeps the plates linked to[6] the computer. If a plate of food has been out on the belt too long, it will be automatically thrown away. At Kura, you won't see waiters busily serving[7] food. Instead, you will see customers use computer touchscreens to order all kinds of delicious items.

What is the point of all of this automation? The decreased number of staff lowers the cost of business. This means Kura can offer cheaper prices to customers without affecting[8] the quality of sushi in expensive Japan.

 Reading Exercises 閱讀隨堂考

____ 1. What is this reading mostly about?

(A) The popularity of sushi around the world.

(B) Automation is quite expensive.

(C) Kura is an unusual type of sushi restaurant.

(D) There are more and more sushi bars in Japan and other places.

____ 2. Which will you NOT see at Kura?

(A) Busy waiters.

(B) Conveyor belts.

(C) Plates.

(D) Touch screens.

Vocabulary & Phrases 單字片語解密

1. **satisfy** [ˈsætɪsˌfaɪ] *vt.* 使滿足
   satisfied [ˈsætɪsˌfaɪd] *a.* 滿足的
   be satisfied with...
   對⋯⋯感到滿意
   例: I was quite satisfied with
   the customer service of that
   company.
   我對那家公司的顧客服務感到相當
   滿意。

2. **advanced** [ədˈvænst] *a.* 先進的，進
   步的
   advance [ədˈvæns] *vi.* & *n.* 進步
   例: Thanks to advances in medical
   science, we can now live a
   longer life.
   由於醫療科學的進步，我們現在才
   能活得更久。
   Our knowledge of the disease
   has advanced considerably
   over the past few years.
   我們對這種疾病的認識在過去幾年
   來有了長足的進展。

3. **deliver** [dɪˈlɪvə] *vt.* 運送
   例: We promise to deliver your
   goods to your office by Friday.
   我們承諾在星期五以前把貨送到您
   的辦公室。

4. **take sb's order** 幫某人點菜
   例: May I take your order, sir?
   我可以替您點餐了嗎，先生？

5. **operation** [ˌɑpəˈreʃən] *n.* 營運
   operate [ˈɑpəˌret] *vt.* 營運
   例: The system has been in
   operation for half a year.
   這套系統營運已經有半年的時間
   了。

I'm learning how to operate
a business under Peter's
guidance.
我在彼得的指導之下正在學習如何
營運一家公司。

6. **be linked to...** 被連結在⋯⋯
   link A to B 把 A 連接到 B 上
   例: Dan linked his PDA phone to
   his computer.
   阿丹將他的 PDA 手機接到了他的
   電腦上。

7. **serve** [sɝv] *vt.* 端上（食物、飲料
   等）
   例: To our satisfaction, the
   restaurant served food quickly.
   令我們滿意的是，這家餐廳上菜上
   得很快。

8. **affect** [əˈfɛkt] *vt.* 影響
   例: Every aspect of Henry's life
   was seriously affected after his
   divorce.
   亨利離婚後，生活中每個層面都受
   到了嚴重影響。

1. **conveyor belt** [kən'veɚ ˌbɛlt] *n.*
輸送帶

2. **chain** [tʃen] *n.* 連鎖店，連鎖集團

3. **automate** ['ɔtəˌmet] *vt.* 使自動化
automatically [ˌɔtə'mætɪklɪ] *adv.*
自動地
automation [ˌɔtə'meʃən] *n.*
自動化（操作）

4. **IC chip** *n.* 積體電路晶片
（integrated circuit chip 的縮寫）

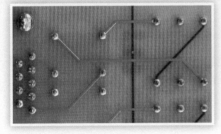

5. **touchscreen** *n.* 觸控式螢幕

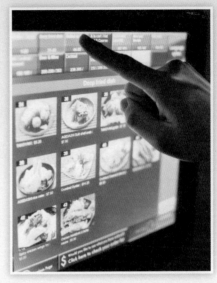

Sentence Structure Analysis   句型分析

Now, not only does a conveyor belt deliver your food, but a computer system (also) takes your order and records how much you have eaten.

▶ 本句採用 "not only...but also..." 的句型，本片語連接對等的主要子句時，若將 not only 置於句首，視為否定副詞，第一個主要子句要倒裝。but also 僅為連接詞，故其後第二個主要子句不須倒裝，但 also 則一定要省略，或移至句中。亦可將 also 省略後在句尾處加 as well。

例: Not only can Mary sing, but she can (also) dance.

= Not only can Mary sing, but she can dance as well.
瑪麗不僅會唱歌，她還會跳舞。

 Grammar Points   重點來了

The decreased number of staff lowers the cost of business.

▶ staff （職員群，幕僚群）一字為集合名詞，不可數。因此要說廿位職員不可說：20 staffs (✕)，而必須說：a staff of 20 或 20 staff members。

例: The company has a staff of 50.

= The company has 50 staff members.
這家公司有五十名職員。

At Kura, you won't see waiters busily serving food. Instead, you will see customers use computer touch screens to order all kinds of delicious items.

▶ 感官動詞（see, hear, listen to）接了受詞後須接原形動詞或現在分詞。原形動詞強調『事實』，現在分詞強調『正在進行的動作』。

例: I saw you put the key in your pocket.
我看見你把鑰匙放進口袋了。

I heard them speaking ill of you behind your back.
我聽見他們正在你背後說你壞話。

1. The new sushi bar doesn't have any waiters!

   新的壽司吧沒有任何服務生！

2. Everything in the restaurant is automated.

   餐廳裡所有東西都是自動的。

3. Food is delivered by a series of conveyor belts.

   食物是用一系列的輸送帶運送的。

4. Automating the service means the restaurant can cut down on expenses.

   使服務自動化意味著餐廳能削減開支。

5. Robots are becoming more common in everyday life.

   機器人在日常生活中變得越來越普遍。

6. My health insurance card has an IC chip with all my medical data on it.

   我的健保卡上有個 IC 晶片，上面有我的就醫紀錄。

7. Do you wish you had a personal robot assistant?

   你希望能有個個人化機器人助理嗎？

8. Have you ever seen a robot vacuum cleaner?

   你曾見過機器人吸塵器嗎？

Situational Dialogue 打開話匣子 04-03

S = Susan; K = Keri

 S: I was reading an old book that had predictions[1] about the future. Boy, were they wrong![2]

 K: Give me an example!

 S: The book said that in the year 2000, everyone would have a personal[3] robot.

 K: Ha! I certainly don't have a robot! But you know, actually my neighbor does have a robot. She has this robot vacuum cleaner[4] that automatically cleans the floors.

 S: That's right! I've seen those! Maybe the book wasn't that far off[5]!

 K: We might not have robots as our personal assistants, but robots are becoming more common. Just the other day[6] a sushi restaurant opened up that doesn't have any waiters!

 S: Really? How do you order food?

 K: The customers type in[7] their order on a computer screen and a system of conveyor belts brings you the dish you ordered! Even the rice balls are made by machines!

 S: I've seen sushi bars with conveyor belts, but robots making rice balls takes it to a whole new level[8]!

 K: Yeah! I guess we really are living in the future!

1. **prediction** [prɪˋdɪkʃən] *n.* 預測
   例: It's difficult to make accurate predictions about earthquakes.
   要精確預測地震相當困難。
   ＊accurate [ˋækjərɪt] *a.* 精確的，準確的

2. **Boy, were they wrong!**
   哇，他們都錯了！
   本句句首 Boy 是感嘆句，相當中文的「哇」或「天啊」，之後採倒裝句構。
   例: Boy, is that girl beautiful!
   哇，那個女孩子真美啊！

3. **personal** [ˋpɝsn̩l] *a.* 個人的
   例: The novel is written from personal experience.
   這本小說是由個人經驗撰述而成。

4. **a vacuum cleaner** 吸塵器
   vacuum [ˋvækjʊəm] *n.* 真空

5. **be not far off / not far out / not far wrong**
   幾乎是正確的 / 不算太離譜
   例: Your guess wasn't far out at all.
   你的猜測幾乎是正確的。

6. **the other day**
   前幾天（與過去式並用）
   例: I ran into an old friend of mine the other day.
   我幾天前偶遇我的一位老友。

7. **type in...** 鍵入……
   = key in...

8. **take sth to a whole new level**
   把某事帶到新的境界

Review Exercises 隨堂小測驗

Part A: Fill in the blanks with the correct answers.

_____ 1. _____ your computer linked to your printer?

    (A) Is

    (B) Does

    (C) Are

    (D) Have

_____ 2. _____ does he like sushi, but he knows how to make it.

    (A) And

    (B) So much

    (C) Not only

    (D) That

_____ 3. This is a very _____ piece of machinery.

    (A) advance

    (B) advancing

    (C) advanced

    (D) advancement

_____ 4. This is cool! The sushi comes to me _____.

    (A) auto

    (B) automated

    (C) automatic

    (D) automatically

_____ 5. Nice try. That guess was not _____.

    (A) so far

    (B) far off

    (C) too far

    (D) far in

Part B: Fill in the blanks by choosing the correct words from the box below.

linked	automated	cut down	take
affect	chain	satisfying	operation

One day, I decided to go to a restaurant (1)_____ that my friend told me

about. I was surprised to find that everything was (2)_____. There were

no waiters to (3)_____ your order! Instead, I entered my order through a

system that was (4)_____ to a computer. I was very impressed by the

(5)_____. I found the food very (6)_____. I'm sure the

automation does (7)_____ on expenses; however, it doesn't

(8)_____ the quality of the food.

Let's All Go Nuts
健康小『堅』兵

1. Do you ever eat any healthy snacks? If so, what do you eat?

2. How many different kinds of nuts can you name?

別看堅果小小一粒，其所蘊藏的營養價值非常豐富，其中最受人注目的成分包含良好的脂肪、膳食纖維及多種維生素和礦物質。

 堅果中的油脂是單元不飽和脂肪酸為主，具有降血脂效能，以減少心血管疾病發生。

 堅果亦含植物纖維，有助於消化和便秘的防治。

 堅果中的維生素和礦物質更是豐富，這些礦物質和維生素在身體的抗氧化功能擔任相當重要的角色。

Topic Reading 主題閱讀 05-01

Lots of articles can be found about healthy snacks and meals. One kind of snack that has gotten a lot of attention[1] lately is nuts. Recent research[2] has shown that there is a link[3] between eating nuts and having a healthy heart. For example, one study found that women who ate nuts more than four times a week were 40 percent less likely to[4] die of[5] heart disease. Scientists are not sure exactly how good nuts are, but there is proof[6] that they are one of the best snack choices.

There are several things in nuts that make them good for us. First of all[7], they are a source[8] of protein and fiber, which are needed for a healthy diet. They also contain omega-3s. These are the "good fats" that can prevent heart attacks.

Another substance in nuts, arginine, keeps artery walls flexible[9] and reduces the chance of blood clots. One of the best qualities of nuts is that they seem to help keep cancer cells from developing. If you really want to try "going nuts[10]," do it wisely. Nuts that are covered with[11] chocolate, salt, or sugar will keep you neither healthy nor[12] fit[13].

 Reading Exercises 閱讀隨堂考

_____ 1. What connection does the reading NOT specifically discuss?
   (A) Between nuts and a healthy heart.
   (B) Between nuts and a longer life.
   (C) Between nuts and blood clots.
   (D) Between nuts and cancer.

_____ 2. What does the reading warn against doing?
   (A) Eating nuts with salt or sugar.
   (B) Eating too many nuts.
   (C) Eating snacks too often.
   (D) Eating too much protein.

Vocabulary & Phrases   單字片語解密

1. **attention** [ə'tɛnʃən] *n.* 注意
   pay attention to...   注意……
   例: You should pay attention to every word I say.
   我所說的每個字你都應注意。

2. **research** ['risɜtʃ] *n.* 研究（集合名詞，不可數）
   do / conduct research about / on...   從事有關……的研究
   例: The scientists did a lot of research about some rare animals on that island.
   科學家針對該島的若干稀有動物做了許多研究。

3. **link** [lɪŋk] *vt.* 產生關聯 & *n.* 關係
   例: The two families are linked by marriage.
   這兩個家庭因通婚而有連繫。
   John has cut off links with all his friends.
   約翰切斷了他與所有朋友的關係。

4. **be likely to V**   可能……
   例: Paul is likely to get married next year.
   = It is likely that Paul will get married next year.
   保羅可能在明年結婚。

5. **die of...**   死於……（多指疾病）
   例: His father died of lung cancer.
   他的父親死於肺癌。

6. **proof** [pruf] *n.* 證明（不可數）
   例: I need proof that he is guilty.
   我需要他有罪的證明。

7. **First of all, ...**   首先 / 第一，……
   例: That man should get the job. First of all, he has a lot of experience.
   那個人應該獲得這份工作。第一點，他有許多經驗。

8. **source** [sɔrs] *n.* 來源
   source of income   收入來源

9. **flexible** ['flɛksəbḷ] *a.* 有彈性的；易彎曲的
   例: Stretching daily will keep you flexible.
   每天做伸展能保持你的柔軟度。

10. **go nuts**   發瘋；變瘋狂
    例: Fans went nuts when Jeremy Lin slam dunked the ball.
    當林書豪把球灌進籃框時，球迷都為之瘋狂。

11. **be covered with / in...**   被……所覆蓋
    例: In winter, the mountain is covered with snow.
    冬天時，整座山被白雪覆蓋。

12. **neither...nor...**   既不……也不……（連接對等的單字或片語）
    例: Neither you nor I am wrong.
    你沒錯，我也沒錯。
    （動詞按最近的主詞變化）

13. **fit** [fɪt] *a.* 健康的（= healthy）
    stay fit   保持健康
    = stay healthy
    例: To stay fit, you should exercise every day.
    要保持健康，每天就應該運動。

1. **snack** [snæk] *n.*（正餐之外的）點心

2. **protein** [ˋprotin] *n.* 蛋白質

3. **fiber** [ˋfaɪbɚ] *n.* 纖維質

4. **omega-3** [oˋmɛɡəˏθri] *n.* 奧米加三脂
肪酸

5. **substance** [ˋsʌbstəns] *n.* 物質

6. **arginine** [ˋɑrdʒənin] *n.* 精氨酸

7. **artery** [ˋɑrtərɪ] *n.* 動脈

8. **clot** [klɑt] *n.*（血液或牛奶中的）凝
塊

9. **cell** [sɛl] *n.* 細胞

Sentence Structure Analysis 句型分析

For example, one study found that women who ate nuts more than four
❶ ❷ ❸ ❹

times a week were 40 percent less likely to die of heart disease .
❺

❶ 為主詞；

❷ 為本句動詞，之後以 that 引導的名詞子句作受詞；

❸ 為名詞子句的主詞；

❹ 為形容詞子句，用以修飾名詞子句中的主詞 women；

❺ 為名詞子句的動詞 were 及主詞補語 40 percent less likely to die of heart
disease。

 Grammar Points 重點來了

One kind of snack that has gotten a lot of attention lately is nuts.

⬤ 空格後有時間副詞 lately。lately, recently, of late, in recent years / months /...
等表『最近（……）』的時間副詞或時間副詞片語常與現在完成式或現在完成進
行式並用。表示到現在為止仍在繼續的動作或狀態時，須使用現在完成式來表
達。表示一直持續到現在且可能仍將繼續下去的動作，則須使用現在完成進行式
來表達。

One of the best qualities of nuts is that they seem to help keep cancer cells
from developing.

⬤ keep sth from V-ing　　阻止某事物……

= prevent sth from V-ing

= stop sth from V-ing

1. A study found that eating nuts can significantly lower your chances of dying from heart disease.

   一項研究發現，吃堅果可以顯著降低因心臟疾病死亡的機會。

2. Everyone likes to eat snacks, but many times we choose unhealthy ones.

   每個人都喜歡吃零食，但很多時候我們選擇了不健康的零食。

3. If you say someone is "nuts," it means they are kind of crazy.

   如果你說某人是「堅果」，這意味著他們有點瘋癲。

4. Do you think chocolate-covered nuts are a health food?

   你覺得包著巧克力的堅果是健康食品嗎？

5. Junk food might be tasty, but it has almost no nutritional value.

   垃圾食物也許很美味，但它幾乎沒有任何營養價值。

6. Do you often tell yourself you'll start eating healthier food tomorrow?

   你是否經常告訴自己，你明天就會開始吃健康食品嗎？

7. Nuts are a good source of fiber and protein.

   堅果是纖維質和蛋白質的良好來源。

8. Did you know that nuts might actually help prevent cancer?

   你知道堅果實際上可能有助於防癌嗎？

Situational Dialogue 打開話匣子 — 🔊 05-03

L = Lisa; S = Sam

L: Honey, I know you're going be working late for the next couple of weeks, so I packed you some healthy snacks. You really need to cut down on[1] the junk food!

S: (sighs) I know that these days I've been stressed a lot. I eat when I'm stressed[2].

L: I didn't want to say anything, but you've gained weight recently. I think it's time for a health food diet[3].

S: Yeah, I guess you're right. I keep telling myself I'll eat something healthy tomorrow – but I know I'm just procrastinating[4].

L: You know I love you and I want you to be healthy. I'm not trying to make your life miserable[5].

S: I know, honey. And I appreciate[6] your efforts. So what snacks did you pack for me? Seaweed and tofu?

L: Actually, I put together a collection of[7] mixed nuts. Nuts are a good source of protein and fiber, and I've recently read that they help prevent[8] heart disease.

S: Well, that's cool! I like nuts, especially chocolate-covered almonds[9] or super salty peanuts[10].

L: Honey...anything chocolate-covered or super salty is not a health food!

S: I know – I'm just kidding!

1. **cut down on...** 削減……

2. **stressed** [strɛst] *a.* 感到有壓力的，感到緊張的

   例: Jack was being stressed before he gave his lecture.
   演講前的那一陣子，傑克感到十分緊張。

3. **diet** [ˋdaɪət] *n.* （為了治療或健康因素所做的）規定的飲食 & *vi.* 節食
   go on a diet　　節食（指動作）
   be on a diet　　節食（指狀態）

   例: The young woman used to diet all the time.
   這位小姐過去一直在節食。

   Mom went on a diet after she had surgery.
   媽媽在手術之後節食。

4. **procrastinate** [proˋkræstəˌnet] *vi.* & *vt.* 延遲

5. **miserable** [ˋmɪzərəbl̩] *a.* 悲哀的

6. **appreciate** [əˋpriʃɪˌet] *vt.* 感激；欣賞

   例: I really appreciate your help.
   我真的很感激你的幫助。

7. **a collection of...** 一批……

8. **prevent** [prɪˋvɛnt] *vt.* 阻止

   例: Vitamin C is supposed to prevent colds.
   維他命 C 被認為能預防感冒。

9. **almond** [ˋɑmənd] *n.* 杏仁

10. **peanut** [ˋpiˌnʌt] *n.* 花生

Part A: Fill in the blanks with the correct answers.

____ 1. _____ a good source of protein.
- (A) Nuts are
- (B) Nut is
- (C) The nuts are
- (D) Nuts be

____ 2. You should stop yourself _____ too much snack food.
- (A) to eat
- (B) of eating
- (C) from eating
- (D) for eating

____ 3. Your eating habits _____ a big problem.
- (A) has got
- (B) have become
- (C) are being
- (D) have gotten

____ 4. "Go nuts" _____ to go crazy.
- (A) mean
- (B) means
- (C) meaning
- (D) will mean

____ 5. Amanda has done a lot of traveling _____.
- (A) recently
- (B) recent
- (C) soon
- (D) almost

Review Exercises 隨堂小測驗

Part B: Fill in the blanks by choosing the correct words from the box below.

lately	cancer	cut down	stress
almonds	diet	prevent	procrastinating

I've really been gaining a lot of weight (1)_____. I know that I should eat less, but it's tough to (2)_____ on the things I like to eat. I keep telling myself that I must go on a (3)_____! But then I always end up (4)_____.

There are many reasons why I should eat healthily. A good diet and exercise can help (5)_____ serious diseases, such as (6)_____. I have a lot of (7)_____ in my life, so I think that's why I eat too much. Instead of eating junk food, I should eat (8)_____ and peanuts.

Bubble, Bubble, Hot Pot Fun
熱騰騰的火鍋趣

1. What do you know about the history of hot pot in Taiwan?

2. What kind of hot pot do you like the most?

現在都市人為求便利，幾乎一年三百六十五天都可以吃涮涮鍋，到了冬天天冷時尤其如此。不過以下這點可要特別小心：

研究顯示，在開始涮火鍋後的半小時內，火鍋湯中亞硝酸鹽的含量是很低的，所以如果要喝湯底，在半小時內喝就不會有太大的問題。某些火鍋湯底燒煮九十分鐘後，亞硝酸鹽含量會增加近十倍之多！雖然我們平常吃的火鍋湯中的亞硝酸鹽含量不至於讓人中毒，但亞硝酸鹽與火鍋湯中的氨基酸分解產物結合，可能形成致癌物亞硝胺，所以我們還是儘量不要在火鍋煮到最後才喝湯才好。

Topic Reading 主題閱讀

E ating hot pot is appealing[1] because it involves[2] three things that everyone loves: food, fire, and friends. This simmering[3] pot which is filled with[4] all kinds of ingredients dates back to the Tang Dynasty. However, it wasn't until the Ching Dynasty that hot pot became popular all over China. In the beginning[5], people just threw meat and vegetables into a big pot and boiled[6] them over a fire. This was a great way to feed a large number of people because the food didn't have to be watched over[7]. Today, hot pot is seen as[8] a joyful meal which is perfect for[9] get-togethers.

The popularity of hot pot and hot pot restaurants in Taiwan is at an all-time[10] high. On any popular food street, there is sure to be many hot pot restaurants

with people who are waiting outside. In the 1970s, lamb hot pot was introduced[11] into Taiwan. The lamb is cooked with Chinese herbs and eaten mostly during the winter. In the 1980s, ginger duck hot pot became a crowd favorite. For this dish, a duck is cooked in ginger, rice wine, and sesame oil, which results in[12] a pot of delicious soup.

Since the 1990s, shabu shabu has been the most popular form of hot pot. This Japanese style of hot pot first appeared[13] in Taiwan in department stores. The reason for its popularity is that each person gets to have their own individual[14] hot pot.

📋 Reading Exercises 閱讀隨堂考

____ 1. Why does the reading mention the Ching Dynasty?
   (A) That's when the first hot pot was made.
   (B) That's when hot pot became popular in Taiwan.
   (C) That's when lamb was introduced into the hot pot.
   (D) That's when hot pot became popular all over China.

____ 2. According to the reading, why is shabu shabu so popular?
   (A) Because it has had a very long history in Taiwan.
   (B) Because people can eat from individual pots.
   (C) Because it has many delicious ingredients.
   (D) Because it is often served in department stores.

Vocabulary & Phrases　單字片語解密

1. **appealing** [əˈpilɪŋ] *a.* 有趣的；有吸引力的（與介詞 to 並用）
   appeal [əˈpil] *vi.* 吸引（與介詞 to 並用）
   例: The idea of spending the whole day on the beach is rather appealing to me.
   整天待在沙灘上這個想法對我來說很有吸引力。
   The design of our logo has to appeal to all ages and social groups.
   我們商標的設計必須要能吸引所有年齡層和社會族群。

2. **involve** [ɪnˈvɑlv] *vt.* 包含（之後接名詞或動名詞作受詞）
   例: The test will involve answering questions about a photograph.
   這項考試將包含回答照片的相關問題。

3. **simmer** [ˈsɪmɚ] *vt. & vi.* 用文火慢煮

4. **be filled with...**　　充滿了……
   = be full of...

5. **In the beginning,...**
   一開始，……
   at the beginning of...
   在……開始時
   例: In the beginning, Tom enjoyed his job, but he's tired of it now.
   一開始，湯姆很喜歡他的工作，但現在他卻厭倦了這一切。
   We're going to Hawaii at the beginning of July.
   我們七月初要去夏威夷。

6. **boil** [bɔɪl] *vt. & vi.* 煮沸

7. **watch over...**　　看管……

例: I felt as if an angel was watching over me.
我覺得好像有天使在守護著我。

8. **be seen as...**　　被視為……
   = be viewed as...
   = be looked upon as...
   例: The little boy was seen as a hero.
   那位小男孩被視為英雄。

9. **be perfect for...**
   很適合從事……
   例: The weather is perfect for outdoor activities.
   這種天氣很適合戶外活動。

10. **all-time** [ˈɔlˌtaɪm] *a.* 前所未有的，空前的
    例: This is my all-time favorite song.
    這是我有史以來最喜歡的歌。
    Profits are at an all-time high / low.
    利潤在新高點 / 新低點。

11. **introduce** [ˌɪntrəˈdjus] *vt.* 引進
    introduce + 物 + into + 地方
    將某物傳入某地
    例: The Europeans introduced cannons into China during the Ming Dynasty.
    歐洲人於明朝時將大砲引入中國。

12. **result in...**　　導致 / 造成……
    = bring about...
    例: The drought resulted in a forest fire.
    旱災引起了森林大火。

13. **appear** [əˈpɪr] *vi.* 出現

14. **individual** [ˌɪndəˈvɪdʒʊəl] *a.* 個別的，單獨的

Bonus Vocabulary 補充單字

1. **ingredient** [ɪnˋgridɪənt] *n.*（烹調用的）材料

2. **joyful** [ˋdʒɔɪfəl] *a.* 充滿喜悅的

3. **get-together** *n.* 聚會

4. **popularity** [ˏpɑpjəˋlærətɪ] *n.* 受歡迎程度

5. **herb** [ɝb] *n.* 藥草；香草

6. **ginger** [ˋdʒɪndʒɚ] *n.* 薑

7. **sesame** [ˋsɛsəmɪ] *n.* 芝麻

Sentence Structure Analysis 句型分析

However, it wasn't until the Ching Dynasty that hot pot became popular all over China.

本句使用 not...until... 的句型，有以下幾種變化：

S1 + not + V + until + S2 + V
= Not until + S2 + V + 倒裝句
= It is / was not until + S2 + V + that + S1 + V

例: I didn't know it until I came back.
= Not until I came back did I know it.
= It was not until I came back that I knew it.
直到我回來後才曉得這件事。

因此本句也可改寫成：

Hot pot didn't become popular until the Ching Dynasty.
或: Not until Ching Dynasty did hot pot become popular.

Grammar Points 重點來了

This was a great way to feed a large number of people because the food didn't have to be watched over.

a large number of + 複數可數名詞　　許多……
a large amount of + 不可數名詞　　大量的……

例: You need to drink a large amount of water after exercising.
你運動後需要喝大量的水。

This simmering pot which is filled with all kinds of ingredients dates back to the Tang Dynasty.

date back to + 明確時間　　回溯至某確切時間點
date back + 一段時間　　回溯一段時間以前

例: This church dates back to 1920.
這座教堂建於一九二〇年。
The clay jars that were discovered here date back thousands of years.
在這裡挖掘出的泥罐可追溯至好幾千年前。

1. Hot pots date back to the Tang Dynasty.

   火鍋可以追溯到唐朝。

2. Today, hot pot is seen as a joyful meal that is perfect for get-togethers.

   今日，火鍋可以被視為充滿喜樂的一頓飯，非常適合聚餐。

3. The popularity of hot pot and hot pot restaurants in Taiwan is at an all-time high.

   火鍋和火鍋餐廳在台灣目前受歡迎的程度創新高。

4. Since the 1990s, shabu shabu has been the most popular form of hot pot.

   自從一九九〇年代以來，涮涮鍋就一直是最受歡迎的火鍋型態。

5. Enjoying a hot pot on a cold winter day is wonderful.

   在寒冷的冬天享受一頓火鍋大餐是很棒的事。

6. Most hot pot restaurants offer buffets and many different flavors of hot pot to choose from.

   大多數火鍋餐廳提供自助無限吃到飽以及許多種不同的火鍋味道可供挑選。

7. The most popular kind right now is spicy hot pot.

   目前最受歡迎的種類是麻辣火鍋。

8. Spicy hot pot can cause stomach trouble and is bad for sore throats.

   麻辣火鍋可能會引起胃病，且對喉嚨痛也有不良影響。

Situational Dialogue 打開話匣子 06-03

K = Kevin; H = Hanna

 K: It's such a cold day. Let's have hot pot for dinner.

 H: That's a good idea.

 K: Did you know that hot pots date back to the Tang Dynasty?

 H: I wasn't aware of[1] that. So, that means they've been popular for a really long time.

 K: That's for sure. And right now the popularity of hot pot and hot pot restaurants in Taiwan is at an all-time high[2]. Enjoying a hot pot on a cold winter day is wonderful.

 H: What's the most popular type of hot pot in Taiwan?

 K: The most popular kind right now is spicy hot pot.

 H: Do Taiwanese people eat hot pot a lot?

 K: Well, during cold weather, they do. But I wouldn't recommend[3] eating it every day.

 H: Why not?

 K: Spicy hot pot can cause stomach trouble and is bad for sore throats[4]. In other words[5], you shouldn't overdo[6] it. In moderation[7], however, eating hot pot is fantastic.

 H: Then what are we waiting for?

 K: You're right. Let's go.

1. **be aware of...**　　知道……

   例: The manager was well aware of the problem.
   經理很清楚那個問題。

   Everybody should be made aware of the risks involved.
   大家都應該要知道這當中所包含的風險。

2. **be at an all-time high / low**
   創新高 / 低

   例: New York Knicks' team morale is now at an all-time high.
   紐約尼克隊的全隊士氣現在創新高。

3. **recommend** [ˌrɛkəˈmɛnd] *vt.* 建議
   recommend + N/V-ing　　建議……

   例: I recommend reading the novel before you watch that movie.
   我建議你看那部電影前先看這本小說。

4. **a sore throat**　　喉嚨痛

5. **In other words,...**
   換句話說，……

   例: They asked Henry to leave. In other words, he was fired.
   他們要求亨利離開。換句話說，他被開除了。

6. **overdo** [ˌovɚˈdu] *vt.* 過度從事

   例: Use illustrations where (they are) appropriate but don't overdo it.
   在適當的地方使用插畫，但不要過度使用了。

   * appropriate [əˈproprɪət] *a.*
   適當的

7. **in moderation** [ˌmɑdəˈreʃən]
   適度地

   例: You should always do things in moderation.
   你做任何事總要適度。

Review Exercises 隨堂小測驗

Part A: Choose the correct answer.

____ **1.** _____ 2008, Dennis has lived in New York.

    (A) Since

    (B) For

    (C) In

    (D) During

____ **2.** The teacher said _____ students will be given a final exam.

    (A) each

    (B) entire

    (C) whole

    (D) all

____ **3.** I didn't find out about the problem _____ I got back home.

    (A) until

    (B) unless

    (C) still

    (D) while

____ **4.** Only a small _____ of cookies were left in the box.

    (A) amount

    (B) number

    (C) sum

    (D) type

____ **5.** The party was a _____ occasion.

    (A) joy

    (B) enjoy

    (C) joyful

    (D) enjoying

Part B: Each sentence has a mistake in it. Correct the mistakes and write the corrected sentences in the blanks below.

1. The popular of that company's products is very high right now.

_____

2. In the begin, Kelly didn't like Ben, but later they became friends.

_____

3. Spending on electronic products is at an all-times high.

_____

4. The theater has full of people today.

_____

5. My job involving a lot of hard work.

_____

Healthy Honey
最甜蜜的保健良方

Warm-up Exercise 暖身練習

1. What are some of the various ways people use honey?
2. In what ways can honey be like a medicine?

相信大家都愛蜂蜜，那種香香甜甜的滋味加在任何飲品裡都是絕佳良伴。但是你知道，蜂蜜除了好吃外，它還有多方面的功效嗎？

蜂蜜中含有葡萄糖、果糖、蛋白質、酶、維生素、和多種礦物質。從所含的礦物質來看，蜂蜜幾乎囊括了元素週期表上的礦物質；蜂蜜也是高熱量食品，對於發育中的兒童有很大的補益。蜂蜜含有對生長可塑性物質起重要作用的蛋白質，也有對兒童和少年不可或缺的葉酸。

《神農本草》上記載：久服蜂蜜可以增強意志、輕鬆身體、保持青春、延年益壽。蜂蜜是絕佳的安神催眠補品，而且沒有其他藥物所具有的如壓抑、疲憊、分神和破壞協調等副作用。

近年來，有許多有關蜂蜜對於燙傷傷口加速癒合的研究，證實蜂蜜對於皮膚的燒燙傷具有降低發炎與紅腫的作用，並可減少結痂的情況。研究人員發現蜂蜜的高含糖量，可吸收傷口滲出的組織液，能使傷口乾燥不會沾染衣物，其高黏稠度可防止傷口感染。此外，蜂蜜可以促進組織再生，刺激新血管及組織的形成。蜂蜜還具有抗發炎作用，能減輕傷口的腫脹。蜂蜜不會附在傷口組織上，在換藥時，不會因撕去新形成的組織引起疼痛。

蜂蜜有如此多的療效，怪不得野熊甘願冒著被蜜蜂螫的危險，也要吃到蜂蜜。我們有養蜂人幫忙採收蜂蜜，讓我們輕鬆就能享受既營養又保健的聖品，因此我們更應該善用此項資源，好好珍惜才是。

Topic Reading 主題閱讀 07-01

Bees do much more than just annoy[1] people during the summer months. In fact, one of their biggest contributions to the environment is the making of honey. Bees leave their hives to gather nectar from flowers and change it into honey. When they get back, they store[2] it in the hive. Beekeepers then take the honey and sell it. Recently, doctors and scientists have found out that honey is actually a very good medicine.

Honey is very helpful in[3] treating[4] infections of the throat. It can be added to medicine and tea to help cure[5] sore throats and ease[6] coughs. Singers have been known to drink tea with honey before they perform. Also, honey can be mixed into gels to be put on wounds that are in the process of[7] healing[8]. This not only helps the wounds heal faster, but also[9] keeps the bandages or clothes from sticking[10] to the wounded area.

Bees can be scary to some people, but they are a very important part of nature. Next time you see a bee, remember that its honey may one day prevent you from[11] being ill.

____ 1. According to the article, what is honey NOT capable of doing?
   (A) Curing sore throats and easing coughs.
   (B) Gathering nectar from flowers.
   (C) Keeping clothes from sticking to wounds.
   (D) Preventing people from being ill.

____ 2. Which of the following is also a good title for the article?
   (A) The Relationship between Bees and Honey
   (B) How Beekeepers Produce Honey
   (C) Honey's Contribution to the Environment
   (D) The Healing Powers of Honey

Vocabulary & Phrases 單字片語解密

1. **annoy** [əˋnɔɪ] *vt.* 使生氣；使煩惱

   例: Charlie really annoyed me this morning.
   查理今天早上真的把我惹惱了。

2. **store** [stɔr] *vt.* 儲存

   例: I store some canned goods in the cabinet in case I get hungry late at night.
   我在廚櫃中存放一些罐頭食品以防深夜時肚子餓。

3. **be helpful in...** 對……有幫助

   例: Teamwork is helpful in developing communication skills.
   團隊工作有助於發展溝通技巧。

4. **treat** [trit] *vt.* 治療；對待

   例: The doctor urged me to use water vapor to treat my sore throat.
   醫生叫我用水蒸氣來治療喉嚨痛。

5. **cure** [kjʊr] *vt.* 治癒
   cure sb of a disease
   治療某人的疾病

   例: The doctor cured him of asthma.
   醫生醫好了他的氣喘。

   ＊asthma [ˋæzmə] *n.* 氣喘病

6. **ease** [iz] *vt.* 減輕，舒緩
   ease one's pain / tension
   減輕痛苦 / 消除緊張

   例: Listening to music can ease my tension.
   聽音樂可以消除我的緊張。

7. **be in the process of V-ing**
   在做……的過程中

   例: My mom is in the process of baking a cake.
   我媽正在烤蛋糕。

8. **heal** [hil] *vi.* 傷口痊癒（cure 則指『醫好』某疾病）

   例: Don't worry. The wound will heal in a week.
   別擔心。這傷口一星期就會好。

9. **not only...but (also)...**
   不僅……也……

   例: Not only can Jane sing, but she can also dance.
   阿珍不但會唱歌，也會跳舞。

10. **stick** [stɪk] *vi.* 黏貼（與介詞 to 並用）
    三態為: stick, stuck [stʌk], stuck

    例: Linda's boyfriend sticks to her like glue.
    琳達的男友像膠一樣黏著她。

11. **prevent sb from V-ing**
    預防 / 阻止某人……

    例: The rain prevented us from going fishing.
    因為下雨而使得我們無法去釣魚。

1. **contribution** [ˌkɑntrəˋbjuʃən] *n.*
   貢獻

2. **hive** [haɪv] *n.* 蜂巢

3. **nectar** [ˋnɛktɚ] *n.* 花蜜

4. **infection** [ɪnˋfɛkʃən] *n.* 感染

5. **sore** [sɔr] *a.* 疼痛的，痠痛的

6. **gel** [dʒɛl] *n.* 凝膠

7. **wound** [wund] *n.* 傷口

8. **bandage** [ˋbændɪdʒ] *n.* 繃帶

Sentence Structure Analysis 句型分析

This not only helps the wounds heal faster, but also keeps the bandages
　　　❶　　　❷　　　　　　　　　　　　　　　　　　　❸

or clothes from sticking to the wounded area.

❶ 為 not only... but also... 為對等連接詞，本句中用來連接兩個對等的單數動詞 helps 及 keeps。

❷ help 後常省略 to 再加原形動詞，構成 help sb/sth (to) V 的結構。

　例: When I'm free, I help my mother (to) do the dishes.
　　有空時，我會幫媽媽洗碗。

❸ keep sb/sth from V-ing　　防止某人 / 某事……

　例: After watching the comedy, Jenny couldn't keep herself from laughing.
　　看完此喜劇後，珍妮無法止住自己大笑。

 Grammar Points 重點來了

Bees leave their hives to gather nectar from flowers and change it into honey.

▸ change A into B　　將 A 變成 B
　= turn A into B
　= transform A into B

　例: The magician changed the mouse into a bird.
　　魔術師把老鼠變成一隻鳥。

...they are a very important part of nature.

▸ nature 的用法：
　(1) 表『大自然』時，之前不可置定冠詞，如上句。
　(2) 也可表『事務的本質』，此時之前須置定冠詞。

　　例: What's the nature of your trip?
　　　你此趟旅遊屬什麼性質？

1. Did you know honey is quite good for you?

你知道蜂蜜對你相當有益嗎？

2. Do you eat honey very often?

你時常食用蜂蜜嗎？

3. Doctors and scientists have found out that honey is actually a very good medicine.

醫生及科學家發現蜂蜜其實是種很好的藥物。

4. Honey is very helpful in treating infections of the throat.

蜂蜜對治療喉嚨所受到的感染大有幫助。

5. You should think about eating honey instead of peanut butter or jam.

你應該考慮改吃蜂蜜，而不是花生醬或是果醬。

6. It can be added to medicine and tea to help cure sore throats and ease coughs.

蜂蜜可加在藥物或茶飲裡，用來幫助治癒喉嚨痛及舒緩咳嗽。

7. Singers have been known to drink tea with honey before they perform.

大家都知道，歌手在表演前會喝加了蜂蜜的茶。

8. Honey can be mixed into gels to be put on wounds that are in the process of healing.

蜂蜜可以混在凝膠裡，用來塗抹在癒合中的傷口上。

Situational Dialogue 打開話匣子 ◀))) 07-03

S = Serina; B = Brent

 S: Is there any peanut butter? I guess I should ask the waitress for some.

 B: Why don't you use honey on your toast instead[1]? Did you know honey is quite good for you?

 S: It's natural[2], but I still prefer[3] peanut butter or jam.

 B: You should think about eating honey instead of peanut butter or jam.

 S: What's so special about honey? It tastes[4] too sweet to[5] be good for you.

 B: Well, for one thing, honey is very helpful in treating infections of the throat. It can be added to medicine and tea to help cure sore throats and ease coughs.

 S: That's good to know, I suppose. Maybe I'll try it the next time I get sick.

 B: Also, singers have been known to drink tea with honey before they perform.

 S: Hmm... I do like to go to karaoke with friends, and sometimes my throat hurts when I sing.

 B: Honey just might be what you need to sing more smoothly[6].

 S: Thanks for the advice[7].

Vocabulary & Phrases 單字片語解密

1. **instead** [ɪnˋstɛd] *adv.* 相反地

   例: Music is not my cup of tea. I like dancing instead.
   音樂不是我的所愛。我反而喜歡跳舞。

   ＊one's cup of tea
   某人喜歡的事

2. **natural** [ˋnætʃərəl] *a.* 自然的

3. **prefer** [prɪˋfɝ] *vt.* 寧願，更喜歡
   prefer A to B　喜歡 A 勝於喜歡 B
   prefer to V rather than V
   比較喜歡……勝過……

   例: I prefer music to movies.
   = I prefer to listen to music rather than go to the movies.
   我比較喜歡聽音樂勝過看電影。

4. **taste** [test] *n.* 品嚐 & *vi.* 嚐起來

   例: May I have a taste of your cake?
   我可不可以嚐一口你的蛋糕？
   This food tastes delicious.
   這道食物嚐起來真好吃。

5. **be too + adj. + to V**
   太……而不……

   例: Mark is too tired to do anything.
   馬克太累而無法做任何事。

6. **smoothly** [ˋsmuðlɪ] *adv.* 順暢地，平滑地

7. **advice** [ədˋvaɪs] *n.* 建議；忠告（集合名詞，不可數）
   an advice　　(×)
   → a piece of advice　一則建議 (○)
   some advice　　一些建議 (○)
   a lot of advice　很多建議 (○)

Review Exercises 隨堂小測驗

Part A: Choose the correct answer.

_____ 1. Tom is _____ the process _____ taking a big exam.
- (A) on; for
- (B) of; with
- (C) in; of
- (D) doing; to

_____ 2. Oranges are not only good for us _____ also delicious.
- (A) but
- (B) and
- (C) though
- (D) however

_____ 3. A bad cold prevented him _____ out with his friends.
- (A) to go
- (B) of going
- (C) from going
- (D) to have gone

_____ 4. Instead of _____ a taxi, why don't you take a bus?
- (A) take
- (B) taking
- (C) took
- (D) takes

_____ 5. I prefer tea _____ coffee.
- (A) to
- (B) than
- (C) from
- (D) rather

Part B: Fill in the blanks by choosing the correct words from the box below.

wound	stick	infections	natural
sore	heal	treat	process

I love honey because it is a very (1)_____ product. Moreover, it can be used to (2)_____ some health problems. Let me give you an example. One day, while I was in the (3)_____ of trying to catch the bus, I fell hard on the street. When I looked at my leg, I saw a huge (4)_____ on it. My mom put some honey on it so it wouldn't (5)_____ to the bandage. She said it would also help my leg to (6)_____ faster. That's not all. Later when I had a (7)_____ throat, Mom put some honey and lemon in hot water. She said the drink was good for fighting throat (8)_____. I drank the honey and lemon and my throat felt a lot better.

Creative Cooking
創意烹飪法

1. How many different types of cooking methods can you name?

2. Which of the methods that you named do you like the most?

　由於現代社會環保意識抬頭，因此許多人都在想該如何節約能源。美國最早有人開始提倡使用太陽能烹煮食物。器材只要使用一片反光板，一個吸熱的黑色金屬鍋子，就能在太陽下煮東西來吃。這當中的原理很簡單，反射板能聚集大量太陽熱能，再傳導到金屬的鍋子內。這種原理也被利用來製造『太陽灶』，其功率相當一千五百瓦的電磁爐，燒一壺四公升的開水約需時十五分鐘，不插電、不燒煤材、不需瓦斯或天然氣。

Topic Reading 主題閱讀 08-01

N owadays, most of the food we eat is cooked in ovens or on stoves. The heat which is needed to cook this food comes from burning wood, gas, or other fuels. However, natural resources are decreasing. When fuel becomes less available[1], people have to become more creative. Some of these creative cooking methods have been around[2] for a long, long time.

Some traditional cooking methods use little or no fuel. One example is an underground oven. This method is done by burying[3] food in the ground under hot stones. In some places, food alone can be buried in sand. It is cooked by the sun heating the sand or by hot gases that rise out of the ground.

When cars became common, people realized[4] they could be used to cook food, too. The heat from a car's engine can cook an entire meal as you drive around. The heat from light bulbs can do the same thing. These creative cooking methods save fuel by using it to do two things at the same time[5]. If you are interested in trying out[6] any of these methods, look online. Many websites can show you how to use these methods to prepare food safely.

Solar cooking has been around for a while. However, it has gained a lot of popularity[7] only in recent years. People are starting to use solar cooking methods for two main reasons. One, it is good for the environment, and two, sunlight is free. In addition, the materials which are used to make solar cookers are often cheap and easily acquired[8]. In Thailand, there is a vendor who uses over 900 mirrors to reflect[9] the sun's light so he can grill chicken. Throughout[10] the day, he has to adjust[11] the mirrors to match the movement of the sun. On sunny days, the chicken cooks in only 10 minutes.

Solar cooking is so easy that anyone can do it at home. Try it yourself and discover that helping the environment can be fun and tasty[12]!

 Reading Exercises　閱讀隨堂考

_____ 1. What is this reading mostly about?
(A) Alternative cooking methods.
(B) The most popular ways to cook.
(C) Modern methods of cooking.
(D) Ways to improve your cooking.

_____ 2. Which of the following is an example of solar cooking?
(A) Using the heat from a car's engine to cook food while driving.
(B) Using mirrors to reflect the sun's light to cook food.
(C) Using a light bulb to cook food slowly over a period of time.
(D) Using heat from the Earth to cook food in an underground oven.

Vocabulary & Phrases 單字片語解密

1. **available** [əˋveləbl] *a.* 可提供的
   例: I'm sorry, but this is the only room available.
   抱歉,這是僅剩的一間空房。

2. **around** [əˋraʊnd] *a.* 存在的
   例: Smart phones have been around for some time now.
   智慧型手機存在已經有一段時間了。

3. **bury** [ˋbɛrɪ] *vt.* 埋藏(不要唸成 [ˋbjʊrɪ])
   例: Those miners were buried alive when the tunnel collapsed.
   隧道倒塌時那些礦工被活埋了。

4. **realize** [ˋrɪəˏlaɪz] *vt.* 體會到
   例: I didn't realize (that) you were not satisfied with the situation.
   我並沒有體會你對情況不滿意。

5. **at the same time** 同時
   例: It is dangerous to drive a car and talk on a cellphone at the same time.
   一邊開車一邊講手機是很危險的一件事。

6. **try out...** 試驗……
   比較:
   try on... 試穿……
   例: Mother tried out her new recipe on us last night.
   老媽昨晚用我們來試驗她的新食譜。
   You should try on the shoes before you buy them.
   妳要買那雙鞋之前應該要先試穿。

7. **popularity** [ˏpɑpjəˋlærətɪ] *n.* 歡迎程度
   gain popularity 受歡迎度增加
   = increase in popularity
   例: Online shopping has gained popularity over the past few years.
   線上購物在過去幾年以來受歡迎的程度已經增加。

8. **acquire** [əˋkwaɪr] *vt.* 取得
   acquisition [ˏækwɪˋzɪʃən] *n.* 取得物
   例: Nick has acquired a reputation for being late.
   尼克是有名的會遲到。

9. **reflect** [rɪˋflɛkt] *vt.* 反射;反映
   例: The window reflected the bright morning sunlight.
   那扇窗戶反射明亮的晨間曙光。
   Our magazine aims to reflect the views of the minority community.
   我們的雜誌目標是要反映出少數社群的觀點。

10. **throughout** [ˏθruˋaʊt] *prep.* 貫穿,從頭到尾
    例: The museum is open daily throughout the year.
    這間博物館全年每天都開放。

11. **adjust** [əˋdʒʌst] *vt.* 調整 & *vt.* & *vi.* (使)適應
    例: You should adjust your language to the age of your audience.
    你應該要按照聽眾的年紀來調整你的用語。

It took me a while to adjust to living in the US.
我花了一段時間才適應在美國的生活。

12. **tasty** [ˋtestɪ] *a.* 美味的

1. **oven** [ˋʌvən] *n.* 烤箱

2. **stove** [stov] *n.* 火爐

3. **natural resources** [ˋrisɔrsɪz] *n.* 自然資源

4. **a light bulb**　　電燈泡

5. **solar** [ˋsolɚ] *a.* 利用太陽能的；太陽的

6. **vendor** [ˋvɛndɚ] *n.* 攤販

7. **grill** [grɪl] *vt.* （用烤架）烤

Sentence Structure Analysis 句型分析

Some of these creative cooking methods...Others are rather new.

❯ 以下介紹一些有關 some 的代名詞用法：

❶ some...others... 一些……另一些……（非限定的兩群）

例: Some of my friends like to play tennis. Others like to play basketball.
我的朋友有些喜歡打網球。另一些則喜歡打籃球。

❷ some...others...still others... 一些……一些……另一些……（非限定的三群）

例: Some of the flowers are red, others are white, and still others are yellow.
有些花是紅色的，有些是白的，另一些則是黃的。

❸ some...the others... 一些……其餘……（用於限定的一個群體）

例: Some of the students in the class failed the test. The others passed.
班上有些學生考試沒過。其他人則都及格了。

Grammar Points 重點來了

Solar cooking is so easy that anyone can do it at home.

❯ 本句使用 "so...that..."（很……所以……）的結構，so（如此）是副詞，之後可置形容詞或副詞，that（以致）是連接詞，引導副詞子句。

例: The teacher is so nice that he is popular among his students.
這位老師人很好，所以他很受學生的歡迎。

比較:

so that 亦是連接詞，表『以便』，引導副詞子句，該子句常與 can, will, may 等助動詞並用。

例: I woke up early so that I could catch the first train.
我早起以便能搭上第一班列車。

1. **How often do you cook your own meals?**

   你通常多久自己煮一次飯？

2. **Do you have any specialties?**

   你有什麼招牌菜嗎？

3. **What cooking methods do you prefer: frying, boiling, baking or steaming?**

   你比較喜歡什麼樣的烹調法：煎、煮、烤還是用蒸的？

4. **Have you ever tried any alternative or unusual cooking methods?**

   你曾嘗試過什麼替代性或不尋常的烹煮方法嗎？

5. **When fuel becomes less available, people have to become more creative.**

   當燃料變得越來越難以取得時，人類就得變得更有創意。

6. **Some traditional cooking methods use little or no fuel.**

   一些傳統的烹煮法幾乎沒什麼使用燃料。

7. **Solar cooking has been around for a while.**

   太陽能烹煮法存在已有一段時間了。

8. **Solar cooking is so easy that anyone can do it at home.**

   太陽能烹煮法很簡便，所以任何人在家都能從事。

Situational Dialogue 打開話匣子 08-03

L = Lulu; A = Allan

 L: I'm curious[1], Allan; how often do you cook your own meals?

 A: Once in a while[2]. Not that often.

 L: Do you have any specialties[3]?

 A: Well, I can heat up[4] a pretty good TV dinner[5], ha! But, seriously[6], I don't really have a specialty when it comes to[7] cooking.

 L: What cooking methods do you prefer: frying[8], boiling[9], baking[10] or steaming[11]?

 A: I usually fry things – it's fast and easy.

 L: Have you ever tried any alternative[12] or unusual cooking methods?

 A: I'm not sure what you mean.

 L: I'm referring to[13] cooking that uses different forms of energy, like solar energy.

 A: Why would people want to do that when they can just use a regular[14] stove or oven?

 L: When fuel becomes less available, people have to become more creative.

 A: I don't know. Solar energy sounds too difficult for me to try.

L: Actually, solar cooking has been around for a while. Solar cooking is so easy that anyone can do it at home.

A: Can you use it to heat up TV dinners?

L: Probably.

 Vocabulary & Phrases 單字片語解密

1. **curious** [ˈkjʊrɪəs] *a.* 好奇的
   be curious about...　　對⋯⋯感到好奇
   例: Babies are curious about everything around them.
   嬰兒對他們四周的東西都感到好奇。

2. **once in a while**　　偶而
   = every now and then
   = from time to time
   = occasionally

3. **specialty** [ˈspɛʃəltɪ] *n.* 招牌菜
   （此處也就等於 a signature dish）

4. **heat up...**　　把⋯⋯加熱
   例: I heated up the leftovers in the microwave for dinner.
   我把剩菜用微波爐加熱當晚餐。

5. **TV dinner**
   電視餐（一種冷凍盒裝食品，加熱後即可食用而不中斷看電視）

6. **seriously** [ˈsɪrɪəslɪ] *adv.* 嚴肅地，正經地
   例: Seriously now, did John really say that or are you just being silly?
   說正經的，約翰真有那麼講或是你亂講的？

7. **when it comes to + N/V-ing**
   提到⋯⋯
   例: When it comes to singing, Frank is second to none.
   提到唱歌，法蘭克真是首屈一指。
   ＊be second to none
   　首屈一指

8. **fry** [fraɪ] *vt.* 煎，炸

9. **boil** [bɔɪl] *vt.* 煮

10. **bake** [bek] *vt.* 烘培

11. **steam** [stim] *vt.* 蒸

12. **alternative** [ɔlˈtɜnətɪv] *a.* 替代性的
    alternative energy resources
    替代性能源

13. **refer to...**　　指的是⋯⋯
    例: When I said that, I was not referring to you.
    我說那件事時，我並不是在說你。

14. **regular** [ˈrɛɡjələ] *a.* 一般的，普通的

Review Exercises 隨堂小測驗

Part A: Choose the correct answer.

_____ **1.** Shirley only cooks once in a _____.
- (A) time
- (B) period
- (C) sometime
- (D) while

_____ **2.** This dish is _____ easy to make _____ anyone can do it.
- (A) too; so
- (B) so; that
- (C) much; but
- (D) very, that

_____ **3.** Some people have trouble doing two things _____ the same time.
- (A) at
- (B) on
- (C) for
- (D) in

_____ **4.** The company _____ around for a long time.
- (A) is
- (B) to be
- (C) has been
- (D) is being

_____ **5.** I think I'll _____ a new recipe tonight.
- (A) try out
- (B) put on
- (C) start to
- (D) get up

Review Exercises　隨堂小測驗

Part B: Match the terms on the left with the definitions on the right by writing the correct letters in the blanks.

____ **1.** tasty

____ **2.** adjust

____ **3.** popularity

____ **4.** available

____ **5.** vendor

____ **6.** acquire

____ **7.** realize

____ **8.** try out

a. to get

b. a seller

c. how much sth or sb is liked

d. to test; to sample

e. delicious

f. able to be used or gotten

g. to change

h. to know; understand

The World's Favorite Goody
世人最愛巧克力

 Warm-up Exercise 暖身練習

1. How much do you like chocolate?
2. What are your favorite chocolate and non-chocolate desserts?

很多人認為吃巧克力容易『上火』，但根據美國有線電視新聞網（CNN）報導，適量食用黑巧克力對控制血壓、抗血栓、保護皮膚都有很大的裨益。但由於巧克力富含熱量和脂肪，如果攝取過量，也會對人體造成負擔。專家建議，一天約兩湯匙（約十公克）的黑巧克力是最適當的量。

巧克力的原產地在墨西哥，主要原料是可可豆。可可豆是一種像椰子般的果實，長在樹幹上會開花結果。後來荷蘭人想到把它做成好喝的可可亞。瑞士人後來發現在可可亞裡加入牛奶，近而成為今日的巧克力。

Topic Reading 主題閱讀
 09-01

How do companies like Hersey get their chocolate? It all starts with the cacao tree. Cacao trees grow fruit, and there are 20 to 40 seeds inside each one. These seeds are cocoa beans and give chocolate its flavor. After the beans are harvested[1], they are left in piles[2] for about a week to ferment[3]. The beans get darker and develop a rich flavor. Then, they are dried, shipped[4] to a chocolate factory, and roasted[5] at high temperatures. Without the roasting, the cocoa beans would not reach their full chocolate flavor.

Once the shells are removed[6], the beans are ground[7] into a thick paste. To get the chocolate we love to eat, sugar and maybe some milk is added. There are many different types of and recipes[8] for chocolate. Belgian chocolates are legendary[9] and viewed as the best in the world. Many other parts of the world have their own special

chocolates. Some are creamy, some are bitter[10], and different ingredients[11] may be added.

Some people mistakenly[12] believe that chocolate truffles contain[13] the expensive and rare fungus that is used in gourmet cooking. In fact, these goodies have creamy chocolate fillings that are coated[14] in

chocolate or cocoa powder, which makes them look similar to the fungus. Another common mistake is thinking that white chocolate is chocolate. Actually, it is mostly milk, sugar, and vanilla. In all its forms, the world loves chocolate!

 Reading Exercises 閱讀隨堂考

____ 1. What is this article mostly about?
    (A) How chocolate is made.
    (B) The history of chocolate.
    (C) Why so many people like chocolate.
    (D) The benefits of eating chocolate.

____ 2. What mistake do some people make about chocolate truffles?
    (A) They are more expensive than other types of chocolate.
    (B) One of the ingredients is a type of expensive fungus.
    (C) They have a very creamy filling in the middle.
    (D) Real truffles are only made in the country of Belgium.

Vocabulary & Phrases   單字片語解密

1. **harvest** [ˈhɑrvɪst] *vt.* 收割，收穫 & *n.* 收成；收成量
   a good / bad harvest
   豐收 / 收成欠佳
   例: The farmers are busy harvesting their crops.
   農夫們正忙著收割他們的作物。
   Farmers are extremely busy during the harvest.
   農夫在收成期間特別忙碌。

2. **pile** [paɪl] *n.* 一堆 & *vt.* 使成堆
   a pile of books / clothes
   一堆書 / 衣服
   例: Mike arranged the documents in neat piles.
   邁可把文件一堆堆整理得很整齊。
   ＊neat [nit] *a.* 整潔的
   Judy piled the boxes one on top of the other.
   茱蒂把箱子一個堆著一個地放好。

3. **ferment** [fɚˈmɛnt] *vi.* & *vt.* （使）發酵
   例: Red wine is made by fermenting grapes.
   紅酒是經由葡萄發酵而製成的。

4. **ship** [ʃɪp] *vt.* 運送
   ship sth to...   將某物運送到……

5. **roast** [rost] *vt.* 烘焙（豆類、堅果）；烤（肉）
   例: Dana roasted some lamb chops for dinner.
   黛娜烤了一些羊排來當晚餐吃。

6. **remove** [rɪˈmuv] *vt.* 移除
   remove A from B
   把 A 從 B 中移除
   例: I used the detergent to remove the stain from the tablecloth.
   我用這款洗滌劑去除桌布上的污漬。

7. **grind** [graɪnd] *vt.* 研磨，碾碎
   （三態為：grind, ground [graʊnd], ground。）
   例: The animal has teeth that grind its food into a pulp.
   這種動物有牙齒能把食物磨成泥狀物。
   ＊pulp [pʌlp] *n.* 果泥，泥狀物

8. **recipe** [ˈrɛsəpɪ] *n.* 食譜（與介詞 for 並用）
   a recipe for chicken soup
   雞湯的食譜

9. **legendary** [ˈlɛdʒəndˌɛrɪ] *a.* 傳說中的；長期以來很出名的

10. **bitter** [ˈbɪtɚ] *a.* 苦的

11. **ingredient** [ɪnˈgridɪənt] *n.* 食材，原料
    例: The key ingredient in this dish is pineapple.
    這道料理的重點材料是鳳梨。

12. **mistakenly** [məˋstekənlɪ] *adv.*
    錯誤地
    mistaken [məˋstekən] *a.* 誤解的
    （與介詞 about 並用）
    例: You're completely mistaken
    about Jane.
    你完全誤解阿珍了。

13. **contain** [kənˋten] *vt.* 包含

14. **coat** [kot] *vt.* 使包裹，使覆蓋
    例: Sal coated the donuts with
    powdered sugar.
    沙爾在甜甜圈上裹了一層糖粉。

1. **cacao tree** [kəˋkɑo ˏtri] *n.* 可可樹
   cocoa bean [ˋkoko ˏbin] *n.* 可可豆

2. **paste** [pest] *n.* 漿糊；糊狀物

3. **truffle** [ˋtrʌfļ] *n.* 塊菌（俗稱松露）

4. **fungus** [ˋfʌŋgəs] *n.*
   真菌（複數為 fungi [ˋfʌndʒaɪ]）

5. **gourmet** [ˋgʊrme] *n.* 美食家 &
   a. 關於美食的

6. **goodies** [ˋgʊdɪz] *n.*
   好吃的東西；吸引人的東西

7. **filling** [ˋfɪlɪŋ] *n.* 內餡，餡料

8. **vanilla** [vəˋnɪlə] *n.* 香草

Sentence Structure Analysis 句型分析

In fact, these goodies have creamy chocolate fillings that are coated in

chocolate or cocoa powder , which makes them look similar to the fungus .

❶ 為主要子句；

❷ 為關係代名詞 that（= which）引導的形容詞子句，修飾先行詞 creamy chocolate fillings；

❸ 為非限定形容詞子句，關係代名詞 which 在本句中代替的是逗點前的整個句子；which 也可用來代替前面句子的部分概念，但不論是哪一種情形，屬非限定形容詞子句時，which 之前都一定要有逗點。

例: Sam did well on his Spanish test, which surprised me.
山姆的西班牙文考得很好，這件事讓我很驚訝。
→ which 代替逗點前的整句
I was asked to give a speech, which I'm good at doing.
有人請我去演講，而這正是我擅長的事。
→ which 代替 give a speech

Grammar Points 重點來了

Then, they are dried, shipped to a chocolate factory, and roasted <u>at</u> high temperatures.

◑ 介詞 at 常與度數／程度／價格／年齡等與數字有關的名詞並用。另外常見的還有：

at the price / cost / expense of + 數字　　以……的價格
at the age of + 年齡　　　　　　　　　　在……歲數時
at the speed of + 速度　　　　　　　　　在……的速度

例: Sandy had her first child at the age of 32.
珊蒂在卅二歲時生了第一個小孩。
Susan drove at the speed of 30 miles an hour.
蘇珊當時以時速卅英里的速度開車。

1. Tom has a sweet tooth, but he also has a lot of cavities.

   湯姆愛吃甜食,但他也有很多蛀牙。
   ＊have a sweet tooth　愛吃甜食

2. I'm a "chocoholic!" I just can't get enough of the stuff.

   我是個『巧克力狂』!那種東西我就是怎麼吃都吃不夠。

3. I kind of go for the sweeter stuff like milk chocolate and even white chocolate.

   我似乎比較喜歡像是牛奶巧克力甚至是白巧克力等較甜一點的東西。
   ＊kind of　　有點兒
   　go for...　喜歡……(＝like...)

4. Real chocolate is quite expensive, so some companies use a chocolate substitute that's full of chemicals.

   真的巧克力相當昂貴,所以有些公司會使用充滿化學物質的巧克力替代品。

5. Some farmers use dogs to sniff out where truffles are buried.

   有些農夫會用狗來嗅出松露埋藏處。
   ＊sniff [snɪf] vt. 嗅

6. Chocolate is said to act as a natural antidepressant.

   巧克力據稱能被用作天然的抗憂鬱藥。
   ＊act as...　作為……

7. Eating chocolate in moderation is good for you.

   適量地吃巧克力對你有好處。
   ＊in moderation　適量地,適度地
   　moderation [ˌmɑdəˋreʃən] n. 適度,節制

8. If you want to taste high-quality chocolate, be ready to pay an arm and a leg!

   如果你想要品嚐高品質的巧克力,準備好要付很多錢吧!
   ＊pay an arm and a leg　付很多錢
   ＝ pay a lot of money

Situational Dialogue 打開話匣子 　　🔊 09-03

W = Willy; A = Anne

 W: I think I have an addiction[1]. I may need to seek[2] professional help!

 A: Really? What are you addicted to?

 W: Chocolate! I'm a "chocoholic." I just can't get enough of the stuff.

 A: I know what you mean. I love chocolate as well.

 W: Last year I took a trip to Brussels and tasted some of the world's best chocolate. It was so good that I actually considered[3] moving to Belgium!

 A: Do you prefer dark chocolate or milk chocolate?

 W: Dark! The darker, the better!

 A: Really? I kind of go for[4] the sweeter stuff like milk chocolate and even white chocolate.

 W: To me, when they add too much sugar and milk, it detracts[5] from the original flavor of the cocoa beans.

 A: You know, I've never really tasted very many darker kinds of chocolate.

 W: OK, tomorrow I'll bring you a dark chocolate that is almost bitter, but the flavor is still amazing!

 A: Cool! I'd love to try that.

Vocabulary & Phrases 單字片語解密

1. **addiction** [əˋdɪkʃən] *n.*
   上癮（與介詞 to 並用）
   addicted [əˋdɪktɪd] *a.*
   上癮的（與介詞 to 並用）
   be addicted to...　　對……上癮
   例: My father is now fighting his
   addiction to alcohol.
   我父親現在正在對抗酒癮。

   Jack is addicted to computer
   games.
   傑克對電腦遊戲上癮了。

2. **seek** [sik] *vt.* 尋求
   = look for...
   = search for...
   例: The girl managed to calm down
   and seek help from a neighbor.
   那個女孩設法鎮定下來並向鄰居求
   援。

3. **consider + V-ing**　　考慮……
   例: I'm considering moving to the
   US.
   我正在考慮要移居到美國。

4. **go for sth**　　選擇 / 喜歡某物
   例: I think I'll go for the fruit salad.
   我想我會選擇水果沙拉。

5. **detract** [dɪˋtrækt] *vi.* 減損，降低
   detract from...
   = take away from...
   例: I won't let anything detract from
   my enjoyment of the trip.
   我不會讓任何事減損我這趟旅程的
   樂趣。

Review Exercises 隨堂小測驗

Part A: Fill in the blanks with the correct answers.

_____ 1. The cocoa beans are roasted _____ high temperatures.
(A) in
(B) for
(C) with
(D) at

_____ 2. All these chocolates look great. May I have _____ ?
(A) another
(B) other
(C) the other
(D) others

_____ 3. I _____ of ordering a piece of chocolate cake.
(A) thinking
(B) think
(C) have thinking
(D) am thinking

_____ 4. As soon as I _____ chocolate, I have to eat it!
(A) am seeing
(B) see
(C) saw
(D) seen

_____ 5. George _____ believed his girlfriend loved all kinds of desserts.
(A) mistake
(B) mistaken
(C) mistook
(D) mistakenly

Review Exercises 隨堂小測驗

Part B: Each sentence has a mistake in it. Correct the mistakes and write the corrected sentences in the blanks below.

1. My brother is addict to chocolate.

   _____

2. Were you knowing that chocolate is made from seeds?

   _____

3. I've never real liked the taste of bitter chocolate.

   _____

4. Chocolate truffles look similar with real truffles.

   _____

5. There are still one chocolate left in the box.

   _____

Slow Food vs. Fast Food
慢食享生活

![warm-up]()**Warm-up Exercise　暖身練習**

1. What kind of fast food do you like to eat?

2. How often do you go to fast food restaurants?

在現代人普遍匆忙、講求速度及效率的社會中，慢食主義正在世界各饕客間逐漸竄紅，蔚為風潮。

而『慢食』，並不只是慢慢吃而已。慢食主張的精神是，我們吃的東西，應該是以更緩和的步調去培植、去烹煮，和食用。佩屈尼（慢食組織的發起人 Carlo Petrini）表示，慢吞吞並非慢食的目標，慢的真義是指你必須能掌握自己的生活節奏，仔細品味、珍惜傳統，領悟食材和物種，感激農民的耕耘，欣賞廚師手藝的態度，這樣世界才會更加豐富。所以，『慢食』是一股思潮，也是一種平衡，更是人對自己生活節奏的自主意識。

也許，只是一碗平凡的牛肉麵、一塊豆腐；也許，只是撇開工作煩憂，從容享受一頓與家人在一起的晚餐，屬於慢食的滋味，其實是來自於內心回歸生命原點；當你找到了，那就是屬於你的好味道。舒特曼曾說：『走急的人看不見地上的釘子，煩惱的人享受不到幸福。』

Topic Reading 主題閱讀 10-01

W hen was the last time you went to a McDonald's or KFC? As life gets busier, more and more of us eat fast food on a regular basis[1]. Although we know this is not the healthiest choice, it often seems like too much trouble to cook for ourselves. In 1986, a group of people in Rome gathered to protest[2] against the opening of the first McDonald's in Italy. They wanted to encourage people to take a greater interest in[3] food and to make eating a more meaningful[4] experience. By 1989, the Slow Food Movement and organization were born.

Members of Slow Food believe that our dependence[5] on fast food is causing local food traditions to disappear. They believe that food represents a people's culture and history, which is something that should be cherished[6]. They also worry that using land to grow only certain vegetables, fruits, or animal breeds for businesses like fast food restaurants will cause many native food sources to disappear completely[7]. This would mean a loss of food variety[8] available to consumers.

Slow Food now has over 83,000 members and 800 offices in 122 countries, such as France, the United Kingdom, Switzerland, Germany, Japan, and Taiwan.

The guiding principle is "Good, Clean, Fair." Good means that taste is a priority. Clean means that the food is healthy and nutritious. Plus, animal welfare[9] and environmental protection must be taken into consideration[10]. Fair is the idea that everyone has a right to eat healthy and delicious foods. It also means that those people who produce the foods should be paid well so that their future generations[11] can carry on[12] their work. They hope that once people rediscover the slow way of eating, an unhealthy fast food lifestyle will be a thing of the past.

 Reading Exercises 閱讀隨堂考

____ 1. According to the reading, why are more people eating fast food these days?
  (A) Because people are very busy.
  (B) Because the food is delicious.
  (C) Because it's a meaningful experience.
  (D) Because other food sources are disappearing.

____ 2. What happened in 1989?
  (A) The Slow Food Movement was born.
  (B) Some countries banned McDonald's.
  (C) Romans protested against KFC.
  (D) The first McDonald's opened in Rome.

Vocabulary & Phrases 單字片語解密

1. **on a regular basis**
   定期地，固定地
   例: Rick gets check-ups on a regular basis.
   瑞克會定期做身體檢查。

2. **protest** [prə`tɛst] *vi.* 抗議，反對
   （與 against 並用）
   例: I strongly protest against the death penalty.
   我極力反對死刑。

3. **take an interest in...**
   對……產生興趣
   例: David is now taking an interest in politics.
   大衛現在對政治感興趣了。

4. **meaningful** [`minɪŋfḷ] *a.* 有意義的，意義深長的
   例: This photo album is very meaningful to me.
   這本相簿對我來說深具意義。

5. **dependence** [dɪ`pɛndəns] *n.* 依賴，依靠
   例: Singapore has been trying to reduce its dependence on imported water.
   新加坡不斷試圖減少對進口水的依賴。

6. **cherish** [`tʃɛrɪʃ] *vt.* 珍愛，珍惜
   例: I'll always cherish my childhood memories.
   我將永遠珍惜我的童年回憶。

7. **completely** [kəm`plitlɪ] *adv.* 完全地，徹底地
   例: Victor completely forgot his mother's birthday.
   維克多把他媽媽的生日忘得一乾二淨。

8. **variety** [və`raɪətɪ] *n.* 種類，品種
   例: The farmer bred many varieties of roses.
   這個農夫培育出許多品種的玫瑰。

9. **welfare** [`wɛl,fɛr] *n.* 福祉；幸福
   例: Dina's only concern is her child's welfare.
   蒂娜唯一關心的事就是她孩子的幸福。

10. **take...into consideration**
    考慮到……
    例: We have to take budget into consideration when planning a trip.
    我們在計劃旅遊時必須要考慮到預算。

11. **generation** [,dʒɛnə`reʃən] *n.* 一代（人）
    例: Our generation gets married at a later age.
    我們這一代的人較晚婚。

12. **carry on...** 繼續做 / 堅持……
    例: Al carried on his business against all odds.
    儘管困難重重，艾爾仍繼續打拼事業。
    ＊against the odds
    不顧一切困難

1. **movement** [`muvmənt] *n.*（政治、社會方面的）運動

2. **guiding principle** *n.* 指導原則

3. **environmental protection** *n.* 環境保護

4. **rediscover** [ˌridɪ`skʌvɚ] *vt.* 重新發現

5. **lifestyle** [`laɪf͵staɪl] *n.* 生活方式

Sentence Structure Analysis 句型分析

Members of Slow Food believe that our dependence on fast food is
❶ ❷ ❸

causing local food traditions to disappear .

❶ 為本句主詞；

❷ 為本句動詞，由於主詞為 Members of Slow Food，故動詞要使用複數動詞；

❸ 為 that 引導的名詞子句。

　　a) 子句中的主詞 our dependence（我們依賴）須與介詞 on 並用。

　　b) cause sb/sth to V，表『造成某人／某事……』。

It also means that those people who produce the foods should be paid
❶ ❷ ❸

well so that their future generations can carry on their work .

❶ 為代名詞，作本句主詞，表前一句所提到『公平的這種概念』；

❷ 為本句動詞；

❸ 為 that 引導的名詞子句，作 means 的受詞。該子句中主詞為 those people，
之後 who produce the foods 則為形容詞子句，修飾之前的先行詞 those
people，子句中述詞為 should be paid well，之後的連接詞 so that 則表『如
此』，引導副詞子句，該副詞子句常與助動詞 can, will, may 等並用。

Grammar Points 重點來了

They believe that food represents a people's culture and history...

▶ people 在本句並不作 person 的複數形用，而是表『民族，種族』，是可數名
詞，此時 people 本身為單數，故須加 -s 以構成複數形。

　　例: All of the English-speaking peoples share a common language.
　　　　所有的英語系民族都使用同一種語言。

...once people rediscover the slow way of eating...

▶ Once + 主詞 + 動詞，主詞 + 動詞　　一……就……

= As soon as + 主詞 + 動詞，主詞 + 動詞

= The instant + 主詞 + 動詞，主詞 + 動詞

= The moment + 主詞 + 動詞，主詞 + 動詞

1. What's your opinion of the food served in fast food restaurants such as McDonald's and KFC?

   你對於麥當勞及肯德基這類速食餐廳所提供的食物有何意見？

2. Do you think people eat too much fast food? What about yourself?

   你認為人們吃太多速食了嗎？你自己本身呢？

3. Do you ever worry about the negative effects of eating fast food?

   你會擔心吃速食所帶來的負面影響嗎？

4. It often seems like too much trouble to cook for ourselves.

   自己做飯往往似乎又太過於麻煩。

5. Have you ever heard of the Slow Food Movement?

   你有沒有聽過慢食運動？

6. Members of Slow Food believe that our dependence on fast food is causing local food traditions to disappear.

   慢食組織的成員相信，我們對速食的依賴會造成地方飲食傳統的消失。

7. They wanted to encourage people to take a greater interest in food and to make eating a more meaningful experience.

   他們想要鼓勵人們對食物產生更大的興趣，並使飲食變成更有意義的體驗。

8. What type of food do you enjoy eating the most?

   你最愛吃什麼類型的食物呢？

Situational Dialogue 打開話匣子 10-03

P = Pauline; S = Stewart

 P: Stewart, what's your opinion of the food served in fast food restaurants such as McDonald's and KFC?

 S: I like it – it's convenient, and it tastes pretty good.

 P: Do you ever worry about the negative effects[1] of eating fast food?

 S: Not really. I know that it can make you fat.

 P: Yes, and it can be unhealthy[2] in other ways.

 S: I'm always too busy to cook at home.

 P: Yes, it often seems like too much trouble to cook for ourselves. But that doesn't mean we need to eat junk food all the time[3]. Have your ever heard of the Slow Food Movement?

 S: No, I haven't.

 P: Members of Slow Food believe that our dependence on fast food is causing local food traditions to disappear. They wanted to encourage people to take a greater interest in food and to make eating a more meaningful experience.

 S: Hey, do you want to go to KFC for lunch?

 P: What do you think?

 S: Hmm... I guess not.

Vocabulary & Phrases 單字片語解密

1. **negative effects**　　負面影響
   positive effects　　正面影響
   effect [ɪˈfɛkt] *n.* 影響

2. **unhealthy** [ʌnˈhɛlθɪ] *a.* 不健康的

3. **all the time**　　一直

Review Exercises 隨堂小測驗

Part A: Fill in the blanks with the correct answers.

_____ 1. _____ soon as Mike learned junk food was unhealthy, he stopped eating it.
(A) So
(B) As
(C) When
(D) Once

_____ 2. The negative _____ of smoking are numerous.
(A) effects
(B) affects
(C) infects
(D) rejects

_____ 3. It was a short but _____ relationship.
(A) meaning
(B) meanings
(C) meanful
(D) meaningful

_____ 4. Robert's wife told him he should _____ a greater interest in his health.
(A) take
(B) make
(C) do
(D) be

_____ 5. When making a difficult decision, many things must _____ taken into consideration.
(A) to
(B) be
(C) have
(D) use

Review Exercises 隨堂小測驗

Part B: Each sentence has a mistake in it. Correct the mistakes and write the corrected sentences in the blanks below.

1. Over time, some animals have completely disappear.

_____

2. What do you think the Slow Food Movement?

_____

3. I'm not sure whether or not most people care environmental protection.

_____

4. Have you take into consideration that traffic might be heavy?

_____

5. Eat healthy means consuming lots of fruit and vegetables.

_____

Danger in the Salad Bowl
沙拉碗中的危機

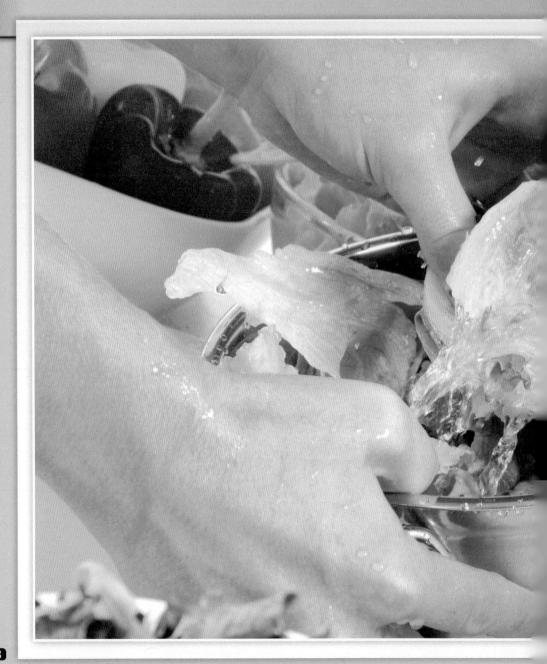

1. Have you ever been sick after eating food? Do you remember what made you sick?

2. What type of uncooked food have you eaten? Did you worry about eating it?

林口長庚醫院毒物科主任林杰樑表示，某些食物之所以被列為危險食物均與食用方式有關，並非食物本身不健康；國外習慣吃生菜拉沙，葉菜類從栽種、運送到食用都容易受到細菌汙染，而國人習慣熟食，只要煮沸，可以殺死絕大多數的細菌。

喜歡吃生菜沙拉的人，應注意清洗過程中要使用臭氧、清水、消毒，將殘留的農藥或細菌清洗乾淨。林杰樑看過有人生菜沒清洗乾淨，上面還有蝸牛，還自解是『這證明是生機飲食』。他警告，蝸牛身上可能有廣東住血線蟲，一旦感染就可能寄生腦部，台灣已發現過病例。

Topic Reading   主題閱讀   11-01

💀 The Ten Riskiest Foods 💀

| 1 Leafy Greens | 2 Eggs | 3 Tuna | 4 Oysters | 5 Potatoes |

| 6 Cheese | 7 Ice Cream | 8 Tomatoes | 9 Sprouts | 10 Berries |

When you think of high-risk foods, the first thing that may come to mind[1] is the beef imported[2] from the US because of mad cow disease or the highly poisonous blowfish in Japan. However, a new study suggests that the riskiest foods are far closer to home. A recent report released by the American consumer watchdog, the Center for Science in the Public Interest[3], names the 10 foods which have caused the largest number of food poisoning cases in the US. The guilty[4] foods are almost all central to[5] the American diet, and some are quite surprising.

Leafy greens, such as lettuce, top[6] the list. According to the report, leafy greens have been linked to[7] more than 350 food poisoning outbreaks[8], affecting[9] more than 13,000 people between

1990 and 2008. The problem is that the leaves can become infected[10], often with the dangerous E. coli bacteria（大腸桿菌）, and can cross-contaminate[11] other foods. Some of the other risky foods are less surprising. It is well known that eggs, number two on the list, can carry salmonella（沙門氏菌）. Oysters are all the way up at number four in spite of being only a small part of most people's diets. However, the other foods listed include such staples as potatoes, which caused nearly 4,000 cases of food poisoning.

The full list also includes tuna, ice cream, cheese, tomatoes, bean sprouts, and berries. Although poor hygiene and lack of cleaning are usually the causes of the problem instead of the actual food, these statistics[12] are worrying. The US has a huge and complex[13] food chain, and it is very easy for bacteria like salmonella or E. coli to enter the cycle. While part of the problem is solvable through legislation, the real solution[14] is to wash and prepare everything you eat carefully.

 Reading Exercises 閱讀隨堂考

_____ 1. What does the reading mainly discuss?
    (A) The dangers of eating certain foods.
    (B) Mad Cow Disease in the US.
    (C) The number of food poisoning cases worldwide.
    (D) Why Americans are not very healthy.

_____ 2. What type of food is NOT mentioned in the reading?
    (A) Cheese.
    (B) Ice cream.
    (C) Chicken.
    (D) Potatoes.

Vocabulary & Phrases 單字片語解密

1. come to mind 浮現在腦海中

例: It just came to mind that I'd forgotten my friend's birthday.

= It just occurred to me that I'd forgotten my friend's birthday.
我剛想起來我忘記朋友的生日了。

2. import [ɪm`pɔrt] *vt.* 進口，引進 &
[`ɪmpɔrt] *n.* 進口

export [ɪks`pɔrt] *vt.* 出口，輸出 &
[`ɛkspɔrt] *n.* 出口

例: Mr. Lin imports coffee from Indonesia into Taiwan.
林先生從印尼進口咖啡到台灣。

3. in the public interest
為了公眾利益

in the interest of... 為了……著想

例: In the interest of safety, smoking is forbidden here.
為了安全考量，此處禁止吸煙。

4. guilty [`gɪltɪ] *a.* 有過失的；有罪的
be guilty of... 有……的罪

例: The evidence shows that Gary is guilty of robbing the bank.
證據顯示蓋瑞犯下搶劫銀行的罪行。

5. be central to...
是……的核心；對……很重要

例: My mother is central to keeping our family together.
我媽媽是維繫我們全家的重心。

6. top [tɑp] *vt.* 位居……的首位；高於
top the list 在名單上位居第一名

例: Our company's sales topped those of our main rival's.
我們公司的銷售量超過我們的主要競爭對手。

7. be linked to + N/V-ing
和……有關

例: Premature aging and other health problems are linked to worrying too much.
提早老化及其他健康問題均與煩惱過度有關。

＊premature [ˌprimə`tʃur] *a.* 早熟的，過早的

8. outbreak [`aʊtˌbrek] *n.* 爆發
break out （戰爭、疾病等）爆發

例: They had escaped to the US shortly before war broke out in 1941.
他們在一九四一年戰爭爆發前不久就逃到了美國。

9. affect [ə`fɛkt] *vt.* （疾病）侵襲；影響

例: The disease affects the central nervous system.
這種疾病會侵害中樞神經系統。

Don't let his criticism affect your mood.
別讓他的批評影響你的心情。

10. infect [ɪn`fɛkt] *vt.* 使感染
be infected with... 感染到……

例: Many people in this area have been infected with the flu.
這一區有很多人都染上流感。

11. cross-contaminate
[ˌkrɔskən`tæməˌnet] *vt.* 交叉污染
contaminate [kən`tæməˌnet] *vt.* 污染

例: Chemical waste from the factory was contaminating the river nearby.
那間工廠排放的化學廢棄物污染了附近的河川。

12. **statistics** [stə'tɪstɪks] *n.* 統計數字
（視為複數）；統計學（不可數）

例: Statistics show / suggest that
women live longer than men.
統計數字顯示女性活得比男性長。

There is a compulsory course in
statistics.
有一堂統計學的必修課。

＊compulsory [kəm'pʌlsərɪ] *a.*
強制的；必修的

13. **complex** ['kamplɛks / kəm'plɛks] *a.*
複雜的

= complicated ['kamplə,ketɪd] *a.*

例: The doctor's explanation
was too complex for me to
understand.
那位醫師的解釋太過複雜了，我無
法了解。

14. **solution** [sə'luʃən] *n.* 解決之道
（與介詞 to 並用）

例: There is no simple solution to
the problem.
這個問題沒有簡單的解決之道。

1. **high-risk** [,haɪ'rɪsk] *a.* 高風險的

2. **mad cow disease**　　狂牛症

3. **poisonous** ['pɔɪzənəs] *a.* 有毒的

4. **blowfish** ['blo,fɪʃ] *n.* 河豚

5. **risky** ['rɪskɪ] *a.* 有風險的

6. **watchdog** ['watʃ,dɔg] *n.* 監察組織

7. **leafy** ['lifɪ] *a.* 多葉的

8. **lettuce** ['lɛtɪs] *n.* 生菜，萵苣

9. **E. coli bacteria**　　大腸桿菌
＊E. coli 為 Escherichia [,ɛskə'rɪkɪə]
coli ['kolaɪ] 的縮寫。

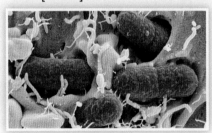

10. **salmonella** [,sælmə'nɛlə] *n.* 沙門氏
菌

11. **oyster** ['ɔɪstɚ] *n.* 蠔，牡蠣

12. **staple** ['stepḷ] *n.* 主食

13. **tuna** ['tunə] *n.* 鮪魚

14. **bean sprout** ['bin ,spraʊt] *n.* 豆芽

15. **hygiene** ['haɪdʒin] *n.* 衛生

16. **food chain** ['fud ,tʃen] *n.* 食物鏈

17. **solvable** ['salvəbḷ] *a.* 可以解決的

18. **legislation** [,lɛdʒɪs'leʃən] *n.* 立法，
法律

Sentence Structure Analysis 句型分析

A recent report (which was) released by the American consumer watchdog ,
❶   ❷

the Center for Science in the Public Interest , names the 10 foods
❸   ❹   ❺

which have caused the largest number of food poisoning cases in the US .
❻

❶ 為本句主詞；

❷ 為形容詞子句化簡而成的分詞片語，用以修飾先行詞 A recent report（最近的一份報導）。released 之前省略了 which was；

❸ 為 the American consumer watchdog（美國消費者權益保護機構）的同位語；

❹ 為本句的動詞；

❺ 為本句的受詞；

❻ 為另一形容詞子句，用以形容先行詞 the 10 foods（那十種食物）。

Grammar Points 重點來了

However, a new study suggests that the riskiest foods are far closer to home.

▶ 可用來修飾比較級形容詞或副詞的通常有下列六個副詞：far, much, a lot, a great deal, still, even。

例: Mary is far more talented in music than her sister.
瑪麗比她姊姊更有音樂天分。

Some of the other risky foods are less surprising.

▶ 要使用比較級描述『較不』時，須使用 less，之後形容詞或副詞不管是幾個音節，都是使用原形。

less + 原級形容詞或副詞　　較不……

例: It is less difficult to learn English than French.
學英語沒學法語那麼難。

1. Do you eat salads very often?

你常吃沙拉嗎？

2. Eating cooked vegetables on a regular basis is good for your health.

經常吃煮熟的菜有益你的健康。

3. A US study shows that eating lettuce can be dangerous to eat.

美國一項研究顯示吃生菜可能有危險。

4. According to the report, leafy greens have been linked to more than 350 food poisoning outbreaks.

根據該報導指出，綠色蔬菜和三百五十多起食物中毒事件有關。

5. The problem is that the leaves can become contaminated.

問題在於蔬菜的葉子可能被感染了。
＊contaminate [kənˈtæməˌnet] *vt.* 感染（物品）

6. Poor hygiene and lack of cleaning are usually the causes of the problem.

衛生條件差以及缺少清洗通常都是問題的根源。

7. It's kind of ironic that salads can be dangerous to eat.

吃生菜沙拉可能會有危險，這件事還真是有點諷刺啊。
＊kind of　　有點（＝ a little）
　ironic [aɪˈrɑnɪk] *a.* 諷刺的

8. The real solution is to wash and prepare everything you eat carefully.

真正的解決之道在於仔細地清洗並準備你要吃的每樣東西。

Situational Dialogue 打開話匣子 11-03

M = Max; A = Annie

 M: Hey, where can you find salads in Taipei? Can you recommend[1] any good restaurants?

 A: Actually, there are a lot of places where you can find salads. Do you eat salads very often?

 M: Yes, I love them. They are so healthy.

 A: In general[2], yes, but I read about a US study that shows eating lettuce can be dangerous to eat.

 M: I didn't know that.

 A: According to the report, leafy greens have been linked to more than 350 food poisoning outbreaks.

 M: Is that right? I wonder why salads can be so dangerous.

 A: The problem is that the leaves can become contaminated. Poor hygiene and lack of cleaning are usually the causes of the problem.

 M: It's kind of ironic[3] that salads can be dangerous to eat.

 A: I agree. The real solution is to wash and prepare everything you eat carefully.

 M: That sounds like good advice[4]. Thanks for the tip[5].

 A: Sure. My pleasure.

1. **recommend** [ˌrɛkə'mɛnd] *vt.* 推薦
   recommend sth to sb
   把某物推薦給某人
   recommend sb for sth
   推薦某人做某事
   例: I recommended the book to all my students.
   我向所有的學生推薦了這本書。
   Cindy was recommended for the job by a colleague.
   辛蒂由同事推薦來從事這份工作。

2. **In general,...** 一般來説，……
   = Generally speaking,...
   = On the whole,...
   = In most cases,...
   例: In general, the more you give, the more you get.
   一般來説，你給的越多，就得到越多。

3. **ironic** [aɪ'rɑnɪk] *a.* 諷刺的
   例: It's ironic Nick went into teaching. He used to hate school.
   尼克會選擇教書真是諷刺。他過去曾經很討厭上學。

4. **advice** [əd'vaɪs] *n.*
   建議（集合名詞，不可數）（之後與介詞 on 並用）
   an advice (×)
   → a piece of advice 一則建議
   some advice 一些建議
   a lot of advice 很多建議
   take / follow sb's advice
   聽從 / 遵循某人的建議
   例: Let me give you a piece of advice on how to prepare for the exam.
   讓我給你一個建議，告訴你該如何準備那個考試。

Take my advice, or you'll regret it for the rest of your life.
聽我的建議，否則你一輩子都會後悔。
You should follow your doctor's advice.
你應該要遵循醫生的建議。

5. **tip** [tɪp] *n.*
   訣竅（與介詞 on 或 for 並用）
   例: I need some useful tips on how to save money.
   我需要一些針對該如何省錢的實用訣竅。

Review Exercises   隨堂小測驗

Part A: Fill in the blanks with the correct answers.

____ 1. This information is very _____.
   (A) worry
   (B) worried
   (C) worrying
   (D) worries

____ 2. I strongly believe Doug is guilty _____ lying to me.
   (A) to
   (B) of
   (C) for
   (D) about

____ 3. We must make sure not to harm the food _____.
   (A) chain
   (B) link
   (C) interest
   (D) solution

____ 4. Disease is often _____ to poor hygiene.
   (A) predicted
   (B) infected
   (C) linked
   (D) protected

____ 5. _____, fried food is not a healthy food choice.
   (A) Top the list
   (B) In general
   (C) According to
   (D) Occurred to me

Review Exercises 隨堂小測驗

Part B: In the sentences below, circle the correct words in the blanks.

1. Ron is the healthier / healthiest person I know.

2. Olive oil is central for / to cooking in Mediterranean countries.

3. Eating certain foods may carry / worry some health risks.

4. Judy got infected / affected with the same illness her friend had.

5. Of all the foods he liked, pizza topped his link / list.

6. Let me give you a piece of advise / advice.

7. The more you learn, the more you know / are knowing.

8. I'm sorry; nothing come / comes to mind right now.

9. Be careful; those wild berries are poisoning / poisonous.

10. These statistic / statistics are really something to worry about.

Industrial Farming: The Pros and Cons
工業農牧：利與弊

Warm-up Exercise　暖身練習

1. Do you worry about all the chemicals in the food you eat? Why or why not?

2. Have you ever been to a farm? What do you remember about the farming methods you saw?

數千年來，許多文化皆仰賴農牧業來提供食物。工業農牧的誕生或多或少受到工業革命的影響而連帶開始發生，並使工業化農牧成為現代農業中重要的一環。科學家發現農作物生長的關鍵要素為氮、鉀和磷，也可成為培育農作物所需的化學肥料主體。在二十世紀的前二十年，也就是直到一九二〇年，科學家發現了維生素及其在動物體內所產生的營養作用。人們深知若能有效使牲畜補充維生素，便能使牲畜開始在室內培養長大，也不需暴露在惡烈的生長環境。而疫苗和抗生素又有助於預防疾病在擁擠的居住環境下蔓延，有效地控制了牲畜在擁擠生活環境下所造成的疾病。

此外，化學製品在二次世界大戰中的頻繁使用、開發，也間接產生了更有效益的合成農藥，配合航運網絡及技術的成長，更能進一步將農產品妥善地運送到各地。工業化農牧為全世界六十億人口提供了食物。但相對的，從事農耕的人口卻從三十年代的百分之二十四驟降至現今百分之一點五。雖然工業農牧的重點是降低生產成本，以創造更多的生產力，但另一方面，除了文章內所提到的負面影響，也造成了從事農業的就業人口慢慢地流失。

Topic Reading 主題閱讀 12-01

M odern industrial farming uses methods that produce the greatest amounts at the lowest cost. That is[1], farmers can produce more food on smaller areas of land, allowing the public to buy cheaper food.

Industrial farming provides food for seven billion people around the world. Many techniques are applied to[2] produce these crops. For example, chemicals are heavily used to help plants grow and to protect them from insects. Also, genetically modified seeds have been created to produce more crops than normal seeds.

Besides crops, industrial farming also involves factory farming of animals. In the 1920s, scientists discovered the benefits[3] of vitamins, vaccines and antibiotics. By giving animals vitamins, farmers can raise them indoors. Vaccines and antibiotics help to prevent the spread of diseases that occur in crowded living conditions[4]. In addition, giving the animals other kinds of drugs helps them to grow bigger and faster.

Though industrial farming provides people with sufficient[5] amounts of food, many of these techniques carry risks[6]. For example, the intensive[7] use of water, energy, and chemicals causes more environmental pollution. In some places, such as Japan and Europe, genetically modified foods are believed to be[8] unsafe to eat and even banned[9]. Factory farming has serious effects on[10] the environment as well as the health of humans. Eighteen percent of all global greenhouse gas emissions is caused by waste from these factory-farmed animals.

Another problem is that the animals are given antibiotics, which can result in[11] bacteria becoming drug-resistant. This can lead to infections in humans. Some of the drugs given to animals have also been linked to[12] serious diseases, such as cancer. Therefore, as consumers, people should be more conscious[13] of the foods they purchase[14]. This way, farming can be set on the right track[15].

Reading Exercises 閱讀隨堂考

____ 1. Why does industrial farming result in cheaper food prices?
 (A) The machines used in farming are cheap to buy.
 (B) People refuse to pay higher prices for this type of food.
 (C) More food is grown on less land.
 (D) Less water is required for crops and animals.

____ 2. What does the reading advise consumers to do?
 (A) To stop buying genetically modified food.
 (B) To be more aware of the food they buy.
 (C) To protest against industrial farming.
 (D) To work hard to stop global warming.

Vocabulary & Phrases 單字片語解密

1. **That is (to say),** 主詞 + 動詞
   換言之⋯⋯

   例: I passed the entrance exam. That is, I got into a top school.
   我通過了入學考。也就是說，我能進頂尖的學校就讀了。

2. **apply** [əˈplaɪ] *vt.* 應用，運用

   例: The new law was applied to reduce crime.
   這條新法規是用來減少犯罪。

3. **benefit** [ˈbɛnəfɪt] *n.* 利益，好處

   例: It will be to your benefit to arrive early.
   早點抵達對你有好處。

4. **living / housing / working conditions**
   生活 / 居住 / 工作環境

   注意: 表示『環境』時，condition 一字常用複數。

5. **sufficient** [səˈfɪʃənt] *a.* 足夠的，充分的

   例: These reasons are not sufficient to justify the ban.
   這些原因不足以成為該禁令的正當理由。

6. **carry risks** 帶有風險

7. **intensive** [ɪnˈtɛnsɪv] *a.* 密集的
   an intensive language course
   密集的語言課程

8. **be believed to V** 被認為⋯⋯

   例: The vases are believed to be worth over $2,000 each.
   那些花瓶被認為每個價值超過兩千美元。

9. **ban** [bæn] *vt.* 禁止
   ban sb from + N/V-ing
   禁止某人從事⋯⋯

   例: Ted was banned from leaving Japan while the case was being investigated.
   在該案進行調查期間，泰德被禁止離開日本。

10. **have a serious / huge effect on...**
    對⋯⋯有很嚴重 / 很大的影響

    例: My high school teacher has a huge effect on me.
    我的高中老師對我有很大的影響。

11. **result in...** 導致 / 造成⋯⋯
    = **lead to...**
    = **bring about...**

    例: Over-exercising can lead to injuries.
    過度運動會造成身體傷害。

12. **be linked to...**
    = **be related to...**
    = **be connected to...**
    與⋯⋯有關連 / 有關係

    例: The accident was linked to the dense fog.
    這場意外的發生與濃霧有關。

13. **conscious** [ˈkɑnʃəs] *a.* 意識到的，注意到的

    例: Henry became conscious of having failed his parents.
    = Henry became aware of having failed his parents.
    亨利意識到他已經辜負了父母的期望。

14. **purchase** [`pɝtʃəs] *vt.* 購買，採購

例: Sally purchased a new car from me three days ago.
莎莉三天前向我買了一輛新車。

15. **on the right track** 方向正確

例: We haven't found a cure yet ─ but we are on the right track.
我們還沒找到解藥──但我們方向正確。

1. **industrial farming**
工業化農牧（即是指在室內進行大規模的畜牧）
= factory farming

2. **technique** [tɛkˋnik] *n.* 技術

3. **genetically modified** *a.* 基因改造的

4. **vaccine** [vækˋsin] *n.* 疫苗

5. **antibiotic** [ˌæntɪbaɪˋɑtɪk] *n.* 抗生素

6. **greenhouse gas** *n.* 溫室氣體

7. **emission** [ɪˋmɪʃən] *n.* 排氣；排放物

8. **bacteria** [ˋbæktɪrɪə] *n.* 細菌

9. **resistant** [rɪˋzɪstənt] *a.* 抗……的
drug-resistant 抗藥性的

Sentence Structure Analysis 句型分析

Another problem ❶ is ❷ that the animals are given antibiotics ❸ ,

which can result in bacteria becoming drug-resistant ❹

❶ 為本句主詞；

❷ 為本句動詞；

❸ 為 that 引導的名詞子句，作主詞補語用。用來補充說明另一個問題所在；

❹ 為 which 引導的形容詞子句，修飾先行詞 antibiotics。

 Grammar Points 重點來了

Industrial farming provides food for seven billion people around the world.

▶ 本句使用句型 "provide sth for sb"，此外也可替換成 "provide sb with sth"，故原句可改寫如下：

Industrial farming <u>provides</u> seven billion people around the world <u>with</u> food.

In addition, giving the animals other kinds of drugs helps them to grow bigger and faster.

▶ 由於本句主詞為動名詞片語 giving the animals other kinds of drugs，故視之為單數，動詞也要使用單數動詞 helps。

1. Do you pay much attention to the ingredients in the food you buy?

   你會重視所購買的食品成份嗎？

2. Sometimes I worry about all the drugs and chemicals in the food we eat.

   我有時候會擔心我們所吃食品內的所有藥物和化學藥品。

3. Industrial farming carries certain risks.

   工業化農牧帶有若干風險。

4. Do you think eating genetically modified food is safe?

   你認為食用基因改良的食品安全嗎？

5. Genetically modified food is banned in some places.

   某些地方禁用基因改良的食品。

6. Maybe I should start buying organic food even though it's more expensive.

   雖然較為昂貴，也許我應該開始購買有機食品了。

7. Factory farming has serious effects on the environment.

   工業農牧對環境有嚴重的影響。

8. Some of the drugs given to animals have been linked to cancer.

   給動物服用的一些藥物和癌症有關。

Situational Dialogue 打開話匣子 12-03

P = Paul; K = Kelly

 P: I'm hungry. Let's get a hot dog.

 K: Yuck! Paul, do you pay much attention to[1] the ingredients in the food you buy?

 P: Sure, if it tastes good, I eat it.

 K: That's not what I mean. Sometimes I worry about all the drugs and chemicals in the food we eat.

 P: Oh, I think most of what we eat is safe. Technology is improving all the time[2], making food better.

 K: I'm not so sure about that. Do you think eating genetically modified food is safe?

 P: I've never really thought much about it. I suppose it is.

 K: Did you know that genetically modified food is banned in some places, such as Japan and Europe? Some of the drugs given to animals have been linked to cancer.

 P: No, I didn't know that. Maybe I should start buying organic[3] food even though it's more expensive.

 K: That's probably a good idea.

1. **pay attention to...**　　注意……
   例: Don't pay any attention to what they say.
   別理會他們說的話。

2. **all the time**　　一直，總是
= **at all times**
   例: Our representatives are ready to help you at all times.
   我們的專員隨時準備好要為您服務。

3. **organic** [ɔrˋgænɪk] *a.* 有機的

 Review Exercises 隨堂小測驗

Part A: Fill in the blanks with the correct answers.

____ 1. Some countries have _____ beef imports from America.
   (A) banned
   (B) burned
   (C) blended
   (D) bent

____ 2. Industrial farming has resulted _____ many benefits to farmers and consumers.
   (A) for
   (B) to
   (C) of
   (D) in

____ 3. Sometimes Dan isn't thoughtful; _____ is, he can be pretty rude.
   (A) it
   (B) that
   (C) what
   (D) this

____ 4. I never pay much _____ to what Sam says.
   (A) effort
   (B) idea
   (C) time
   (D) attention

____ 5. _____ Lucy conscious of the fact she insulted you?
   (A) Has
   (B) Does
   (C) Is
   (D) Will

Part B: Match the terms on the left with the definitions on the right by writing the correct letters in the blanks.

_____ **1.** modify   a. connected with

_____ **2.** ban   b. to cause

_____ **3.** vaccine   c. small living things that may cause illness

_____ **4.** emission   d. to change

_____ **5.** result in   e. sth, such as gas or heat, sent into the air

_____ **6.** bacteria   f. not damaged or affected by

_____ **7.** resistant to   g. to not allow

_____ **8.** linked to   h. sth that helps protect against disease

One Less Hamburger

週一無肉日　減碳救地球

 Warm-up Exercise 暖身練習

1. Do you think being a vegetarian is a good idea? Why or why not?

2. Some people refuse to eat meat. What are some reasons people do so?

―― ○○七年諾貝爾和平獎得主帕卓里博士
―― （Dr. Pachauri）隔年九月在倫敦發表以
『肉品生產與肉食對氣候變遷的影響』為題發表演
講，強調改變飲食習慣的重要性。

　　研究中顯示，生產一公斤的肉，會排放出
三十六點四公斤的二氧化碳。帕卓里博士認為對抗
氣候變遷最輕而易舉的事，就是少吃肉！因此，他
強調要以少吃肉來縮小畜牧業的規模，進而減少溫
室氣體的排放。

　　肉食也導致了食物資源分配的不公。畜牧業
生產一公斤牛肉需要十公斤的飼料，目前全球三分
之一的穀糧和超過百分之九十的大豆用以餵養牲畜
以生產肉類，以供富國消費，這麼做不但嚴重浪費
食物資源，更造成窮國的糧荒問題。

Topic Reading 主題閱讀 13-01

S ome people think that there's nothing better than biting into a juicy burger or tearing apart[1] a tasty chicken wing. Unfortunately, there's a dark side to[2] the consumption of meat—what it does to the environment. According to studies, cattle production is the biggest producer of carbon pollution. To put it simply[3], raising animals for meat is creating more pollution than vehicles, air conditioners, or factories.

One way to approach such a big problem is to take it one step at a time[4]. An idea that has been suggested is having one day of the week when everyone eats a vegetarian diet. If everyone cooperated with this simple step, it would mean a 15 percent reduction in total meat

consumption. The result would be that fewer animals would have to be raised[5] for food, which in turn[6] would contribute to[7] carbon pollution reduction. With just one day a week without meat, the lungs of the Earth would breathe a little easier.

Two Taiwanese authors are excited about the idea of Meatless Monday. Su Hsiao-huan and Hsu Jen-hsiu are launching[8] a campaign[9] to bring Meatless Monday to Taiwan. They argue that[10] Meatless Monday should be promoted[11] by environmental groups and that all restaurants should start providing menus with vegetarian options[12]. They hope that the government will eventually[13] make it a law that Mondays are meat-free. Su and Hsu are not alone. Meatless Monday is being discussed in other countries like Belgium. One day a week is just one step in fixing a very serious problem, but it will help. Why not start thinking about changing your diet today?

 Reading Exercises 閱讀隨堂考

_____ 1. What is this reading mainly about?
(A) A campaign to reduce meat consumption.
(B) The health benefits of being a vegetarian.
(C) The reasons being a vegetarian is difficult.
(D) What type of food people in Taiwan eat.

_____ 2. What do Su Hsiao-huan and Hsu Jen-hsiu want the government to do?
(A) To make it a law not to eat meat on Mondays.
(B) To encourage restaurants to serve only vegetarian dishes.
(C) To stop farmers from raising so many animals for food.
(D) To create more environmental groups.

Vocabulary & Phrases 單字片語解密

1. **tear apart... / tear...apart**
將……撕裂；使……分裂
例: The civil war tore the small country apart for decades.
內戰使得那個小國分裂了數十年。

2. **There's a dark side to sth.**
某事物有其黑暗的一面。
例: There's a dark side to everything, so you should be optimistic but cautious.
每件事都有其黑暗面,所以你應該樂觀而謹慎。

3. **To put it simply,...**
= Simply put,...
= Put simply,...
簡單地說,……
＊put 在此表『表達,陳述』的意思。
例: Put simply, we either accept their offer or go bankrupt.
簡而言之,我們要麼接受他們的提議,要麼就破產。

4. **數字 + at a time** 一次若干個數目
例: After the incident, everyone involved was called into the principal's office one at a time.
事件發生後,相關人等一次一個被叫進校長室。

5. **raise** [rez] *vt.* 飼養(動物);養育(小孩)
例: They were raised on a diet of hamburgers.
他們是吃漢堡長大的。

6. **in turn** 因此,進而(多置於句中,前後以逗點隔開)
例: Increased production will, in turn, lead to increased profits.
增加生產,進而導致利潤增加。

7. **contribute to + N/V-ing**
= lead to + N/V-ing
= bring about + N/V-ing
促成 / 導致……
例: The driver's carelessness may have contributed to the accident.
司機的疏失可能是這起意外的肇因。

8. **launch** [lɔntʃ] *vt.* 發起(活動等)
例: We decided to launch an ad campaign to promote our products.
我們決定要發起一項廣告宣傳活動來促銷產品。

9. **campaign** [kæm`pen] *n.* (政治、社會等)活動

10. **argue + that 子句**
主張 / 辯稱……
例: Scholars argue that the ancient documents should be preserved and not sent on international museum tours.
學者們主張這些古老文獻不應該送去國際間各博物館作巡迴展,而應好好保存起來。

11. **promote** [prə`mot] *vt.* 促銷,推廣

12. **option** [`ɑpʃən] *n.* 選擇
have no option but to V
= have no choice but to V
= have no alternative but to V
別無選擇只好……
例: We had no option but to let John go because he was lazy.
我們別無選擇只好把約翰炒魷魚,因為他很懶惰。

13. **eventually** [ɪˋvɛntʃʊəlɪ] *adv.* 最後，終於（= finally）

例: The suspect was eventually proven innocent in court.
那名嫌犯最後在法庭上被證明是無辜的。

1. **juicy** [ˋdʒusɪ] *a.* 多汁的

2. **tasty** [ˋtestɪ] *a.* 美味的

3. **chicken wing**　雞翅

4. **consumption** [kənˋsʌmpʃən] *n.* 吃，喝；消耗

5. **cattle** [ˋkætḷ] *n.* 牲口；牛（群）
a herd of cattle　一群牛
注意:
cattle 如同 people，視作複數名詞，可被 two 以上的數詞（如 three、four、many 等）修飾。

6. **carbon** [ˋkɑrbən] *n.* 碳

7. **vehicle** [ˋviɪkḷ] *n.* 車輛

8. **vegetarian** [ˏvɛdʒəˋtɛrɪən] *a.* 素食的 & *n.* 素食者

9. **reduction** [rɪˋdʌkʃən] *n.* 減少

10. **lung** [lʌŋ] *n.* 肺臟（因有兩片肺，故本字常用複數）

Sentence Structure Analysis 句型分析

An idea　that has been suggested　is　having one day of the week
　❶　　　　　　❷　　　　　　❸　　　　❹

when everyone eats a vegetarian diet .
　　　　　　　❺

❶ 為本句的主詞；

❷ 為關係代名詞 that（＝ which）形容詞子句，修飾之前先行詞 An idea；

❸ 為本句的動詞，因為主詞為單數名詞 An idea，故此處使用 is；

❹ 為動名詞片語，作主詞補語，補充説明主詞 An idea；

❺ 為關係副詞 when（＝ on which）引導的形容詞子句，修飾之前的 one day of the week（一星期當中的一天）。

Grammar Points 重點來了

They hope that the government will eventually make <u>it</u> a law that Mondays are meat-free.

▶ 本句劃線的 it 是代名詞，作虛受詞，之後的 a law 是受詞補語。it 代替之後的 that 子句（即 that Mondays are meat-free），該 that 子句是真受詞。本句採用下列句型：

主詞 + 動詞 + 虛受詞 it + 形容詞 / 名詞 + ⎰ to V
　　　　　　　　　　　　　　　　　　⎱ that + S + V

注意: 其他常與虛受詞並用的類似動詞有：consider（考慮）、find（發現）、think（認為）、believe（認為）、feel（感覺）等字。

例: I find it difficult <u>to communicate</u> with that stubborn guy.
我發現要和那個固執的傢伙溝通很困難。
Jack makes <u>it</u> a rule <u>to take a walk</u> after dinner.
傑克習慣在晚餐後去散步。

1. **Are you or any of your friends vegetarian?**

   你或是有什麼朋友是吃素的嗎？

2. **Is there any type of food that you don't eat?**

   有什麼種類的食物是你不吃的嗎？

3. **Cattle production is the biggest producer of carbon pollution.**

   肉牛生產是碳污染的最大元兇。

4. **Raising animals for meat is creating more pollution than vehicles, air conditioners, or factories.**

   為肉類食品飼養動物所製造的污染比車輛、冷氣機或工廠還多。

5. **What's your opinion of Meatless Monday?**

   你對於無肉星期一有什麼看法？

6. **If everyone cooperated with this simple step, it would mean a 15 percent reduction in total meat consumption.**

   如果大家都配合此一簡單的步驟，那會意味能減少百分之十五的肉類總消耗量。

7. **How do you think people would react if Meatless Monday were made law?**

   如果無肉星期一被制定成了法律，你認為大家會有怎樣的反應？

8. **I imagine it could really help the problem, but would everyone agree to it?**

   我可以想像這麼做能真正解決問題，但大家會同意這個做法嗎？

Situational Dialogue 打開話匣子　　🔊 13-03

S = Suzie; L = Larry

S: Larry, are you or any of your friends vegetarian?

L: I'm not, but I do have a few friends who are. Why do you ask?

S: Well, I've read that cattle production is the biggest producer of carbon pollution.

L: You're not trying to make me give up meat and become a vegetarian, are you?

S: Why not? Raising animals for meat is creating more pollution than vehicles, air conditioners, or factories.

L: That sounds serious, but I'm not ready to give up[1] hamburgers and steak yet.

S: How about just once a week? What's your opinion of Meatless Mondays?

L: I think I've heard of that. I suppose I could try giving up meat for one day a week.

S: That's the spirit[2]. If everyone cooperated[3] with this simple step, it would mean a 15 percent reduction in total meat consumption.

L: I imagine it could really help solve the problem, but would everyone agree to it?

S: Perhaps not at first[4], but I think that could happen eventually.

Vocabulary & Phrases 單字片語解密

1. **give up + N/V-ing** 放棄……

   例: They had given up hope of ever having children.
   他們已經放棄要生小孩的希望了。

   You should give up smoking.
   你應該要戒煙。

2. **That's the spirit.**
   這就對了。/ 好樣的。

   例: A: I'll keep trying until I get the hang of it.
   B: That's the spirit, Jeremy.
   甲：我會繼續努力，直到我抓到竅門。
   乙：這就對了，傑若米。

   ＊get the hang of sth
   抓到某事的竅門

3. **cooperate** [koˋɑpə͵ret] *vi.* 合作
   cooperate with sb 與某人合作

   例: The two companies refused to cooperate with each other.
   那兩家公司拒絕彼此合作。

4. **at first** 起先

   例: At first, they didn't like each other. However, they ended up getting married.
   起先，他們互看彼此不順眼。然而，他們最終卻結婚了。

✏ Review Exercises 隨堂小測驗

Part A: Choose the correct answer.

_____ 1. Study harder and you will get good grades. This, _____, will make your parents happy with you.

    (A) in contrast
    (B) instead
    (C) in opposition
    (D) in turn

_____ 2. There was a 10 percent _____ in sales last month.

    (A) reduce
    (B) reducing
    (C) reduction
    (D) reduced

_____ 3. To _____ it _____, some people really need to lose weight.

    (A) take; simple
    (B) go; easy
    (C) put; simply
    (D) be; convenient

_____ 4. Eventually, if you keep eating too much, you _____ weight.

    (A) have gained
    (B) will get
    (C) are getting
    (D) will gain

_____ 5. There's nothing better _____ having a nice cold drink on a hot day.

    (A) to
    (B) for
    (C) than
    (D) then

Part B: Match the terms on the left with the definitions on the right by writing the correct letters in the blanks.

____ 1. reduce

____ 2. tasty

____ 3. launch

____ 4. promote

____ 5. dark side

____ 6. campaign

____ 7. option

____ 8. tear apart

a. to separate by force

b. delicious

c. a negative part

d. to begin

e. a choice

f. to lower

g. an organized effort

h. to encourage

Fortune Telling and Soda Selling
無所不能，無所不賣的日本販賣機

1. Why do you think vending machines are so popular around the world?

2. Do you remember the last time you bought something from a vending machine? What was it? When was it?

日本法律規定，二十歲以上才能吸菸。根據二〇〇八年七月的新規定，全日本的香菸販賣機必須確定買者是否成年。為此，日本富士高公司研發出從臉部特徵辨識年齡的系統。販賣機附設數位相機，買香菸的顧客看著鏡頭，這套系統會把顧客臉上的特徵，像是眼睛四周的皺紋、骨額結構和鬆弛的皮膚，與十萬多人的臉部特徵做比對。這套系統的準確度達百分之九十，剩下的百分之十就是『灰色地帶』，比方説有皺紋的未成年人，或是娃娃臉的成年人。這時消費者會被要求插入駕照以辨識年齡。

Topic Reading 主題閱讀 14-01

"They are so convenient, I wish I had one in my room," says an 18-year-old in Tokyo. She's talking about vending machines, and she's not the only one. Vending machines are hugely popular in Japan, with about one for every 50 people and 2.5 million units for drinks alone. That figure doesn't even include the ones that sell other products like cigarettes, toys, flowers, cold bananas, cooked meals, and just about anything else you can think of[1].

With so many variations, companies really have to be imaginative[2] to make their vending machines stand out[3]. Showing that they care, Coca-Cola made some that give out[4] free drinks in case of[5] an earthquake. The newest development in vending machine technology, however, comes from a machine at a train station in Tokyo. It has a camera and software that figures out[6] a shopper's age and sex. With that information, the machine guesses what the shopper wants to buy almost as though it were trying to read his or her mind[7].

For example, one shopper reported[8] that the vending machine offered her three different choices, with one being her favorite. She also said that it would come in handy[9] when she couldn't make a decision. According to the company that operates[10] the machine, consumers' pictures are deleted[11] immediately, but general[12] information about who is buying from the machine is gathered[13] and used by the company. However, this doesn't seem to bother[14] customers because they are so excited about[15] the strange new machine. With this kind of technology, it seems anything is possible with vending machines.

 Reading Exercises 閱讀隨堂考

_____ 1. According to the reading, how can companies make their vending machines "stand out?"
    (A) By being creative.
    (B) By offering cheap prices.
    (C) By selling toys.
    (D) By operating in Japan.

_____ 2. In the last paragraph, what are the customers not bothered by?
    (A) Having their pictures taken by the machine.
    (B) Being given only three choices to choose from.
    (C) Having personal information collected about them.
    (D) Letting the vending machine "read their mind."

Vocabulary & Phrases   單字片語解密

1. think of...   想到……

例: Can you think of a reason to explain why we are late?
你能想出一個理由來解釋我們遲到的原因嗎？

2. imaginative [ɪˋmædʒəˏnetɪv] *a.* 富於想像力的

imaginary [ɪˋmædʒəˏnɛrɪ] *a.* 想像中的

imaginable [ɪˋmædʒɪnəbļ] *a.* 想像得到的（常與最高級並用）

例: Dean Koontz is an imaginative writer of horror stories.
狄恩‧昆斯是個富有想像力的恐怖小說作家。

Luke's imaginary friend Bob disappeared when he grew up.
路克長大後，他幻想出來的朋友鮑伯就消失了。

For me, the most terrifying creatures imaginable are crying babies.
對我來說，可以想像得到的最可怕的生物就是哭個不停的嬰兒。

3. stand out   脫穎而出，引人注目

例: The red dress you're wearing will definitely stand out at the party.
妳身上穿的紅色洋裝絕對會在派對上引人注目。

4. give out...   分發……

例: Sarah helps by giving out food to people at the homeless shelter.
莎拉會去遊民之家幫忙分發食物給他們。

5. in case of...
萬一／以防／倘若……

例: In case of a fire, calmly walk to the emergency exits.
萬一發生火災，要冷靜地走向往緊急逃生門。

6. figure out...   弄懂……

例: The scientists are trying to figure out how the mysterious disease spreads.
科學家們正設法找出這怪病的傳染途徑。

7. read sb's mind / thoughts
知道某人心中在想什麼

例: A: How about going to the movies after work?
B: You can read my mind!
甲：咱們下班後去看電影如何？
乙：你還真知道我在想什麼耶！

8. report [rɪˋport] *vt.* 報導，描述（後接 that 引導的名詞子句）

例: Employers reported that college graduates these days lack problem-solving skills.
雇主們描述現今的大學畢業生缺乏解決問題的能力。

9. come in handy
隨時會用得到／派上用場

例: You should always carry an umbrella in your handbag; it may come in handy one day.
你應該隨身在包包裡放把傘，因為有一天可能派上用場。

10. operate [ˋɑpəˏret] *vt.* 操作

11. **delete** [dɪˋlit] *vt.* 刪除

例: I accidentally deleted an important document from my laptop.
我不小心刪掉筆電裡一份重要的文件。

12. **general** [ˋdʒɛnərəl] *a.* 一般的

13. **gather** [ˋgæðɚ] *vt.* 蒐集

14. **bother** [ˋbɑðɚ] *vt.* 煩擾；打擾；費心

例: What bothers me most about the manager is that he loses his temper over the smallest matters.
我最受不了我們經理的地方是他會因極小的瑣事而發脾氣。

Sorry to bother you, but there's a call for you on line two.
抱歉要打擾你，二線有你的來電。

Mike didn't even bother to let me know he was coming.
邁可甚至不想費心讓我知道他要來。

15. **be excited about...**
對……感到興奮

例: My brother and I were excited about getting a new puppy.
我和我弟弟因為收到新的小狗而興奮不已。

1. **vending machine** [ˋvɛndɪŋ məˏʃin] *n.* 自動販賣機

2. **unit** [ˋjunɪt] *n.* 單位

3. **figure** [ˋfɪgjɚ] *n.* 數字
sales figures　銷售數字

4. **variation** [ˏvɛrɪˋeʃən] *n.* 變化

Sentence Structure Analysis 句型分析

<u>Showing that they care</u>, Coca-Cola made some that give out free drinks in case of an earthquake.

> 畫底線為分詞結構。原句原為 "Coca-Cola showed that they care"。由於如此一來兩個子句之間就無連接詞連接，屬錯誤句構。改正之道有以下三種方法：

a) 將逗點改成分號，即成：Coca-Cola showed that they care; they made some that give out free drinks in case of an earthquake.

b) 加連接詞 so，即成：Coca-Cola showed that they care, so they made some that give out free drinks in case of an earthquake.

c) 將第一個子句改為分詞片語。首先刪除相同的主詞，再將一般動詞改為現在分詞（即 V-ing）

~~Coca-Cola showed~~ that they care, Coca-Cola made some that give out free drinks in case of an earthquake.

→ <u>Showing</u> that they care, Coca-Cola made some that give out free drinks in case of an earthquake.

 Grammar Points 重點來了

<u>I wish (that) I had</u> one in my room.

> wish 表『但願』，之後所接 that 引導的名詞子句中，動詞必須使用假設語氣，因此與現在事實相反時動詞要使用簡單過去式；與過去事實相反時，動詞要使用過去完成式。此句中，該少女表示『希望現實生活中真能有一台這樣的販賣機在她房內』，故與現在事實相反，動詞因而使用 has 的過去簡單式 had。

例: I wish you <u>had been</u> there at the party last night.
但願你昨晚在派對上。（你昨晚並不在派對上，與過去事實相反）

With that information, the machine guesses what the shopper wants to buy almost <u>as though it were</u> trying to read his or her mind.

> as if / as though 表『彷彿』，該子句中動詞也必須與假設語氣並用。唯在與現在事實相反的假設語氣中，I 及 it 等單數主詞仍是要使用 were。

例: You talked as if you <u>had been</u> there.
你說起來彷彿當時在那兒似的。

1. What do you usually buy from vending machines?

   你通常從自動販賣機買什麼東西？

2. Are vending machines popular in your country?

   自動販賣機在你們國家流行嗎？

3. Vending machines are hugely popular in Japan.

   自動販賣機在日本相當受歡迎。

4. You can buy almost anything from vending machines in Japan.

   你從日本的自動販賣機當中幾乎能買到任何東西。

5. Isn't technology amazing?

   科技是不是很神奇呢？

6. Coca-Cola made some machines that give out free drinks in case of an earthquake.

   可口可樂生產了一些機器，那些機器能在發生地震時免費供應飲料。

7. With this kind of technology, it seems anything is possible with vending machines.

   有了這種技術，自動販賣機似乎什麼都有可能賣了。

8. I sometimes wonder if there's too much technology in our lives.

   我有時候會想我們生活中是否充斥著太多科技了。

Situational Dialogue 打開話匣子 14-03

B = Barry; L = Lana

B: Do you mind if I just grab[1] something from this vending machine?

L: No, go ahead[2]. What are you getting?

B: Just a Coke.

L: What do you usually buy from vending machines?

B: Oh, you know—pop, chocolate bars, chips.

L: Are vending machines popular in your country?

B: Sure; just like everywhere, I suppose[3].

L: When it comes to vending machines, I think Japan takes the cake[4], though.

B: What do you mean?

L: You can buy almost anything from vending machines in Japan.

B: That's cool. I think it's very convenient to buy things this way.

L: Isn't technology amazing[5]?

B: You can say that again[6].

 L: Did you know that Coca-Cola made some machines that give out free drinks in case of an earthquake?

 B: That's a good idea for a place like Japan that has a lot of earthquakes.

 L: With this kind of technology, it seems anything is possible with vending machines. I sometimes wonder if there's too much technology in our lives, though.

 Vocabulary & Phrases 單字片語解密

1. **grab** [græb] *vt.* 匆匆購買
   例: Let's grab a sandwich before we go.
   咱們出發前趕快去買個三明治吧。

2. **go ahead** 許可進行
   go-ahead [ˋgoˏʌhɛd] *n.* 許可
   例: A: May I start now?
   B: Yes, go ahead.
   甲：我現在可以開始了嗎？
   乙：是的，可以開始了。
   We've been given the go-ahead to start building.
   我們已經獲得許可，可以開工了。

3. **suppose** [səˋpoz] *vt.* 猜想（後接 that 引導的名詞子句）
   例: To tell you the truth, I don't suppose for a minute that he'll agree.
   老實説，我絲毫都不認為他會同意。

4. **take the cake**
   突出，令人驚訝；令人生氣
   例: You say Linda opened your letters? Oh, that really takes the cake!
   你説琳達開了你的信？喔，那真是太令人氣憤了！

5. **amazing** [əˋmezɪŋ] *a.* 令人驚嘆的

6. **You can say that again.**
   我非常同意。
   例: A: Tony is the smartest student I've ever seen.
   B: You can say that again.
   甲：湯尼是我見過最聰明的學生了。
   乙：我非常同意你。

✎ Review Exercises 隨堂小測驗

Part A: Choose the correct answer.

_____ 1. I can't figure _____ how to use this machine.
 (A) up
 (B) to
 (C) out
 (D) on

_____ 2. Kelly wishes she _____ a vending machine in her living room.
 (A) has
 (B) had
 (C) will have
 (D) having

_____ 3. _____ it rains later, you should take an umbrella.
 (A) Case
 (B) The case
 (C) In case of
 (D) In case

_____ 4. My friend acts _____ she were my boss.
 (A) such as
 (B) as though
 (C) like that
 (D) it seems

_____ 5. Technology is amazing, _____?
 (A) is it
 (B) isn't it
 (C) has it
 (D) not it

Part B: In the sentences below, circle the correct words in the blanks.

1. As the best student in the class, Pam really stands out / up.

2. The flashlight on my key chain often comes in hand / handy.

3. Artists need to be very imaginary / imaginative.

4. Being in an earthquake is a terrifying / terrify experience.

5. Did / Have you deleted the file already?

6. Wake / Waking up late, Carl had to run to catch the bus.

7. Bill didn't know where to find more information / informations on the topic.

8. I don't know what you are refer / referring to.

9. The store gave out / to free chocolates to customers.

10. Jim was huge / hugely embarrassed when his pants fell down.

Heat from Peppers Bursts with Flavor and Boosts Your Health

辣得讓人哇哇叫的辣椒還能促進你的健康

Warm-up Exercise 暖身練習

1. What type of spicy food do you enjoy?
2. Why do you think a lot of people like spicy food?

根據研究顯示，辣椒有以下功用：

常吃辣椒可預防膽結石

辣椒富含維生素 C，可使體內多餘的膽固醇轉為膽汁酸，從而預防膽結石。

辣椒能改善心臟功能

辣椒配上大蒜、山楂及維生素 E，食用後能改善心臟功能，促進血液循環。此外，常食辣椒可降低血脂，減少血栓形成，對心血管系統疾病有一定的預防作用。

辣椒能降血糖

實驗證明，辣椒素能顯著降低血糖標準。

辣椒有減肥作用

辣椒含有某種成分，能有效地消耗人體脂肪，促進新陳代謝，從而達到減肥的效果。

Although there are many people that do not appreciate[1] the painful[2] effect chili peppers inflict[3] on the tongue, archaeological evidence[4] found in the Americas suggests that the plant has been cultivated[5] since prehistoric times. This proves that it has been part of the human diet for nearly[6] 10,000 years. Chili peppers were first encountered[7] by Christopher Columbus in the West Indies in the 15th century. Soon after, they quickly spread[8] across Europe and Asia, becoming a staple ingredient in many cooking traditions.

Chili peppers are used in a variety of[9] ways in different national cuisines. In India, chilies are used in dishes[10] ranging from[11] fried snacks to complex[12] curries, whereas crushed chili pepper flakes are often sprinkled[13] on pizzas and other dishes in Italian cuisine. In Turkey and Mexico, chilies are used to make hot sauces and red pepper pastes. In North African cooking, they are used as both a seasoning and a table condiment. In Asian cooking, the peppers are used to make kimchi and other pickled dishes, while the leaves are sometimes cooked as greens.

The reason chili peppers are spicy in taste is due to a compound called capsaicin（辣椒素）, which is mostly found in the seeds. Studies show that capsaicin not only adds zest, but it also has many health benefits, including relieving headaches and combating[14] nasal congestion[15]. Capsaicin is also effective in lowering high blood pressure and even fighting prostate cancer. In addition to capsaicin, chili peppers also contain large amounts of[16] vitamin B and C as well as carotene, potassium, magnesium, and iron, which are all good for the body. To make the heat of the chili peppers more bearable[17], serve them with cooling accompaniments, such as yogurt or cucumbers. You might just learn to appreciate red hot chili peppers.

 Reading Exercises 閱讀隨堂考

_____ 1. According to the reading, where are fried chili peppers used in snacks?
(A) In America
(B) In Italy
(C) In India
(D) In Mexico

_____ 2. Which is NOT mentioned in the reading?
(A) Columbus loved to eat chili peppers on his travels.
(B) Chili peppers have been eaten for almost 10,000 years.
(C) Eating chili can help relieve headaches and fight cancer.
(D) Chili peppers are spicy mainly because of the seeds inside.

Vocabulary & Phrases 單字片語解密

1. **appreciate** [əˈpriʃɪˌet] *vt.* 欣賞、

2. **painful** [ˈpenfəl] *a.*（身體部位）
   疼痛的
   例: My left ankle is too painful to
   walk on.
   我的左腳踝痛得走不了了。
   注意:
   painful 是指身體某部位疼痛，如果要
   表示『人感到疼痛』，要使用 pain 一
   字。
   例: I felt a lot of pain in my left
   ankle.
   我感覺到左腳踝劇烈疼痛。

3. **inflict** [ɪnˈflɪkt] *vt.* 使遭受，強加
   inflict A on B　　施加 A 於 B
   例: They inflicted a defeat on the
   home team.
   他們使地主隊遭受了失敗的結果。

4. **evidence** [ˈɛvədəns] *n.* 證據（集合
   名詞，不可數）
   a piece of evidence　　一則證據
   some evidence　　　　一些證據
   a lot of evidence　　　很多證據

5. **cultivate** [ˈkʌltəˌvet] *vt.* 耕種
   （土地）；栽培（作物）；培養
   例: The local people cultivate
   mainly rice and beans.
   當地人主要栽種稻米和豆子。
   It takes time, thought and effort
   to cultivate your mind.
   陶冶心性需要時間、心思和努力。

6. **nearly** [ˈnɪrlɪ] *adv.* 幾乎
   （= almost，之後須接 every、any、
   　no、all 等四個涵蓋性完全的形容詞）

   例: Almost all the students knew
   the answer to the question.
   = Nearly all the students knew the
   answer to the question.
   幾乎所有學生都知道這個問題的答
   案。

7. **encounter** [ɪnˈkaʊnkɚ] *vt.* 意外遇見
   （本文即此用法）；遭遇（困難）
   例: We encountered a number of
   difficulties in the initial phase of
   the project.
   我們在專案初期遭遇了一些困難。

8. **spread** [sprɛd] *vi.* & *vt.* 散播（三態
   同形）

9. **a (wide) variety of...**
   各式各樣的……
   （= a wide range of...）
   例: The hotel offers a wide variety
   of facilities.
   那家飯店提供各式各樣的設施。

10. **dish** [dɪʃ] *n.* 菜餚

11. **range from A to B**
    範圍從 A 到 B 都有
    例: I've had a number of different jobs,
    ranging from chef to teacher.
    我做過一些不同的工作，範圍從廚
    師到老師都有。

12. **complex** [ˈkɑmplɛks] *a.* 複雜的
    （= complicated [ˈkɑmpləˌketɪd]）

13. **sprinkle** [ˈsprɪŋkl̩] *vt.* 撒；灑

14. **combat** [ˈkɑmbæt] *vt.* 抵抗；與……
    戰鬥
    例: To combat the sun's harmful
    rays, Tim used sunscreen.
    為了抵擋陽光中的有害輻射，提姆
    擦防曬乳液。

Vocabulary & Phrases 單字片語解密

15. **congestion** [kənˈdʒɛstʃən] *n.* 阻塞
    traffic congestion　　交通阻塞

16. **large / small amounts of +** 不可
    數名詞　　大量的 / 少量的……
 = a large / small amount of + 不可數
    名詞
    比較:
    large / small numbers of + 複數名詞
    多數的 / 少數的……

 = a large / small number of + 複數名
    詞
    例: I drank a large amount of water
    after exercising.
    我運動後喝了大量的水。
    Large numbers of people buy
    lottery tickets each day.
    每天都有許多人買樂透彩。

17. **bearable** [ˈbɛrəbl̩] *a.* 可以忍受的

 Bonus Vocabulary 補充單字

1. **archaeological** [ˌɑrkɪəˈlɑdʒɪkl̩] *a.*
   考古學的

2. **prehistoric** [ˌprihɪsˈtɔrɪk] *a.* 史前的

3. **chili pepper** [ˈtʃɪlɪ ˌpɛpɚ] *n.* 辣椒

4. **staple** [ˈstepl̩] *a.* 主要的；經常需要的

5. **ingredient** [ɪnˈgridɪənt] *n.*
   （烹煮的）原料

6. **cuisine** [kwɪˈzin] *n.* 菜餚

7. **crushed** [krʌʃt] *a.* 壓碎的

8. **flake** [flek] *n.* 小薄片

9. **sauce** [sɔs] *n.* 醬汁；調味料

10. **paste** [pest] *n.* 醬，膏；糊狀物

11. **seasoning** [ˈsizn̩ɪŋ] *n.* 調味料

12. **condiment** [ˈkɑndəmənt] *n.*
    （辛辣）調味料

13. **kimchi** [ˈkɪmtʃi] *n.* 韓國泡菜

14. **pickled** [ˈpɪkl̩d] *a.* 醃漬的

15. **green** [grin] *n.* 青菜，菜葉（多用複
    數）

16. **compound** [ˈkɑmpaʊnd] *n.* 化合
    物；複合物

17. **capsaicin** [kæpˈsesən] *n.* 辣椒素

18. **zest** [zɛst] *n.* 風味，滋味

19. **nasal** [ˈnezl̩] *a.* 鼻子的

20. **prostate** [ˈprɑsˌtet] *n.* 前列腺

21. **carotene** [ˈkærəˌtin] *n.* 胡蘿蔔素

22. **potassium** [pəˈtæsɪəm] *n.* 鉀

23. **magnesium** [mægˈnɪʃɪəm] *n.* 鎂

24. **cooling** [ˈkulɪŋ] *a.* 冷卻的（本文指
    減輕辣味的）

25. **accompaniment** [əˈkʌmpənɪmənt]
    n. 佐餐物；伴隨物

Sentence Structure Analysis 句型分析

Although there are many people that do not appreciate the painful effect (that) chili peppers <u>inflict</u> on the tongue,...

 此副詞子句中含有一個由關係代名詞 that (= which) 引導的形容詞子句，即 that chili peppers inflict on the tongue。該修飾先行詞 the painful effect 的關代 that 由於在形容詞子句中作為動詞 inflict 的受詞，故可省略。

Soon after, they quickly <u>spread</u> across Europe and Asia, <u>becoming</u> a staple ingredient in many cooking traditions.

 一個句子中若有兩個動詞，所表示的動作同時發生時，且該兩個動詞之間並無連接詞 and 連接時，第二個動詞應改成現在分詞。因此，上列句中 spread 是動詞，另一動詞 became 因之前無 and 連接，故改成現在分詞 becoming。

例: David <u>sat</u> in the corner, <u>reading</u> a newspaper.
大衛坐在角落看報紙。

 Grammar Points 重點來了

In India, chilies are used in dishes ranging from fried snacks to complex curries, <u>whereas</u> crushed chili pepper flakes are often sprinkled on pizzas and other dishes in Italian cuisine.

In Asian cooking, the peppers are used to make kimchi and other pickled dishes, <u>while</u> the leaves are sometimes cooked as greens.

注意:

whereas [hwɛrˋæz] 相當於 while，中文譯成『而』，用來連接兩個意思相對的主要子句。

例: I love vanilla ice cream, <u>whereas</u> my sister loves chocolate.
= I love vanilla ice cream, <u>while</u> my sister loves chocolate.
我喜歡香草冰淇淋，而我妹妹則喜歡巧克力口味的。

1. Chili peppers were not part of European cooking until the "Columbian exchange" in the 15th century, when Christopher Columbus first visited the West Indies.

   辣椒直到西元十五世紀『哥倫布交流』時才成為歐洲烹飪的一部分,當時正值克里斯多福‧哥倫布首次探訪西印度群島。

2. Some people aren't big fans of spicy food, but actually chili peppers have a lot of health benefits.

   有些人並不熱衷於辛辣的食物,但實際上辣椒確實有很多健康上的好處。

3. Did you know that some doctors use capsaicin as a drug to relieve pain?

   你知道有些醫生會使用辣椒素來作止痛藥使用嗎?

4. Not all animals think chili peppers are spicy; birds, for example, cannot taste capsaicin.

   並非所有動物都認為辣椒是辣的;舉例來說,鳥類就無法品嚐出辣椒素。

5. *The Guinness Book of World Records* says the world's hottest chili peppers are called "scorpion peppers" and they come from the Islands of Trinidad and Tobago.

   《金氏世界紀錄大全》載明全世界最辣的辣椒被稱為『蠍子辣椒』,那是來自於千里達和多巴哥島國。

6. "Scorpion chili peppers" are so strong that you have to wear protective gloves and a chemical mask when you handle them.

   『蠍子辣椒』辣勁非常強烈,所以你在處理時必須戴防護手套和化學面具。

Situational Dialogue 打開話匣子 15-03

C = Cindy; T = Trevor

C: Hey, Trevor. Do you like spicy food? I'm hosting[1] a dinner at my place this weekend, but I warn you: this food is not for the faint of heart[2]!

T: Cool, I like spicy[3] food a lot. In fact, one of my favorites is Sichuan cuisine.

C: Ha! The stuff we are cooking makes that seem like baby food! My mother's family is from Korea and my dad's side is Mexican. The food we eat tastes like fire! Can you handle[4] it?

T: Sounds like a challenge! Yeah, I'm up for[5] it. Do you guys mainly use chili peppers?

C: You got it! Red hot chili peppers! The peppers we use have a really high amount of capsaicin; many of the dishes we serve contain habanero chilies.

T: I've heard of those! They're some of the spiciest chilies on the planet! Uh... oh, now I'm starting to worry!

C: You'll be fine! Besides, chili peppers are good for you. The compounds contained in chili peppers help relieve[6] nasal congestion, are high in[7] vitamins, and can even help lower[8] blood pressure!

T: You make them sound like medicine.

C: They are natural medicine! And don't worry: if the spices get too hot, you can always cool down[9] your mouth and throat with some yogurt or cucumbers.

T: All right, count me in[10]! I'm ready for this weekend's chili adventure!

1. **host** [host] *vt.* 主辦 & *n.* 主持人

2. **not for the faint of heart**
   不是給膽小人的
= **not for the faint-hearted** [ˋfɛntˏhɑrtɪd]
   例: The climb is not for the faint-hearted.
   這趟登山之旅不是給膽小人爬的。

3. **spicy** [ˋspaɪsɪ] *a.* 辣的

4. **handle** [ˋhændḷ] *vt.* 承受
   例: I can't seem to handle it anymore.
   我似乎再也承受不住了。

5. **be up for sth**
   願意參加（某活動）
   例: We're going to a pub tonight. Are you up for it?
   我們今晚要去酒吧。你要加入嗎？

6. **relieve** [rɪˋliv] *vt.* 減輕，緩和
   例: Being able to tell the truth relieved my guilt.
   能夠說出實話減輕了我的內疚。

7. **be high in...**   ……的含量高
   be low in...   ……的含量低
   例: This kind of fruit is high in Vitamin C.
   這種水果富含維他命 C。

8. **lower** [ˋloɚ] *vt.* 使降低

9. **cool down...**   冷卻……
   例: Drink plenty of cold water to cool yourself down.
   大量喝冷水好讓你自己冷卻下來。

10. **Count me in.**   算我一份。
    Count me out.   不要算我一份。
    例: I hear you're organizing a trip to London. Count me in!
    我聽說你在籌辦一趟倫敦之旅。算我一份！

    I can't go out with you tonight. You'll have to count me out.
    我今晚沒辦法和你外出。你不要把我算進去。

Review Exercises 隨堂小測驗

Part A: Fill in the blanks with the correct answers.

_____ 1. Chili peppers _____ shown to have health benefits.
    (A) has been
    (B) is being
    (C) have
    (D) have been

_____ 2. I like American food, such _____ hamburgers.
    (A) as
    (B) like
    (C) has
    (D) be

_____ 3. Tony ate _____ all the potato chips in the bag.
    (A) barely
    (B) completely
    (C) nearly
    (D) every

_____ 4. _____ to a bowl of chili, I would like to order a salad.
    (A) As well as
    (B) Apart from
    (C) Instead of
    (D) In addition

_____ 5. Our menu ranges _____ Italian food _____ Indian food.
    (A) with, and
    (B) for, of
    (C) to, yet
    (D) from, to

Part B: In the sentences below, circle the correct words in the blanks.

1. After eating a huge meal, my stomach started feeling a bit <u>painful / pain</u>.

2. Sometimes at night, I feel a <u>painful / pain</u> in my leg for some reason.

3. My favorite restaurant has a good <u>variety / various</u> of food.

4. There are <u>variety / various</u> reasons why I like spicy food.

5. Can I interest you in another <u>pickle / pickled</u>, Theresa?

6. Do you like to eat <u>pickle / pickled</u> onions?

7. Is this medicine very <u>effective / effect</u>?

8. What will the <u>effective / effect</u> be of eating too many chili peppers?

9. Do you ever put <u>crush / crushed</u> nuts on ice cream?

10. Ben wanted to <u>crush / crushed</u> the can, but he couldn't.

Urban Oases:
Convenience Stores Transform[1] Taiwan
城市綠洲：便利商店改變台灣

 Warm-up Exercise 暖身練習

1. How often do you buy things at 7-Eleven or other convenience stores?
2. What do you usually buy there?

統一超商自從一九七八年成立並經營 7-ELEVEN 便利商店。由於 7-ELEVEN 全年無休且二十四小時不打烊,因此在這個以服務消費者為主的年代便快速竄紅,從一開始的十四家到現在早已超過四千多家。就連在南投清境農場這樣的高度都有 7-ELEVEN 的設點。該便利商店具體落實深耕台灣市場後,決定朝向無國界、多角化、更多元的模式來經營,為消費者帶來更快速且便利的服務。

　　7-ELEVEN 早期隸屬於美國達拉斯的南方公司,名稱來自於營業初期是從早上七點至晚上十一點,7-ELEVEN 進駐台灣後營業時間才有了重大的變革。某次颱風夜裡,門市人員因為受阻於颱風而無法回家,因此在店裡等待著,想不到三更半夜顧客反而越來越多,因而才發現有延長營業時間至全天二十四小時不打烊的必要。

Topic Reading 主題閱讀 16-01

S trolling[2] through the streets of Taipei, even if you stop at random[3] and look around, you will surely see several convenience stores only a short walk away. The huge number of convenience stores in Taiwan is not only a source of wonder to foreign visitors but also one of the things that Taiwanese who go abroad[4] miss most about home.

Taiwan is ranked first in the world for having the most convenience stores per capita, reflecting[5] an obsession[6] with immediacy because the Taiwanese hate to wait. Since time is a scarce resource, convenience stores can be seen as a revolution in time—no matter when you enter, the shelves are fully stocked[7] and the lights are on. You can pick up or send packages, get cash from the ATM, pay bills, photocopy

documents, grab[8] a pre-packaged fantuan for breakfast or a bedtime snack, or simply buy a latte and sit in the shop flipping through[9] a magazine. There is no distinction[10] between day and night. Without your even realizing it, the scope of your day is expanded[11] and you have broken free of[12] the restraints of the clock.

Moreover, in contrast to[13] the "early to bed, early to rise" constraints imposed[14] by a nine-to-five society, the boundary between work time and play time has been blurred[15], and the demand for nightlife is high in post-modern society. People in Taiwan already commonly use the term 7-Eleven as a metaphor for a working pattern where the sun never sets. When everything becomes dark and quiet late at night, you can still see city life carrying on[16] at the convenience store, making it the standardized image of a city that never sleeps.

 Reading Exercises 閱讀隨堂考

_____ 1. Which characteristic of convenience stores is highlighted in the reading?
    (A) They only offer cheap products.
    (B) They are not popular with foreigners.
    (C) They are very convenient to shop at.
    (D) They have been in Taiwan for five years.

_____ 2. Which of the following is NOT mentioned in the reading?
    (A) Taiwan has the most convenience stores based on population.
    (B) Convenience stores have bank machines.
    (C) Convenience stores only have a limited selection.
    (D) Taiwanese people are impatient when it comes to waiting.

Vocabulary & Phrases   單字片語解密

1. **transform** [trænsˋfɔrm] *vt.*
   使改變，使轉換
   transform A into B   將 A 轉變成 B
   = turn A into B
   = change A into B
   例: They have transformed the old
   train station into a museum.
   他們已經把那個舊火車站改建成一
   座博物館。

2. **stroll** [strol] *vi.* & *n.* 散步
   take a stroll   散步
   = take a walk
   = go for a stroll
   = go for a walk
   例: My parents usually take a stroll
   in the park after dinner.
   我爸媽通常在晚餐後會去公園散
   步。

3. **at random**   隨便地，任意地
   (= randomly [ˋrændəmlɪ] *adv.*)
   例: Lisa opened to a page in the
   magazine at random and
   started reading.
   麗莎隨意翻開雜誌的一頁並開始閱
   讀。

4. **abroad** [əˋbrɔd] *adv.* 在國外
   go abroad / travel abroad
   出國 / 出國旅行
   例: Whether we'll travel abroad this
   year depends on how much
   money we have.
   我們今年是否出國玩要看我們有多
   少錢而定。

5. **reflect** [rɪˋflɛkt] *vt.* 反映；反射
   例: My teacher always says that our
   behavior reflects our thoughts.
   我的老師總說，我們的行為反應我
   們的思想。

6. **obsession** [əbˋsɛʃən] *n.*
   著迷，縈繞不去的念頭 / 想法
   obsess [əbˋsɛs] *vt.* 使著迷
   be obsessed with...
   對……著迷；滿腦子想的都是……
   例: I just can't figure out why people
   are so obsessed with money
   and power.
   我就是想不透為何人們對金錢和權
   力如此著迷。

7. **stock** [stak] *vt.* 貯存 & *n.* 存貨，
   庫存
   have...in stock   有……的存貨
   例: We have three blue shirts in
   stock, but they are all mediums.
   我們有三件藍襯衫的庫存，但都是
   M 號的。

8. **grab** [græb] *vt.* 抓取，攫取
   grab a bite to eat
   隨便吃點東西果腹
   例: Let's grab a bite to eat before
   we go to the movies.
   我們去看電影前先隨便吃點東西
   吧。

9. **flip through...**
   快速瀏覽（書、雜誌）
   例: Lisa flipped through the travel
   brochure.
   麗莎翻了一下旅遊手冊。
   ＊brochure [broˋʃur] *n.* 小冊子

10. **distinction** [dɪˋstɪŋkʃən] *n.*
    區別，差別
    例: It is important to make the
    distinction between right and
    wrong.
    區分對與錯很重要。

11. **expand** [ɪkˋspænd] *vt.* & *vi.* 擴張，擴大

12. **break free of...** 掙脫 / 逃脫……

    例: Feminists are still trying to break free of a male-dominated society.
    女性主義者仍然試圖從父權主導的社會中掙脫出來。

    ＊**dominate** [ˋdɑmə͵net] *vt.* 統治，主宰

13. **in contrast** [ˋkɑntræst] **to...** 和……成對比

    例: The kitten appears small in contrast to its mother.
    這隻小貓和母貓比起來體型小多了。

14. **impose** [ɪmˋpoz] *vt.* 施加，加諸
    impose A on B
    把 A 施加 / 加諸於 B

    例: The government has imposed a ban on smoking in public places.
    政府已下達不准在公共場所吸菸的禁令。

15. **blur** [blɝ] *vt.* 使模糊不清，使朦朧

    例: The author tried to blur the lines between fact and fiction.
    這名作者試圖模糊事實和虛構的界線。

16. **carry on** 繼續
    carry on with sth 繼續做某事

    例: Life will carry on even if I lose my loved ones.
    即使我失去所愛，日子還是要過下去。

    I'll carry on with this project, even at the risk of losing my reputation.
    即使冒著名譽受損的危險，我仍然要繼續這項企劃。

1. **urban** [ˋɝbən] *a.* 城市的
   rural [ˋrʊrəl] *a.* 鄉村的

2. **oases** [oˋesiz] *n.* 綠洲（複數形）
   oasis [oˋesɪs] *n.* 綠洲（單數形）

3. **rank** [ræŋk] *vt.* 名列

4. **per capita** [pɚˋkæpɪtə] *adv.* 每人（平均）地

5. **immediacy** [ɪˋmidɪəsɪ] *n.* 即時，立刻

6. **revolution** [͵rɛvəˋluʃən] *n.* 革命

7. **shelf** [ʃɛlf] *n.* （書櫃等的）架子

8. **ATM** 自動櫃員機
   （為 automated teller machine 的縮寫）

9. **photocopy** [ˋfotə͵kɑpɪ] *vt.* 影印

10. **pre-packaged** [͵priˋpækɪdʒd] *a.* （食品販售前）預先包裝的

11. **scope** [skop] *n.* 範圍，領域

12. **restraint** [rɪˋstrent] *n.* 限制，控制

13. **constraint** [kənˋstrent] *n.* 約束，限制

14. **boundary** [ˋbaʊndrɪ] *n.* 界線，邊界

15. **post-modern** [͵postˋmɑdɚn] *a.* 後現代的

16. **metaphor** [ˋmɛtəfɚ] *n.* 隱喻

17. **standardized** [ˋstændɚ͵daɪzd] *a.* 標準化的

Sentence Structure Analysis 句型分析

The huge number of convenience stores in Taiwan｜is｜not only a source of
❶ ❷ ❸

wonder to foreign visitors but also one of the things｜that Taiwanese who go
❹

abroad miss most about home .

❶ 為本句主詞；

❷ 為本句動詞。由於主詞為 The huge number（這個大的數量），故動詞要使用
單數動詞 is；

❸ 為主詞補語，當中使用了 "not only...but also..."（不僅……而且……）的結構；

❹ 為關係代名詞 that（= which）引導的形容詞子句，用來修飾先行詞 the
things。

 Grammar Points 重點來了

Since time is a scarce resource, convenience stores can be seen as a
revolution in time...

▶ 上述句子使用了以下句型：

see A as B 把 A 視為 B
= view A as B
= regard A as B
= think of A as B
= consider A (to be) B
= deem A (to be) B

例: The little girl was seen as a hero.
那個小女孩被視為英雄。
The party was considered (to be) a great success.
那場派對被視為一大成功。

1. In my neighborhood there are two 7-Eleven convenience stores directly across the street from each other!

   在我家附近有兩間 7-ELEVEN 就隔著馬路正對著彼此！

2. Family Mart, 7-Eleven and OK Mart are just a few of Taiwan's many convenience store chains.

   全家便利商店、7-ELEVEN 和 OK 便利商店只是台灣許多家便利連鎖商店的其中幾家而已。

3. Prices at a convenience store are slightly higher than at a larger supermarket, but many are willing to pay a bit extra because of its convenience.

   便利商店商品的價格要比較大型超市的商品價格稍微高一些，但許多人還是願意為了它的便利性多付一些錢。

4. There's a convenience store just a stone's throw away.

   就在不遠處有一家便利商店。
   ＊a stone's throw away　不遠處

5. Go down to the next traffic light and make a left; you'll see several convenience stores located next to the MRT station.

   沿街走到下一個紅綠燈處再左轉；你會看到幾間便利商店就位在捷運站旁。

6. Several convenience store chains have started offering food for the more health-conscious, including fresh salads.

   一些連鎖便利商店已經開始為那些更講求健康的人提供食物，包括新鮮的沙拉。
   ＊health-conscious [ˈhɛlθˌkɑnʃəs] a. 講究健康的，有健康意識的
   　the health-conscious = health-conscious people　講求健康的人

7. In my home state of Florida, we have to drive for around 30 minutes to get to the nearest convenience store.

   在我家鄉佛羅里達州，我們必須開車約三十分鐘才能抵達最近的便利商店。

8. Some people like to hang out at a convenience store when they need a break from work.

   有些人在工作上需要休息時，他們喜歡在便利商店裡閒晃。

Situational Dialogue 打開話匣子 🔊 16-03

C = Chuck; J = Jasmine

 C: Wow, I'm going to be really busy today! I have to go to the post office and mail a package, go to the bank and pay a few bills, go find an ATM machine and get some cash and go to a photocopy shop and copy some documents. Then finally, I have to go grocery shopping!

 J: Um, you could do all those things at the convenience store across the street.

 C: What? You're joking¹, right?

 J: Nope. In Taiwan, convenience stores are truly convenient. All those things you mentioned are easily accomplished² at any of the major convenience store chains in the city.

 C: But I'll still have to go to a post office to pick up³ something I ordered online.

 J: Nope. You can have the package sent to a convenience store and pick it up there as well! I even buy my concert tickets from a machine at a convenience store.

 C: Wow! That's incredible⁴! But I suppose I'll still have to go down to the train station to buy my high-speed rail tickets to Kaohsiung.

 J: Nope again! I can help you book⁵ your ticket online and then – once again – you just go down to the convenience store and pick it up.

 C: That's amazing! It seems you can go to a convenience store for everything in Taiwan.

 J: You said it!⁶ I can pay parking charges⁷ and even speeding tickets⁸ there.

Vocabulary & Phrases 單字片語解密

1. **You're joking.**　　你在開玩笑吧。
= You're kidding.
= You're kidding me.
注意：
千萬不能說：You're joking me. (×)

2. **accomplish** [əˋkɑmplɪʃ] *vt.* 完成
例: I don't feel I've accomplished very much today.
我覺得今天完成的事情不多。

3. **pick sth up**
領取某物；購買某物；自然學習到某事
例: I picked up my coat from the cleaners.
我去乾洗店領取外套。

Please pick up some milk on your way home.
在回家的路上請買一些牛奶。

Linda picked up Spanish when she was living in Mexico.
琳達住在墨西哥時學到了西班牙語。

4. **incredible** [ɪnˋkrɛdəbḷ] *a.*
令人難以置信的

5. **book** [bʊk] *vt.* 預訂（= reserve）
例: I'd like to book a table for five for 7 o'clock.
我想預訂七點的五人座桌位。

6. **You said it.**　　你說的沒錯。
例: A: To me, John is the greatest cook in the world.
B: You said it.
甲：對我而言，約翰是全世界最棒的廚師。
乙：你說的沒錯。

7. **charge** [tʃɑrdʒ] *n.* 費用 & *vt.* 索費
例: Delivery is free of charge.
送貨免費。

We won't charge you for delivery.
我們不會向您索取送貨費。

8. **a speeding ticket**　　超速罰單

✎ **Review Exercises** 隨堂小測驗

Part A: Fill in the blanks with the correct words.

_____ 1. No matter how hard he tried, George could never break free _____ his habit of smoking.

(A) of
(B) to
(C) with
(D) for

_____ 2. Nina is a hard worker. In _____ , Simon is lazy.

(A) conclusion
(B) response
(C) between
(D) contrast

_____ 3. Why don't we _____ a stroll after dinner?

(A) go
(B) invite
(C) take
(D) make

_____ 4. While waiting in line at the store, Ralph _____ through a sports magazine.

(A) twisted
(B) saw
(C) flipped
(D) wandered

_____ 5. I was just _____ when I said I once ate ten hamburgers at one meal.

(A) joking
(B) joked
(C) joker
(D) jokes

Review Exercises 隨堂小測驗

Part B: Match the terms on the left with the definitions on the right by writing the correct letters in the blanks.

_____ **1.** reflect   a. to change

_____ **2.** expand   b. by chance

_____ **3.** carry on   c. to show

_____ **4.** impose   d. related to the countryside

_____ **5.** rural   e. to reserve

_____ **6.** transform   f. to grow

_____ **7.** at random   g. to continue

_____ **8.** book   h. to force

The Mediterranean Diet
地中海飲食　還你健康好身材

1. Have you ever been on a diet? Did you lose much weight?

2. What do you usually eat for lunch and dinner?

地中海飲食泛指希臘、西班牙、法國和義大利南部等位處地中海沿岸各國,以大量的蔬菜、水果、海鮮、五穀雜糧、堅果和橄欖油,以及少量的牛肉和乳製品、酒類融合而成,形成當地特有的飲食風格。

這種型態的飲食文化對健康有非凡的助益。因為地中海飲食的主要特點就是低脂與高纖,可預防許多人類的疾病,包括心血管疾病、肥胖症與糖尿病等。

科學家發現,地中海飲食其實就是充滿多酚的健康組合。地中海居民的餐桌上都會擺滿豐富多彩的食物,餐食內容包括各式各樣富含抗氧化物質及多酚的蔬果,而烹調時的橄欖油和用餐時搭配的紅酒,也都富含多酚。水果中葡萄、蘋果、草莓、蔓越莓等均含高量的多酚,而各類蔬菜則以花椰菜、洋蔥為佼佼者。另外,飲料中的綠茶,也富含各類的多酚。多酚是一種植物中的化學物質,與部分植物的色彩有關。目前普遍認為多酚對於健康的維持和延緩老化,皆扮演重要的關鍵角色。從這裡我們就可以看出這也是地中海居民健康的主要原因。

The Mediterranean[1] diet is the gold standard for healthy eating.

New diet and weight loss programs are constantly being brought up[2] in response to[3] the global epidemic of obesity. Which ones should be taken seriously, and which are mere fads? Dieting for most people is just another way of taking away the pleasures of dining at a time[4] when they should be enjoying their food.

The Mediterranean diet, however, stands out[5] in the crowd[6]. Rather than make you feel deprived[7], it encourages you to enjoy a balanced assortment of high quality foods. It is not a specific diet plan with rigid rules, but a set of dietary habits and preferences[8] shared by countries that border the Mediterranean Sea including Greece, southern Italy, southern France, and Spain. Scientists have found that people in these countries have a higher average life expectancy[9] and better quality of life than most people in other Western countries.

There are three key features of the Mediterranean diet. First, people should take in[10] a lot of fruits, legumes, unrefined cereals, and vegetables to get fiber and nutrients. Second, a moderate[11] consumption of dairy products, fish, and wine provides healthy fats and antioxidants. The final feature of the diet is a limited intake of meat products.

Olive oil is the major source of fat in Mediterranean cooking as it is used in practically everything, ranging from pastas and breads to salads and stews. Olive oil not only adds flavor but also helps regulate[12] cholesterol and reduce the risk of heart disease and high blood pressure.

Because of its many health benefits and disease-preventing qualities, the Mediterranean diet is often regarded as[13] the gold standard for healthy eating. It's no wonder that Mediterranean eating habits are now being adopted in all corners of the world.

 Reading Exercises　閱讀隨堂考

_____ 1. Which is NOT true about the Mediterranean Diet?
(A) It includes eating lots of fruits.
(B) It is believed to be better than many other diets.
(C) It has several strict procedures to follow.
(D) It doesn't make people feel deprived.

_____ 2. What is the main source of fat in Mediterranean cooking?
(A) Fruits and vegetables.
(B) Pasta.
(C) Pork and lamb.
(D) Olive oil.

Vocabulary & Phrases　單字片語解密

1. **Mediterranean** [ˌmɛdətəˈrɛnɪən] *a.*
   地中海的 & *n.* 地中海

2. **bring up...**
   提出……（建議、想法等）

   例: Marcus brought up many
   creative ideas during the
   meeting.
   馬可仕在會議中提出許多很有創意
   的想法。

3. **in response to...**
   回應……，響應……

   response [rɪˈspɑns] *n.* 回應，響應

   例: The change in operating hours
   was in response to customer
   complaints.
   營運時間的調整是為了因應消費者
   的抱怨。

4. **at a time**　每次

5. **stand out**　脫穎而出；顯眼

   例: Barry's academic performance
   stood out among his peers.
   貝瑞的課業表現在同儕中脫穎而
   出。

6. **in the crowd**
   本片語在本文指『在眾多飲食法中』。

7. **deprived** [dɪˈpraɪvd] *a.* 被剝奪的
   deprive [dɪˈpraɪv] *vt.*
   剝奪（與介詞 of 並用）
   deprive sb of sth　剝奪某人某物

   例: The court deprived the suspect
   of his civil rights.
   法院褫奪這名嫌犯的公民權。

8. **preference** [ˈprɛfərəns] *n.* 偏好
   have a preference for...
   偏好 / 偏愛……

例: Bill has a preference for outdoor
activities such as hiking and
biking.
比爾喜好戶外活動，像是健行和騎
腳踏車。

9. **life expectancy**　　壽命
   = lifespan [ˈlaɪfˌspæn] *n.*
   expectancy [ɪkˈspɛktənsɪ] *n.* 期望，
   預期

   例: The average life expectancy for
   women is higher than that for
   men.
   女人的平均壽命比男人長。

10. **take in...**　　攝取……，吃……

   例: The doctor suggested that
   David take in more fruits and
   vegetables to help his digestion.
   醫生建議大衛多吃水果和蔬菜來幫
   助消化。

11. **moderate** [ˈmɑdərɪt] *a.* 適度的
    moderation [ˌmɑdəˈreʃən] *n.*
    適度；節制
    in moderation　適度地；有節制地

    例: You can have some wine as
    long as you drink in moderation.
    只要適度，你喝點酒也無妨。

12. **regulate** [ˈrɛgjəˌlet] *vt.* 調節；控制

    例: It's getting colder in here. Please
    regulate the temperature of the
    room.
    這裡面愈來愈冷了。麻煩調一下房
    裡的溫度。

13. **be regarded as...**　　被視為……

    例: I regard David as my brother.
    我把大衛當作兄弟。

1. **epidemic** [ˌɛpəˈdɛmɪk] *n.* 流行，盛行；流行病

2. **obesity** [oˈbisətɪ] *n.* 肥胖症
   obese [oˈbis] *a.* 肥胖的

3. **fad** [fæd] *n.* 一時的流行，風尚

4. **dine** [daɪn] *vi.* 用餐

5. **balanced** [ˈbælənst] *a.* 均衡的，平衡的
   a balanced diet　均衡的飲食

6. **assortment** [əˈsɔrtmənt] *n.* 類別；各式各類
   an assortment of...
   各式各類的⋯⋯

7. **specific** [spɪˈsɪfɪk] *a.* 特殊的；特定的

8. **rigid** [ˈrɪdʒɪd] *a.* 嚴密的，嚴格的

9. **dietary** [ˈdaɪəˌtɛrɪ] *a.* 飲食的

10. **legume** [ˈlɛɡjum] *n.* 豆類；豆科植物

11. **unrefined** [ˌʌnrɪˈfaɪnd] *a.* 未精製的；未提煉的

12. **cereal** [ˈsɪrɪəl] *n.* 穀類食品（指燕麥片、玉米片等早餐食品）

13. **fiber** [ˈfaɪbə] *n.* 纖維

14. **nutrient** [ˈnjutrɪənt] *n.* 營養物（可數名詞）
    nutrition [njuˈtrɪʃən] *n.* 營養（不可數名詞）

15. **consumption** [kənˈsʌmpʃən] *n.* 攝取（食物）

16. **dairy** [ˈdɛrɪ] *a.* 乳製品的

17. **antioxidant** [ˌæntɪˈaksədənt] *n.* 抗氧化劑

18. **intake** [ˈɪnˌtek] *n.* （食物的）攝取

19. **stew** [stju] *n.* 燉肉，燉菜

20. **cholesterol** [kəˈlɛstəˌrol] *n.* 膽固醇

21. **benefit** [ˈbɛnəfɪt] *n.* 好處

22. **standard** [ˈstændəd] *n.* 標準
    a / the gold standard　黃金守則

23. **adopt** [əˈdɑpt] *vt.* 採用

Sentence Structure Analysis 句型分析

Dieting for most people 　is　 just another way of taking away the pleasures
　　　❶　　　　　　 ❷　　　　　　　　　　❸

of dining 　at a time when they should be enjoying their food .
　　　　　　　　　　　❹

❶ 動名詞片語，作為本句主詞；

❷ 為本句動詞，由於主詞為動名詞片語，視作單數，故動詞要使用單數 be 動詞 is；

❸ 為主詞補語；

❹ 為介詞片語，作副詞用，修飾之前的動名詞 dining（用餐）。when 為關係副
詞，等於 at which，修飾前面的先行詞 a time。

 Grammar Points 重點來了

▶ Olive oil is the major source of fat in Mediterranean cooking as it is used
in <u>practically everything</u>, ranging from pastas and breads to salads and
stews.
practically [ˈpræktɪkəlɪ] *adv.* 幾乎，差不多（= almost）

注意: practically 及 almost 通常用來修飾涵蓋性完全的詞類，計有四個：
every、no、all 和 any，此處的 practically everything 表『幾乎每樣東
西』。

例: You can see that chain store in practically every city.
你幾乎可以在任何一座城市中看到那家連鎖商店。
Almost all students in this class passed the exam.
幾乎本班所有的學生都考試及格了。

▶ <u>It's no wonder that</u> Mediterranean eating habits are now being adopted in
all corners of the world.
It is no wonder + that 子句　　難怪……
= No wonder + S + V

例: Bobby is naughty. It is no wonder that he is often punished for
misbehaving.
巴比很頑皮，難怪他常會因不乖受到處罰。

1. Have you ever heard of the Mediterranean Diet?

   你聽過『地中海飲食』嗎?

2. Following the Mediterranean Diet seems to make a lot of sense.

   遵循地中海飲食似乎很有道理。

3. Do you follow any particular diet?

   你遵循哪一種特定的飲食習慣呢?

4. I think it's important to get a regular checkup.

   我認為定期接受健康檢查是很重要的。

5. I really should include more fruits and vegetables into my diet.

   我的確應該在我的飲食中多加一點水果及蔬菜了。

6. It's tough to find sufficient time to exercise.

   要找到足夠的時間運動很困難。

7. Junk food is so delicious and tempting to eat.

   垃圾食物是如此美味且誘人。

8. Do you think people are more overweight today than in the past?

   你認為現代人較從前的人更容易過胖嗎?

Situational Dialogue 打開話匣子 🔊 17-03

R = Roberta; M = Matt

 R: I'm sick and tired of¹ dieting². I try to watch what I eat, but I still seem to put on weight³.

 M: Have you heard of the Mediterranean Diet? It's become pretty popular.

 R: Yes, I know it's about eating a lot of fruits and vegetables and cooking food in olive oil.

 M: To me, following the Mediterranean Diet seems to make a lot of sense⁴.

 R: Do you follow⁵ any particular⁶ diet?

 M: Not really; however, I do try to eat fruit and vegetables regularly⁷. Junk food⁸ is so delicious and tempting to⁹ eat, but I try not to eat too much of it.

 R: I guess I really should include more fruits and vegetables into my diet.

 M: Don't forget about exercise – that's important, too.

 R: It's tough to find sufficient time to exercise.

 M: Roberta, that really sounds like a poor excuse not to exercise. You can always find some time, no matter how busy you are.

 R: Yeah, I guess you're right.

1. **be tired of...** 對……感到厭倦
= be bored with...
   例: I was tired of doing the same work every day.
   我對每天做同樣的事感到厭倦。

2. **diet** [ˈdaɪət] *vi.* 依規定的飲食；節食

3. **put on weight** 胖了，增重
= gain weight
   lose weight 瘦了，減肥
   例: You've put on weight recently; you need to go on a diet.
   你最近胖了，需要節食了。

4. **make sense** 有意義
   例: What Peter said doesn't make sense.
   彼得剛才的話沒有意義。

5. **follow** [ˈfɑlo] *vt.* 遵循，採用；聽從
   例: Follow my orders, or you'll be sorry.
   聽從我的命令，否則你會後悔。

6. **particular** [pəˈtɪkjələ] *a.* 特別的；特有的

7. **regularly** [ˈrɛgjələlɪ] *adv.* 有規律地；定期地；經常地

8. **junk food**
   垃圾食物（一般指速食店的食物）

9. **tempting** [ˈtɛmptɪŋ] *a.* 誘惑人的；吸引人的
   tempt [tɛmpt] *vt.* 誘惑，引誘
   tempt sb to V 引誘某人從事……
= tempt sb into V-ing
   例: Nothing would tempt me to live here.
   什麼也吸引不了我來這裏居住。

Review Exercises 隨堂小測驗

Part A: Fill in the blanks with the correct answers.

_____ 1. I _____ a very strict diet in order to lose weight.
    (A) deny
    (B) decide
    (C) eat
    (D) follow

_____ 2. The AIDS _____ began in the 1980s.
    (A) epidemic
    (B) obesity
    (C) assortment
    (D) expectancy

_____ 3. It's _____ that he's fat: he eats all the time.
    (A) about time
    (B) no wonder
    (C) stand out
    (D) in moderation

_____ 4. I recommend you increase your _____ of fruits and vegetables.
    (A) take in
    (B) in take
    (C) intake
    (D) takein

_____ 5. Has Sally put _____ weight?
    (A) on
    (B) off
    (C) to
    (D) with

Review Exercises 隨堂小測驗

Part B: Match the terms on the left with the definitions on the right by writing the correct letters in the blanks.

____ **1.** obese

____ **2.** consumption

____ **3.** stand out

____ **4.** moderate

____ **5.** rigid

____ **6.** adopt

____ **7.** deprived

____ **8.** regulate

a. not having things that are necessary

b. firm; inflexible

c. to be noticeable / special

d. to use

e. eating

 f. to control

g. overweight

h. medium

Bustle[1], Not Romance: Taiwan's Night-Market Culture

非浪漫傳奇——台灣夜市文化

1. What is your favorite night market in Taiwan? Why do you like it the most?

2. What do you eat at night markets? What else have you bought there?

台灣夜市舉世聞名，來訪的遊客許多都指名要參觀各大夜市，連旅居國外的僑胞們最懷念的也都是台灣各鄉鎮隨處可尋的夜市景點。美國有線電視新聞網（CNN）的一則報導列舉出以下重點台灣夜市小吃。下次有空經過這些地方時，不妨停下你的腳步，讓這些食物挑動你的味蕾吧。

一、台北饒河夜市的臭豆腐（Stinky tofu）

二、台北饒河夜市的胡椒餅（Baked black pepper pork）

三、台中豐原夜市的釀魷魚筒（Squid stuffed with risotto）

四、台中逢甲夜市的燒烤（Barbecued anything）

五、台南小北夜市的棺材板（Coffin bread）

六、台南小北夜市的炸蝦捲（Deep fried prawns）

七、高雄瑞豐夜市的大腸包小腸（Rice / Taiwanese sausage）

八、高雄代天宮的滷肉飯（Stewed pork rice）

九、高雄六合夜市的蔥油餅（Scallion pancakes）

十、高雄六合夜市的涼圓（Sweet glass rice dumplings）

When foreign tourists come to Taiwan, where do they want to go? It may surprise you to learn that night markets have surpassed[2] the National Palace Museum and Taipei 101 as the island's hottest tourist attractions[3].

Night markets have at least 200 years of history in Taiwan, dating back to[4] the days when peddlers gathered[5] to create markets. Nowadays, they provide an economic boost[6] to their locales and help preserve[7] traditional snack culture, but they also undeniably[8] take up[9] space, block[10] traffic, create big messes[11], and negatively affect[12] the appearance of cities.

Since the late 1990s, department stores and large supermarkets in Taiwan have even tried to copy the strengths[13] of night markets, with snack stalls brought into basement-level food courts. Although these air-conditioned places are modern and comfortable, department store food courts have had no impact on[14] alfresco markets. Famous night markets are still doing brisk[15] business.

What are the special characteristics[16] of the consumer culture at night markets? Why have food courts not replaced[17] them? "When people walk in night markets, their motivations[18] aren't just to eat snacks and shop. They also want to indulge in[19] the special consumer pleasures and feelings that arise from[20] being amid the hubbub[21] and chaos of crowds," says Yu Shuen-de, an associate research fellow at Academia Sinica's Institute of Ethnology.

The cuisine of Taiwan has absorbed[22] a multitude of[23] foreign influences, but it has also innovated[24] and created many of its own "snacks," or *xiao chi* in Mandarin. While you don't need to go to a night market to eat these snacks, the ambience of night markets makes eating *xiao chi* there especially meaningful.

 Reading Exercises 閱讀隨堂考

_____ 1. Which of the following points is NOT mentioned in the reading?
   (A) Night markets cause some problems.
   (B) Some night markets have disappeared.
   (C) Night markets have a long history in Taiwan.
   (D) A good variety of food is available at night markets.

_____ 2. According to the reading, why do people prefer night markets to department stores?
   (A) Because the prices are cheaper in night markets.
   (B) Because night markets are more modern.
   (C) Because food courts are in the basement level.
   (D) Because people like shopping in large crowds.

Vocabulary & Phrases 單字片語解密

1. **bustle** [`bʌsl̩] *n.* 喧囂
   hustle [`hʌsl̩] *n.* 喧鬧
   the hustle and bustle　熙熙攘攘

2. **surpass** [sə`pæs] *vt.* 勝過
   例: Jeremy Lin's success has surpassed all expectations.
   林書豪的成功已經超越了眾人的期待。

3. **attraction** [ə`trækʃən] *n.* 吸引的東西
   a major tourist attraction
   重要旅遊景點

4. **date back to + 時間**
   追溯到……（時間）
   date back + 一段時間
   追溯到……（一段時間）前
   例: This vase dates back to the Ming Dynasty.
   這個花瓶的年代可以追溯到明朝。
   That relic is very old. It dates back 500 years.
   那座遺跡相當古老，可追溯至五百年前。

5. **gather** [`gæðə] *vi.* 聚集
   例: The kids gathered round to listen to my stories.
   小朋友們聚集在一起聽我講故事。

6. **boost** [bust] *n.* & *vt.* 幫助，促進；一舉，一推
   例: Getting that job did a lot to boost my confidence.
   獲得那份工作對於增加我的自信很有幫助。
   Jack gave me a boost over the fence.
   傑克一把將我舉起越過籬笆。

7. **preserve** [prɪ`zɝv] *vt.* 保護；維護
   例: We all must do our best to preserve the natural habitat.
   我們都必須盡力保護這個自然棲息地。

8. **undeniably** [ˌʌndɪ`naɪəblɪ] *adv.* 不可否認地

9. **take up...**
   佔用／佔據……（空間或時間）
   例: The project took up most of Bill's time.
   那個專案佔去比爾大部分的時間。

10. **block** [blɑk] *vt.* 阻礙，阻擋
    例: The man in front of me is blocking my view of the stage.
    我前方的男子擋住了我看舞台的視線。

11. **mess** [mɛs] *n.* 凌亂，髒亂
    例: Henry's room is always in a mess and full of trash.
    亨利的房間總是一團亂，裡面到處都是垃圾。

12. **affect** [ə`fɛkt] *vt.* 影響

13. **strength** [strɛŋθ] *n.* 長處

14. **have no / an impact on...**
    對……沒有／有影響
    = have no / an influence on...
    = have no / an effect on...
    例: The writer's style had a deep impact on his literary successors.
    這位作家的風格對後世文人有深遠的影響。

15. **brisk** [brɪsk] *a.* 興旺的，繁榮的
    brisk business　生意興隆

Vocabulary & Phrases 單字片語解密

16. **characteristic** [ˌkærɪktəˈrɪstɪk] *n.*
特徵

17. **replace** [rɪˈples] *vt.* 取代，代替
replace A with B　　以 B 取代 A
例: We're going to replace our old
car with a new one next month.
我們下個月要買一部新車來汰換舊
車。

18. **motivation** [ˌmotəˈveʃən] *n.* 動機；
幹勁
例: What is the motivation behind
this sudden change?
這項突然改變的背後動機為何？

19. **indulge (oneself) in...**
（使某人自己）沉溺於 / 沉浸在……
indulge [ɪnˈdʌldʒ] *vi. & vt.* （使）沉
溺於
例: For my birthday, I indulged in a
day at the spa.
我生日那天，享受了一整天的水療。

20. **arise from...**　　起因於……
= result from...
例: Obviously, the accident arose
from the driver's carelessness.
這起意外很顯然起因於駕駛人的粗
心。

21. **hubbub** [ˈhʌbʌb] *n.* 喧鬧聲

22. **absorb** [əbˈsɔrb] *vt.* 汲取；吸收

23. **a multitude of...**
許多 / 眾多……
multitude [ˈmʌltəˌtjud] *n.* 許多
例: The scientists encountered a
multitude of problems while
carrying out the research.
那些科學家進行這項研究時遇到了
許多問題。

24. **innovate** [ˈɪnəˌvet] *vt.* 革新，創新
innovative [ˈɪnəˌvetɪv] *a.* 創新的
例: Our company is innovating new
products all the time.
我們公司不斷創新產品。

 Bonus Vocabulary 補充單字

1. **peddler** [ˈpɛdlɚ] *n.* 小販

2. **locale** [loˈkæl] *n.* （事情發生的）場
所，地點

3. **stall** [stɔl] *n.* 攤位；隔間

4. **food court** [ˈfud ˌkɔrt] *n.* （購物中
心內的）美食街

5. **alfresco** [ælˈfrɛsko] *a.* 戶外的，露
天的

6. **amid** [əˈmɪd] *prep.*
在……之中（= among）

7. **chaos** [ˈkeas] *n.* 混亂

8. **associate** [əˈsoʃɪɪt] *a.* 副的

9. **Academia Sinica's Institute of
Ethnology**　　中研院民族所
Academia Sinica [ˌækəˈdimɪəˈsɪnɪkə]
中央研究院
ethnology [ɛθˈnɑlədʒɪ] *n.* 民族學

10. **cuisine** [kwɪˈzin] *n.* 美食

11. **ambience** [ˈæmbɪəns] *n.* 氛圍；格
調

Sentence Structure Analysis   句型分析

Since the late 1990s , department stores and large supermarkets in Taiwan

❶   ❷

have even tried to copy the strengths of night markets , with snack stalls

❸   ❹

brought into basement-level food courts.

❶ 為時間副詞片語，由於是 Since（自從）引導，故主要子句動詞要使用現在完成式或現在完成進行式，本句中為現在完成式 have even tried（甚至嘗試）；

❷ 為主要子句的主詞；

❸ 為主要子句的動詞（have even tried）及受詞（to copy the strengths of night markets）；

❹ with 為情狀介詞，表狀態。結構為：

with + 受詞 + 形容詞 / 介詞片語 / 分詞

例: Tom was sitting there <u>with</u> his arms <u>open</u>.
                                            形容詞

湯姆雙臂張開坐在那兒。

Mike was talking to me <u>with</u> a pipe <u>in his mouth</u>.
                                          介詞片語

邁可嘴裡含著煙斗跟我說話。

 Grammar Points   重點來了

Nowadays, they provide an economic boost to their locales and help preserve traditional snack culture.

▶ preserve 一字表『保存（食物、文化等）』；務必分辨此字與以下幾個字的差別：conserve（保育、節省）、reserve（預約；預訂）。

例: To conserve electricity, we are cutting down on our central heating.
為了節約用電，我們在削減中央暖氣系統的使用量。
I've reserved a room in the name of Jones.
我用瓊斯的名字預訂了一個房間。

1. Do you enjoy going to night markets in Taiwan?

   你喜歡去逛台灣的夜市嗎？

2. Which night markets have you been to? What did you do / eat there?

   你去過哪些夜市？你在那兒做了什麼／吃了什麼？

3. Night markets have surpassed the National Palace Museum and Taipei 101 as the island's hottest tourist attractions.

   夜市已經超越故宮博物院及台北一零一，成為島上最熱門的旅遊景點。

4. Night markets have at least 200 years of history in Taiwan.

   夜市在台灣至少有兩百年的歷史。

5. What's your opinion of Taiwanese food?

   你對台灣食物有什麼看法？

6. Have you ever tried some Taiwanese food you didn't like? Do you remember the name of it?

   你曾經嘗試過什麼台灣食物是你不喜歡的嗎？你記得那道菜的名稱嗎？

7. Taiwanese cuisine has innovated and created many of its own "snacks," or *xiao chi*.

   台灣的美食已經創新並創造出許多自身的「點心」，或稱為「小吃」。

8. The ambience of night markets makes eating *xiao chi* there especially meaningful.

   夜市的氛圍使得在那兒吃小吃變得特別有意義。

Situational Dialogue 打開話匣子 🔊 18-03

F = Freda; G = Glen

 F: Glen, do you enjoy going to night markets in Taiwan?

 G: Yes, it's one of the things I really like about living here.

 F: Did you know that night markets have surpassed the National Palace Museum and Taipei 101 as the island's hottest tourist attractions?

 G: I didn't know that. That's interesting.

 F: Which night markets have you been to?

 G: I especially like the one on Raohe Street and the Shilin Night Market, which is gigantic[1].

 F: What did you do there?

 G: Mostly, I ate some snacks that street vendors had available.

 F: What's your opinion of Taiwanese food?

 G: I like it a lot – there's a lot of variety[2].

 F: Have you ever tried some Taiwanese food you didn't like?

 G: Well, I'm not too fond of[3] stinky tofu or pig intestines[4], that's for sure[5].

F: So besides eating, did you do anything else at the night markets?

G: Actually, yes; I bought a backpack[6] at a really cheap price[7]. I don't think it's very good quality, but at least the price was right.

 Vocabulary & Phrases 單字片語解密

1. **gigantic** [dʒaɪˋgɛntɪk] *a.* 巨大的

2. **variety** [vəˋraɪətɪ] *n.* 種種;多樣性
   例: There is a wide variety of patterns to choose from.
   有很多種樣式供選擇。
   We all need variety in our diet.
   我們大家都需要在飲食上有多樣性的變化。

3. **be fond of + N/V-ing**　喜歡……
   例: I'm not fond of telling people what to do.
   我不喜歡告訴別人要做什麼事。

4. **intestine** [ɪnˋtɛstɪn] *n.* 內腸(常用複數)

5. **That's for sure.**　那是肯定的。
   例: One thing is for sure—the test is not going to be easy.
   有一件事是可以肯定的——那次的考試不會太容易。

6. **backpack** [ˋbæk͵pæk] *n.* 背包

7. **at a cheap price**　以便宜的價格
   注意:
   與數字有關的名詞常與介詞 at 並用,如:at the age of five(五歲時)、at the speed of 100 km / hr(時速一百公里)、at that rate(以那樣的速度)。

Review Exercises 隨堂小測驗

Part A: Choose the correct answer.

____ 1. The bright colors and flowers give this restaurant a nice _____.
  (A) idea
  (B) chaos
  (C) confusion
  (D) ambience

____ 2. What is your opinion _____ German food?
  (A) of
  (B) for
  (C) in
  (D) with

____ 3. _____ the food is delicious, it is pretty oily and fattening.
  (A) Even
  (B) While
  (C) Despite
  (D) However

____ 4. This tradition _____ back to the 18th century.
  (A) date
  (B) dates
  (C) dated
  (D) dating

____ 5. I decided to treat _____ to some fantastic dessert.
  (A) me
  (B) myself
  (C) my
  (D) I

Review Exercises 隨堂小測驗

Part B: Each sentence has a mistake in it. Correct the mistakes and write the corrected sentences in the blanks below.

1. Night markets have many interesting characteristic that people enjoy.

_____

2. Night markets are great places to visit, what many cheap prices available.

_____

3. The decision will have a big impact many people.

_____

4. During the past few decades, night markets become very popular.

_____

5. Do you enjoy to go to night markets in Taiwan?

_____

The Instant Noodle Guru
泡麵達人駕到

1. Do you like eating instant noodles? Why or why not?

2. Would you ever buy instant noodles in a restaurant?

泡　麵達人館的泡麵合計有一百一十款不同口味及特色的速食麵，不知道如何選擇的顧客，店長特別推薦，若您喜歡吃清淡的口味，可以選擇日本麵，想吃份量多的話可以選擇韓國麵，因為韓國麵的麵體大約是東南亞的兩倍大，最重要的是，韓國口味雖然重但是卻不油膩。

　　店長傳授煮泡麵的訣竅就是，火要大、水要滾，還要加上青菜及肉，最後打上一顆蛋，煮到八分熟，短短三分鐘，美味滿分的泡麵就完成了。

TOP PHOTO

R estaurants featuring[1] Western or Asian cuisines are everywhere in Taiwan, but have you ever heard of[2] restaurants that specialize[3] in instant noodles? The idea of running a restaurant that sells instant noodles may sound absurd[4], especially when they are cheap and can easily be cooked at home. Then, what's the point in[5] going to a restaurant? To pour hot water into a bowl of instant noodles is one thing, but to fix a delicious meal out of instant noodles is quite another[6].

For those non-believers, Pao Mian Da Ren Guan, which literally[7] means Instant Noodle Guru's Restaurant, is ready to convert[8] you with its instant noodle specialties. The restaurant offers a wide variety of[9] instant noodles, ranging from local brands to[10] ones imported from Japan, Korea, Singapore, and Indonesia. Customers can pick their preferred brands and tell the chef what ingredients they want to add to their noodles. Choices include eggs, vegetables, pork, beef, golden needle mushrooms, and other common[11] hot pot ingredients. There's a separate[12] price for each individual ingredient, but the restaurant also provides a range of pre-set meals.

In fact, the idea of putting instant noodles on the menu is nothing new. Food stalls in South Korea and tea restaurants in Hong Kong and Macau have been offering meals made with instant noodles for years. Even though their potential[13] health risks have been a public concern[14], the low prices, variety of flavors, and easy preparation of instant noodles make them widely popular in Asia.

 Reading Exercises 閱讀隨堂考

_____ 1. In the first paragraph, what does "absurd" mean?
    (A) Illogical.
    (B) Expensive.
    (C) Fun.
    (D) Boring.

_____ 2. According to the reading, which is NOT true?
    (A) Putting instant noodles in restaurants is a new idea.
    (B) Pao Mian Da Ren Guan offers many types of instant noodles.
    (C) Eating instant noodles may hurt your health.
    (D) The ingredients have different prices.

Vocabulary & Phrases　單字片語解密

1. **feature** [ˈfitʃɚ] *vt.* 以……為特色；主打

   例: The boutique features fashion designers from all over the world.
   那家精品店有世界各地服裝設計師的作品。

2. **hear of...**　　聽說過……

   hear from sb
   得到某人的消息 / 回音

   例: Have you heard of the movie *Beauty and the Beast*?
   你聽過《美女與野獸》這部電影嗎？

   I haven't heard from Ted since he got married.
   自從泰德結婚後我就沒收過他的音信。

3. **specialize** [ˈspɛʃəˌlaɪz] *vi.* 專攻，專門從事

   specialize in...
   專門從事 / 專精於……

   例: Mike specializes in creating web pages for companies in Taiwan.
   邁可專為台灣各公司架設網頁。

4. **The idea of running a restaurant that sells instant noodles may sound absurd.**

   ＊run [rʌn] *vt.* 經營（ = operate [ˈɑpəˌret]）
   absurd [əbˈsɝd] *a.* 荒謬的

5. **What's the point in...?**
   ……有什麼意義 / 用處？

   There's no point (in) + V-ing
   = There's no sense (in) + V-ing
   = There's no use (in) + V-ing
   ……沒有什麼意義 / 用處

   例: If the boss is not coming in today, then what's the point in our meeting?
   如果老闆今天不來，我們開這個會有何意義？

   There's no point (in) worrying about things you can't control.
   擔心你無法掌控的事是沒有用的。

6. **...is one thing, but / and...is another**
   ……是一回事，而……又是另一回事

   例: Falling in love is one thing, but getting married is another.
   談戀愛是一回事，結婚又是另一回事。

7. **literally** [ˈlɪtərəlɪ] *adv.* 字面上地；真正地

   例: Literally translated, the term karoshi means death from overworking.
   從字面上直譯，『過勞死』的意思就是因工作過度而死亡。

8. **convert** [kənˈvɝt] *vt.* 轉變，轉換
   convert A into B　將 A 轉化成 B
   = change A into B
   = turn A into B

   例: They converted the theater into a supermarket.
   他們把戲院改裝成超市。

9. **a (wide) variety of...**
   = a (wide) range of...
   各式各樣的……

   例: There are a variety of ways to save money, but they all involve hard work and discipline.
   存錢有很多種方法，但都和努力工作與有自制力脫不了關係。

10. **range from...to...**
    範圍從……到……都有
    例: Hank's taste in music ranges from country to heavy metal.
    漢克喜愛的音樂類型從鄉村音樂到重金屬都有。

11. **common** [ˈkɑmən] *a.* 常見的

12. **separate** [ˈsɛprɪt] *a.* 個別的 & [ˈsɛpəˌret] *vt.* 分隔；使分離
    separate A from B
    將 A 與 B 分隔／隔開
    例: Teddy and Andy went their separate ways when the partnership ended.
    泰迪與安迪合夥關係結束後便分道揚鑣了。
    The Atlantic Ocean separates America from Europe.
    大西洋把美洲與歐洲隔開了。

13. **potential** [pəˈtɛnʃəl] *a.* 潛在的 & *n.* 潛能
    例: The new shop across the street is a potential rival to our business.
    對街的那間新店對我們的生意是潛在的對手。
    The boss thinks Terry is full of potential.
    老闆認為泰瑞充滿潛力。

14. **concern** [kənˈsɜn] *n.* 擔心
    例: There is growing concern about violence on television.
    世人對電視上的暴力日漸感到憂心。

1. **cuisine** [kwɪˈzin] *n.* 料理

2. **instant noodles**　速食麵，泡麵

3. **pour** [pɔr] *vt.* 倒，灌，注入

4. **fix** [fɪks] *vt.* 準備（飯菜）
   fix a meal　準備一頓飯
   = prepare a meal
   = cook a meal

5. **guru** [ˈɡʊru] *n.*（某一領域的）專家，大師

6. **specialty** [ˈspɛʃəltɪ] *n.* 招牌菜；名產

7. **import** [ɪmˈpɔrt] *vt.* 進口
   export [ɪksˈpɔrt] *vt.* 出口

8. **preferred** [prɪˈfɜd] *a.* 偏好的，合意的

9. **ingredient** [ɪnˈɡridɪənt] *n.* 食材

10. **pre-set** [priˈsɛt] *a.* 事先準備好的

11. **on the menu**　在菜單上

12. **stall** [stɔl] *n.* 攤位

13. **flavor** [ˈflevɚ] *n.* 口味

Sentence Structure Analysis 句型分析

The restaurant offers a wide variety of instant noodles, <u>ranging</u> from local brands to ones <u>imported</u> from Japan, Korea, Singapore, and Indonesia.

> 原句原為：

The restaurant offers a wide variety of instant noodles, <u>which range</u> from local brands to ones <u>which are imported</u> from Japan, Korea, Singapore, and Indonesia.

注意:
形容詞子句可化簡為分詞片語，原則如下：
(1) 去除作主詞的關係代名詞；
(2) 之後的動詞改為現在分詞；
(3) 動詞若為 be 動詞則改為 being，且 being 可省略。

> 故原句中 "which range" 化簡為 "ranging" 而 "which are imported" 化簡為 "imported"。

 Grammar Points 重點來了

Customers can pick their preferred brands and tell the chef what <u>ingredients</u> they want to <u>add</u> <u>to</u> their noodles.

注意:
(1) 此處使用 add A to B 的句型：
I added sugar to the coffee.
我把糖加到咖啡裡。
(2) 在本句中，add 的受詞是之前的 ingredients，之後加介詞 to，再接另一個受詞 their noodles。

1. Do many people eat instant noodles in the West?

在西方會有很多人吃泡麵嗎？

2. There's a restaurant called Pao Mian Da Ren Guan that specializes in gourmet instant noodles.

有一家餐廳名為『泡麵達人』，那家餐廳專售美食泡麵。
＊gourmet [ˈgʊrme] *n.* 美食家 & *a.* 美味的

3. The restaurant offers a wide variety of instant noodles.

那家餐廳提供各式各樣的泡麵。

4. What's the point in going to a restaurant to eat instant noodles?

去餐廳吃泡麵有什麼意義呢？

5. Don't knock it till you've tried it.

你沒試過就不要批評。
＊knock [nɑk] *vt.* 批評

6. I wonder if it's just a fad or something that will be popular for a long time.

我想知道這只會是一個短期的風潮，又或者這會流行很長一段時間。
＊fad [fæd] *n.* 一時的流行

7. I guess time will tell.

我猜時間會證明一切。

8. Do you have a favorite restaurant in Taiwan that you often go to?

你在台灣有沒有哪家最喜愛的餐廳是你常去的？

Situational Dialogue 打開話匣子 🔊 19-03

G = Gary; J = Jasmine

 G: Hi, Jasmine. What are you eating?

 J: Oh, just some instant noodles. Do many people eat instant noodles in the West?

 G: Some people do, but they aren't as popular as they are in Asia. I've had them before, but I find them kind of plain[1] and boring.

 J: In Taiwan, there's a restaurant called Pao Mian Da Ren Guan that specializes in gourmet instant noodles.

 G: What's the point in going to a restaurant to eat instant noodles? You can just pour water on them and eat them at home.

 J: Hey, don't knock it till you've tried it. Some of my friends have gone there, and they say the food's pretty good.

 G: I wonder if it's just a fad[2] or something that will be popular for a long time.

 J: It's hard to say. I guess time will tell. Do you have a favorite restaurant in Taiwan that you often go to?

 G: Yeah, it's called McDonald's.

 J: Gary! You should experience more Taiwanese food while you're here.

 G: I suppose you're right.

1. **plain** [plen] *a.* 平淡無奇的
   plain food　　平淡的食物

2. **fad** [fæd] *n.* 一時的流行
   例: There is a fad for physical
   fitness.
   有一股健身的熱潮。

Review Exercises 隨堂小測驗

Part A: Fill in the blanks with the correct answer.

____ 1. That store has a good _____ of products.
   (A) category
   (B) variety
   (C) select
   (D) total

____ 2. They specialize _____ Thai food.
   (A) in
   (B) about
   (C) for
   (D) with

____ 3. The old house _____ into a museum.
   (A) has convert
   (B) was converted
   (C) is converting
   (D) been convert

____ 4. I wonder _____ Helen will make dessert tonight.
   (A) that
   (B) if
   (C) though
   (D) who

____ 5. Randy's _____ drink is milk tea.
   (A) prefer
   (B) preferred
   (C) preferring
   (D) preferable

Review Exercises　隨堂小測驗

Part B: In the sentences below, circle the correct words in the blanks.

1. What's / Why's the point of eating ice cream on a cold day?

2. Prices range from / for $180 to $920.

3. I haven't hear / heard of that restaurant before.

4. Tim often eats at the Golden Crown Restaurant, which / that is near his home.

5. I think more onions need to be adds / added to the chili.

6. These noodles are too plane / plain.

7. Running a business is one thing; running a successful one is another / the other.

8. Make sure to separate the documents into / to different piles.

9. There are various / variety ways to cook eggs.

10. Are these candies import / imported?

The Pearl of Taiwan

一口珍珠，一口奶茶，口口透心涼

台灣早期的珍珠奶茶誕生於泡沫紅茶店,多半強調奶茶必須新鮮現搖。自從連鎖式珍珠奶茶出現後,為了口味管理與加快生產速度,不少連鎖店改用事先調好的奶茶。事先調好的奶茶多半也不是在開店前以紅茶跟奶精調出,而是總店直接以奶茶粉的形式提供到店裡,加水即可。為了將奶茶製作成奶茶粉的形式,勢必直接把紅茶磨碎,所以味道與傳統現搖的奶茶會有落差。這種奶茶若靜放幾小時,會發現粉末完全沉澱,上面是透明的糖水,證明這樣調出來的奶茶,紅茶成分並不溶於水中。因此,有部份愛好者堅持喝現調的珍珠奶茶。

台灣珍珠奶茶一般採用粉狀奶精,由於粉狀奶精熱量較高,且木薯珍珠也具有極高熱量(一顆約數十大卡不等),有專家指出,一杯 500cc 珍珠奶茶的熱量,相當於一個普通排骨便當的熱量,對於致力於減輕體重的人們,不宜經常飲用。

O n a hot summer day, there is nothing quite as refreshing[1] as the taste of milk tea combined[2] with bite-sized tapioca balls to cool you down. How did someone come up with[3] this brilliant idea? In the early 1980s, an employee at Chun Shui Tang Teahouse in Taichung started experimenting[4] with adding different kinds of fruits, syrups, and yams to tea. Eventually, she put tapioca balls in the bottom of the cup and nicknamed it pearl milk tea. Around the same time in Tainan, the owner of Hanlin Teahouse was working on expanding[5] his recipes and developed what he also called pearl milk tea.

While many people in southern Taiwan liked pearl milk tea, it didn't really catch on[6] everywhere until a Japanese television show profiled[7] the Chun Shui Tang Teahouse. Soon, people of all ages were lining up[8] for this strange mixture of eating and drinking. Other teashops copied Chun's idea and added small pieces of candy or jelly to the tea. Recently, teashop owners have even been adding colored tapioca balls to milk tea to attract customers and be different from other shops.

Pearl milk tea is one of Taiwan's most famous treasures, and many people around the world drink it whenever they can get their hands on[9] a cup. Bubble teashops have been opened in places with big Asian populations like California, Toronto, New York, and even some countries in Europe.

 Reading Exercises 閱讀隨堂考

____ 1. In the first paragraph, what does "come up with" mean?
    (A) Take away.
    (B) Lose.
    (C) Think of.
    (D) Steal.

____ 2. Which of the following is true?
    (A) Pearl milk tea balls didn't have different colors originally.
    (B) Pearl milk tea started in Japan before it came to Taiwan.
    (C) Pearl milk tea was popular everywhere in Taiwan immediately.
    (D) Pearl milk tea was developed around 2000.

Vocabulary & Phrases   單字片語解密

1. **refreshing** [rɪˈfrɛʃɪŋ] *a.* 提神的

    例: I always enjoy refreshing glasses of iced tea on hot summer afternoons.
    在炎熱的夏日午後，我總是喜歡喝清涼有勁的冰茶。

2. **combine** [kəmˈbaɪn] *vt.* 使結合

    combine A with B
    結合／混合 A 與 B

    例: The chef combined mayonnaise with mustard to create a special sauce.
    那位主廚把美乃滋和芥末混在一起，調配出一種特殊醬料。

3. **come up with...**
    想出／提出⋯⋯

    例: John came up with a creative slogan to advertise the new product.
    約翰想出一個有創意的口號來廣告新產品。

4. **experiment** [ɪkˈspɛrəmənt] *vi.*
    實驗；試驗

    experiment with...
    用⋯⋯做實驗／試驗

    experiment on...
    對⋯⋯做實驗

    例: The students experimented with several different chemicals.
    學生們用幾種不同的化學物品做實驗。

    Scientists have to be careful when they do experiments on people.
    科學家用人體做實驗時必須非常小心。

5. **expand** [ɪkˈspænd] *vt.* & *vi.* 擴展，擴充

    例: The company is expanding its factory's production capabilities.
    這家公司正在擴展其工廠的生產力。

6. **catch on**   流行

    例: Jazz is catching on in Taiwan.
    = Jazz is getting popular in Taiwan.
    爵士樂在台灣正在流行。

7. **profile** [ˈprofaɪl] *vt.* 為⋯⋯作簡介 & *n.* 側面像

    例: The author was profiled in The New York Times last week.
    上星期的《紐約時報》有那名作家的簡介。

8. **line up**   排隊
    = stand in line

    例: Hundreds of fans were lining up to get the singer's autograph.
    好幾百位歌迷在排隊等候這名歌手的親筆簽名。

9. **get one's hands on...**
    獲取／得到⋯⋯

    例: How do I get my hands on one of those free T-shirts?
    我要如何才能獲得一件那些免費的 T 恤呢？

Bonus Vocabulary 補充單字

1. **pearl** [pɝl] *n.* 珍珠

2. **bite-sized** [ˈbaɪtˌsaɪzd] *a.* 一口大小的；很小的

3. **tapioca** [ˌtæpɪˈokə] *n.* 樹薯粉

4. **cool sb down/cool down sb**
   使某人涼爽下來；使某人冷靜下來

5. **employee** [ˌɛmplɔɪˈi] *n.* 雇員
   employer [ɪmˈplɔɪɚ] *n.* 雇主

6. **syrup** [ˈsɪrəp] *n.* 糖漿

7. **yam** [jæm] *n.* 蕃薯、甘薯

8. **nickname** [ˈnɪkˌnem] *vt.* 給……起綽號 & *n.* 綽號

9. **work on...** （著手）進行……

10. **recipe** [ˈrɛsəpɪ] *n.* 配方；食譜

11. **jelly** [ˈdʒɛlɪ] *n.* 果凍

12. **customer** [ˈkʌstəmɚ] *n.* 顧客

13. **bubble** [ˈbʌbḷ] *n.* 泡沫，氣泡

Sentence Structure Analysis　句型分析

..., the owner of Hanlin Teahouse　was working　on expanding his recipes

❶ ❷

and　developed　what he also called pearl milk tea .

❸ ❹

❶ 為本句主詞；

❷ 為本句的動詞；

❸ 為對等連接詞，在此連接前後兩個過去進行式及過去式的動詞 was working 及 developed；

❹ 為以 what 引導的名詞子句作 developed 的受詞。

Grammar Points　重點來了

Pearl milk tea is one of Taiwan's most famous treasures, and many people around the world drink it whenever they can get their hands on a cup.

▶ whenever 前後皆為完整的子句，可知它是副詞連接詞以連接兩句。此時 whenever 等於 every time（每當）。

While many people in southern Taiwan liked pearl milk tea, it didn't really catch on everywhere until a Japanese television show profiled the Chun Shui Tang Teahouse.

▶ while 在此表『雖然』，等於 although。while 也有其他意思：

(1) 表示『當』：

例: I'll take care of your children while you are away.
你不在時我會照顧你的孩子。

(2) 表『而』，用以對比兩事物（= whereas）：

例: John is smart, while his brother is stupid.
約翰聰明，而他弟弟很笨。

1. Have you ever tried pearl milk tea / bubble tea? Do you like it?

你有沒有試過珍珠奶茶 / 泡沫紅茶？你喜歡嗎？

2. On a hot summer day, there is nothing quite as refreshing as the taste of milk tea.

在炎熱的夏日裡，沒有什麼比奶茶的味道更讓人感到清新了。

3. Pearl milk tea didn't really catch on everywhere at first.

珍珠奶茶一開始沒有真正到處流行。

4. It was only until a Japanese TV show featured bubble tea that it became really popular.

直到日本電視節目特別介紹泡沫紅茶，它才真正變得受歡迎。

5. Soon, people of all ages were lining up for this strange mixture of eating and drinking.

很快地，各個年齡層的人為了這種飲食的奇怪混合物而排隊購買。

6. Pearl milk tea is one of Taiwan's most famous treasures.

珍珠奶茶是台灣最有名的珍寶之一。

7. Bubble teashops have been opened in places with big Asian populations like California, Toronto, New York, and even some countries in Europe.

泡沫紅茶店已在有眾多亞洲居民的地方如加州，多倫多，紐約，甚至是歐洲的一些國家開張營業了。

8. Are there any bubble teashops in your country?

貴國有泡沫紅茶店嗎？

Situational Dialogue 打開話匣子 20-03

D = Donnie; M = Mary

 D: I'm thirsty. Let's get something to drink.

 M: What do you suggest[1], Donnie?

 D: Have you ever tried pearl milk tea?

 M: If that's the same as bubble tea, then, yes, I have. I think it's great!

 D: Me, too. On a hot summer day, there is nothing quite as refreshing as the taste[2] of milk tea.

 M: Has pearl milk tea been popular for a long time in Taiwan?

 D: Pearl milk tea didn't really catch on everywhere at first. It was only until a Japanese TV show featured[3] it that it became really popular.

 M: Is that so? I guess that shows the power of the media.

 D: Today, pearl milk tea is one of Taiwan's most famous treasures. And its popularity[4] has also spread[5] elsewhere. Bubble teashops have been opened in places with big Asian populations[6] like California, Toronto, New York, and even some countries in Europe.

 M: Yes, I think I saw one in Vancouver, Canada, too.

 D: OK, well, let's go get some pearl milk tea.

1. **suggest** [səgˋdʒɛst] *vt.* 建議；暗示
   suggest 若表『建議』時，屬意志動
   詞，其後 that 子句中應使用助動詞
   should，而 should 往往予以省略。
   suggest 若表『暗示』時，之後 that
   子句的動詞則採一般時態。

   例: I suggest that this plan (should)
   be called off.
   我建議取消該計劃。

   His words suggested that he
   was getting angry.
   他的話暗示他在生氣了。

2. **taste** [test] *n.* 滋味（可數）；品味
   （不可數）；嗜好（常用單數）

3. **feature** [ˋfitʃɚ] *n.* 特徵 & *vt.* 以……
   為主要特徵；特別介紹

   例: This book features the beauty
   of nature.
   這本書以大自然的美為主題。

4. **popularity** [ˌpɑpjəˋlærətɪ] *n.* 流行；
   名望

   grow / increase in popularity
   名聲逐漸響亮；逐漸流行起來

   例: Rock music is growing in
   popularity in Taiwan.
   搖滾音樂在台灣正逐漸流行。

5. **spread** [sprɛd] *vt.* & *vi.* 流傳；蔓延
   （三態同形）& *n.* 流傳；擴張

   例: The rumor spread like wildfire.
   謠言很快像野火般蔓延開來。

   The rapid spread of SARS
   left the whole city in a state of
   panic.
   SARS 的快速蔓延使整個城市陷入
   一片恐慌。

6. **population** [ˌpɑpjəˋleʃən] *n.*（某地
   域的）全部居民

   例: Only ten percent of the
   population here is illiterate.
   這裡只有百分之十的居民是文盲。

Review Exercises 隨堂小測驗

Part A: Choose the correct answer.

_____ 1. Jim wanted to know where he could get his hands _____ a good used car.
(A) on
(B) for
(C) in
(D) of

_____ 2. The company has _____ with a great new product.
(A) came up
(B) come up
(C) been come up
(D) coming up

_____ 3. If I _____ to start a business, I would open up a coffee shop.
(A) would
(B) were
(C) was
(D) will

_____ 4. A lot of people were _____ up waiting to get a seat in the restaurant.
(A) stood
(B) delaying
(C) lining
(D) waiting

_____ 5. This drink is really _____.
(A) refreshed
(B) refresh
(C) refreshes
(D) refreshing

Review Exercises 隨堂小測驗

Part B: Put the words in the following sentences in order in the blanks below.

1. not sure / will catch on / I'm / this new flavor / if

_____

2. like / A lot / pearl milk tea / of people

_____

3. you find / Do / very refreshing? / this drink

_____

4. bubble tea / in your country? / Are there / any stores / that sell

_____

5. is quite famous / Taiwan / of / This drink / the island / on

_____

Unit 1

 主題閱讀

某人的垃圾是另一人的寶物。沒有什麼比世上最昂貴的咖啡——kopi luwak——更能驗證這句話了。kopi 這個字在印尼文裡指的是咖啡，而 luwak 則是指只在夜間覓食的稀有貓類動物：亞洲麝香貓。你想出關聯了嗎？基本上，麝香貓的糞便已經成為各地咖啡愛好者最渴望的珍寶了。

麝香貓咖啡有什麼特別之處呢？第一個部分就在於麝香貓。牠們只吃最成熟、最美味的咖啡果實。當果實進入牠們的胃之後，果肉會被消化掉。而其種子，也就是咖啡豆，則會經過發酵然後排出體外。發酵過後的豆子則是第二個部份。經過清洗以及輕度烘焙後，這些豆子會產生出一種口味滑順、有巧克力香且不帶苦味的咖啡。由於亞洲麝香貓只棲息於印尼及菲律賓的若干區域，因此收集到的咖啡豆數量有限。所以，當你看到麝香貓咖啡每磅高達三百美金的標價時可別太驚訝。這些垃圾還真是昂貴啊！

 打開話匣子

史蒂芬：嗨，艾波！妳去印尼旅行好玩嗎？

艾　波：太好玩了！那邊的沙灘好玩到真是沒話説。

史蒂芬：聽起來真好玩！我想我不久會嘗試計劃去那旅行。

艾　波：我還帶了一點紀念品回來給你。一些土產咖啡！

史蒂芬：太棒了！妳是知道我有多麼愛咖啡的！

艾　波：我不確定是否應該先讓你嚐嚐，還是先告訴你它的秘密。

史蒂芬：呃？有秘密的咖啡？

艾　波：好吧，我來告訴你。這就是所謂的

『麝香貓咖啡』，而且這咖啡豆真的有通過一種叫做麝香貓的消化系統。

史蒂芬：等一下……妳是説『通過』消化系統？

艾　波：對呀。

史蒂芬：所以這些咖啡豆確實是從動物屁屁出來的？

艾　波：是啊……從麝香貓出來的。牠棲息在樹上，而且看起來有點像貓。

史蒂芬：妳確定這安全可以喝？

艾　波：不僅是安全，它還是世上最昂貴的咖啡。你看到這個袋子了嗎？它花了我將近三百美元！

史蒂芬：哇！這可是我曾聽説過最古怪的事情之一，不過咱們來嚐嚐看吧！

Unit 2

 主題閱讀

台灣的夏天是盛產芒果的季節。此時出產的芒果最為新鮮美味。同時，這個季節也是某些人在森林或山間遊走時，手臂或腿部會碰觸到氣根毒藤的時候。而這兩件事有什麼共通點呢？有時候當某人吃芒果時，他嘴巴的周圍最後會起紅疹。這樣的狀況之所以會發生是因為芒果和氣根毒藤皆屬同一科。

當人們觸摸芒果的表皮時，他們會接觸到一種叫做漆酚的天然化學物質。這種物質正是造成紅疹的原因。如果某人對漆酚過敏的話，他的手上或嘴巴四周會有發癢的紅腫反應。在嚴重的病例中，這樣的紅腫現象甚至會散佈到身上的其餘部位。然而專家們表示芒果中毒的狀況很罕見，而且只觸碰或食用芒果的果肉即可避免這樣的情形發生。由於芒果富含維生素 A 和 C，人們仍應把握時機好好享用這種美味的夏季水果。

打開話匣子

艾芙琳：我不敢相信我居然會因為吃芒果而
　　　　長疹子。你曾經吃完芒果後長疹子
　　　　嗎？

邁　可：不，其實我沒那種經驗。但是我聽
　　　　說有人因為吃芒果而長疹子的。我
　　　　姐告訴我那是因為芒果和氣根毒藤
　　　　屬同一植物科。

艾芙琳：真的嗎？我不知道有那回事。我想
　　　　那說明了為什麼我會長疹子的原
　　　　因。也許我不該再吃芒果了。

邁　可：芒果富含維他命 A 及 C，所以吃
　　　　芒果對身體有益。妳只要觸碰和食
　　　　用芒果內部果肉即可避免長疹子。

艾芙琳：那個主意真不賴。你對水果過敏
　　　　嗎？你對任何東西有過敏反應嗎？

邁　可：我不會對任何食物過敏。然而，我
　　　　對巧克力過敏。

艾芙琳：對巧克力過敏。那多糟啊！

邁　可：對啊，我也是這麼覺得。妳還喜歡
　　　　吃其他什麼種類的水果嗎？

艾芙琳：我本身偏愛草莓和櫻桃。

邁　可：我也喜歡那些食物耶，我還喜歡釋
　　　　迦。

Unit 3

 主題閱讀

在十二響禮炮，以及由德國慕尼黑市長
為啤酒桶裝上開關之下，啤酒節便正
式展開。這個為期十六天的節慶於九月下旬
舉行。啤酒節是德國最重要的節慶之一，現
已舉世聞名。每年有六百多萬的德國人和遊
客參與啤酒節，一同吃喝玩樂與慶祝。傳統
的德國食物，如香腸、馬鈴薯和起司等，會
搭配各式各樣的啤酒進食。

在啤酒節期間，許多人因喝太多啤酒而

昏迷不醒。這些人被戲稱為『啤酒屍體』，
常被帶至醫療帳棚內接受協助。但自二〇〇
五年起，有人為了『安靜的啤酒節』而搭設
了特別的帳棚。這主要是為那些不喝酒及有
年幼孩童的家庭。啤酒節的佔地面積一百零
三英畝裡，總共有十四座主帳棚及十萬個座
位。女服務生穿著傳統服飾工作，而且每人
一次最多可端上八杯啤酒給賓客。因此，不
論你是喜愛啤酒，或只是想體驗德國最盛大
的節慶，參加九月底的啤酒節就對了。

 打開話匣子

馬　克：我不敢相信終於要開始了！我拿到
　　　　票，而且只要再等一個星期！

安　娜：去渡假？

馬　克：類似……我將要去德國慕尼黑的啤酒
　　　　節！我多年以來一直很想去看看！

安　娜：原來是這樣。啤酒節是個啤酒的節
　　　　慶，對嗎？

馬　克：沒錯。而且也是德國最大的節慶！
　　　　六百多萬人會來參與此項作為一種
　　　　讚揚德國啤酒的年度活動。

安　娜：呃，我是喜歡德國食物，尤其是香
　　　　腸，但我想啤酒節不會是我該待的
　　　　地方，因為我不喝酒。

馬　克：其實，自二〇〇五年以來，他們開
　　　　始為家庭與那些不喝酒的人搭建特
　　　　別的帳棚。妳還是可以去，並且品
　　　　嚐一些當地美食！

安　娜：呃……我想我不參加。六百萬酒醉
　　　　的旅客聽起來不像我想的那麼好
　　　　玩。我能想像有些人真的會酩酊大
　　　　醉。

馬　克：是呀！他們被戲稱為『啤酒屍
　　　　體』，但是會有醫療帳蓬，在那裡
　　　　他們會照顧非常醉的人。現場的護
　　　　士會確保沒有人變成真的屍體。

安　娜：那麼，馬克，你好好玩吧！別忘了
　　　　要拍一些照片喔。

Unit 4

 主題閱讀

在數千間的迴轉壽司吧裡，輸送帶上一盤盤美味的壽司滿足了許多飢腸轆轆的饕客。藏壽司這家遍佈全日本且廣受歡迎的連鎖迴轉壽司吧則比這更為先進。店裡大部分的工作都是由機器代勞。如今，不僅會由輸送帶來為您送上餐點，而且還有一套電腦系統替您點菜並記錄您吃了多少東西。

藏壽司裡的其它業務也已自動化。首先，所有的壽司飯糰都是由機器所捏製。其次，每個盤子的底部都有使餐盤和電腦系統連結的晶片。如果放有食物的餐盤在輸送帶上擱置過久，食物就會自動被丟棄。您在藏壽司不會看到忙著上菜的服務生。相反地，您將看到客人使用電腦觸控螢幕來點選各種令人垂涎三尺的餐點。

這所有的自動化過程究竟是為了什麼呢？職員人數一旦減少，營運成本就會降低。這就意謂著藏壽司能在樣樣皆昂貴的日本，以不影響其壽司品質的前提下，提供顧客更便宜的價格。

 打開話匣子

蘇　珊：我在閱讀一本舊書，書中提到關於未來的預言。哇，他們都錯了！

克　里：舉個例子來聽聽吧！

蘇　珊：書上說到了西元兩千年，屆時大家都會配備一台個人機器人。

克　里：哈！我當然沒有機器人啦！但妳知道的，其實我的鄰居確實有機器人。她那台機器人吸塵器會自動清理地板。

蘇　珊：沒錯！我看過那些機器人！也許那本書並沒有錯得太離譜！

克　里：我們也許沒有機器人來當私人助理，但機器人變得越來越普及了。

就在前幾天新開幕了一家壽司餐廳，裡頭沒有任何服務生耶！

蘇　珊：真的嗎？那要怎麼點餐？

克　里：顧客在電腦螢幕上鍵入他們的餐點，而一系列的輸送帶就會把你點的菜送過來！甚至連米飯糰都是機器做的呢！

蘇　珊：我看過有輸送帶的壽司吧，但會做米飯糰的機器人還真能把這一切帶到更新的境界呢！

克　里：對啊！我想我們還真是活在未來呢！

Unit 5

 主題閱讀

關於健康點心和膳食的文章俯拾皆是。近來廣受矚目的一種點心就是堅果。最近的研究顯示食用堅果和擁有強健的心臟有所關聯。舉例來說，一份研究發現一週吃堅果四次以上的女性可能死於心臟疾病的機率會減少四成。科學家並不十分確定堅果到底有多好，但有證據顯示它們是最好的點心選擇之一。

堅果中含有多種使其對我們有益的物質。首先，它們是攝取蛋白質和纖維質的來源之一，這些是健康飲食所需的成分。它們也含有奧米加三脂肪酸。這些則是能預防心臟病發的『好脂肪』。堅果中的另一項物質是精氨酸，它能使動脈壁保持彈性，並且減少血栓形成的機率。堅果最棒的特性之一就是它們似乎能抑制癌細胞的成長。如果您真的想嘗試『瘋堅果』，可得要聰明地進行。裹著巧克力、鹽、以及糖衣的堅果既不會讓您身體健康，也不會使您身材苗條。

麗　莎：親愛的，我知道你接下來幾個星期
　　　　都要加班，所以我給你打包了一些
　　　　健康零食。你真的要少吃點垃圾食
　　　　物了。

阿　三：（嘆氣）我知道這幾天我壓力一直
　　　　很大。我有壓力時會吃東西。

麗　莎：我不想多說什麼，但你最近體重增
　　　　加。我想是採用健康飲食的時候
　　　　了。

阿　三：是啊，我想你說的對。我一直告訴
　　　　自己明天我要吃些健康食物──但
　　　　我知道我只是在拖延。

麗　莎：你知道我愛你，我要你健健康康
　　　　的。我並不想使你的生活苦不堪
　　　　言。

阿　三：我知道，親愛的。我感激妳的努
　　　　力。那麼妳幫我打包了什麼零食
　　　　呢？海帶和豆腐嗎？

麗　莎：事實上，我把一批綜合堅果放在一
　　　　起。堅果是蛋白質和纖維質的良好
　　　　來源，我最近在文章上看到它們有
　　　　助於預防心臟病。

阿　三：嗯，這太酷了！我喜歡堅果！特別
　　　　是包上巧克力的杏仁或是超鹹的花
　　　　生。

麗　莎：親愛的……任何包上巧克力或是超
　　　　鹹的食物都不是健康食品！

阿　三：我知道──我只是在開玩笑啦！

Unit 6

📖 主題閱讀

吃 火鍋令人趣味盎然，因為它跟大家都
喜歡的三件事有關：食物、爐火和朋
友。這個裝滿各種食材、細火慢煮的鍋品可
回溯至唐朝。然而一直到清代，火鍋才在全

中國受到歡迎。人們最初僅是將肉類和蔬菜
丟進大鍋子裡，然後放在火上煮。要餵飽一
大群人，這可是一個好方法，因為這鍋食物
毋須費神照料。如今，火鍋被視為令人充滿
喜悅的餐點，最適合眾人聚餐食用。

　　在台灣，火鍋及火鍋店受歡迎的程度已
到達前所未有的地步。在任何人氣旺的小吃
街上，一定有許多火鍋店，外頭排滿了等候
用餐的民眾。羊肉爐於一九七〇年代引進台
灣。當中的羊肉是和中藥一起燉煮，而且多
於冬天食用。一九八〇年代，薑母鴨則成了
眾人的最愛。這種鍋物裡的鴨肉是放在薑、
米酒及麻油裡烹調，這也使得所有食料都融
成一鍋鮮美的湯。

　　自一九九〇年代以來，涮涮鍋便成為人
們最為喜愛的火鍋種類。在台灣，這種日式
火鍋首先出現於百貨公司裡。它受歡迎的
原因是因為每個人都能夠獨享屬於自己的一
鍋。

凱　文：今天好冷喔。咱們晚餐吃火鍋吧。

漢　娜：那個主意真不賴。

凱　文：妳知道最早的火鍋可以追溯到唐代
　　　　嗎？

漢　娜：這我不知道耶。所以那表示火鍋已
　　　　經流行了很長一段時間囉。

凱　文：沒錯。在台灣現在火鍋和火鍋餐廳
　　　　受歡迎的程度創新高。在寒冷的冬
　　　　天吃火鍋真是棒極了。

漢　娜：台灣最流行什麼類的火鍋？

凱　文：現在最受歡迎的種類是麻辣鍋。

漢　娜：台灣人很常吃火鍋嗎？

凱　文：呃，在冬天是如此沒錯。但我不會
　　　　建議每天吃火鍋。

漢　娜：為什麼不行呢？

凱　文：麻辣鍋可能會造成胃病，而且也不
　　　　利於喉嚨痛。換句話說，妳不應該

吃得過量。然而，如果適量的話，火鍋是很棒的。

漢　娜：那我們還在等什麼呢？

凱　文：妳說得沒錯。咱們出發吧。

Unit 7

 主題閱讀

夏季月份期間，蜜蜂會做的豈止是騷擾人們而已。事實上，牠們對自然環境最大的貢獻之一便是製造蜂蜜。蜜蜂離開蜂巢到花群中採花蜜，再將花蜜轉化成蜂蜜。牠們回巢後便將蜂蜜貯存在蜂巢裡。養蜂人接著將蜂蜜取出來販賣。最近，醫生及科學家發現蜂蜜其實是種很好的藥物。

蜂蜜對治療喉嚨所受到的感染大有幫助。蜂蜜可加在藥物或茶飲裡，用來幫助治癒喉嚨痛及舒緩咳嗽。大家都知道，歌手在表演前會喝加了蜂蜜的茶。此外，蜂蜜可以混在凝膠裡，用來塗抹在正在癒合的傷口上。這樣做不僅能幫助傷口更快痊癒，還可以防止繃帶或衣物沾黏在受傷處。

蜜蜂對某些人來說很可怕，但牠們卻是大自然中相當重要的一環。下次你看到蜜蜂時，記得牠們的蜂蜜或許有天能防止你生病。

 打開話匣子

賽琳娜：這裡有花生醬嗎？我想我應該跟女服務生要一點。

布倫特：妳為什麼不改用蜂蜜塗在吐司上？妳知道蜂蜜對妳相當有益嗎？

賽琳娜：是很天然沒錯，但是我仍較喜歡花生醬或是果醬。

布倫特：妳應該考慮改吃蜂蜜，而不是花生醬或是果醬。

賽琳娜：蜂蜜有什麼特別的？蜂蜜嚐起來太甜，反而對你不太好。

布倫特：呃，首先，蜂蜜對治療喉嚨所受到的感染大有幫助。蜂蜜可加在藥物或茶飲裡，用來幫助治癒喉嚨痛及舒緩咳嗽。

賽琳娜：我想能知道這點真不錯。或許下次生病我會試試看。

布倫特：還有，大家都知道，歌手在表演前會喝加了蜂蜜的茶。

賽琳娜：嗯……，我是喜歡跟朋友去唱卡拉OK，而且唱歌時，我的喉嚨有時候會痛。

布倫特：或許蜂蜜正是妳所需要的，讓妳唱得更順暢。

賽琳娜：謝謝你的建議。

Unit 8

 主題閱讀

今日，我們吃的大多數食物是放在烤箱裡烤的或是爐子上煮的。烹飪這些食物的熱能來自於燃燒木柴、瓦斯或是其它燃料。然而，自然資源正逐漸減少中。燃料變得較不易取得時，人們就得變得更有創意。這些創意烹調法中，有些早就存在已久。

一些傳統烹飪法使用的燃料量很少，甚或沒有。烓窯便是一例。這種烹飪法是將食物埋於地底，放在燒熱的石塊之下。在某些地方，可以只把食物單獨埋在沙裡就好。食物是由陽光將沙子加熱所煮好，或是由地底冒出的滾燙氣體所煮熟。

當汽車變得普及之際，人們明白車子也可以拿來作為烹飪之用。當您開車四處兜風時，來自汽車引擎的熱能就可煮好整頓飯。電燈泡所發出的熱能也能做到同樣的事。這些饒富創意的烹調方法之所以節省燃料，是利用它來同時做兩件事。如果您對試驗這些方法中的任何一種感到興趣，請上網查看。許多網站能為您示範如何安全地利用這些方法來料理食物。

太陽能烹調法已存在好一些日子。不過這種方法僅在近幾年才流行開來。人們為了兩個主要的理由才開始使用太陽能烹調法。對環境有益是其一，陽光是免費的則為其二。除此之外，用來做成太陽能爐具的材料通常價格低廉，而且也容易取得。泰國有一名小販利用九百多面鏡子反射陽光來烤雞。一整天下來，他得經常調整鏡子以配合太陽的移動。在晴朗的日子裡，他只需花十分鐘就可以把雞烤好。

太陽能烹調法非常簡單，每個人在家中都可以這麼做。請您自己動手嘗試，便會發覺幫助環境也能這麼地有趣及美味！

打開話匣子

露　露：我很好奇耶，艾倫；你多久自己煮一次菜？

艾　倫：偶爾啦。並不是經常煮。

露　露：你有什麼招牌菜嗎？

艾　倫：呃，我在加熱電視餐這方面相當厲害，哈哈！但說正經的，談到烹飪我還真沒有什麼招牌菜呢。

露　露：你比較喜歡什麼樣的烹調方法？煎的、煮的、烘烤的或是蒸的？

艾　倫：我通常會用煎的——那樣又快又容易。

露　露：你曾經嘗試過任何替代性或不尋常的烹飪方式嗎？

艾　倫：我不確定妳說的話是什麼意思。

露　露：我指的是用不同型態的能源來做飯，像是太陽能。

艾　倫：人們只要有一般的火爐和烤箱能用時，又為什麼會想要那麼做？

露　露：當燃料變得越來越難以取得時，人們就得變得更具創意。

艾　倫：我不知道耶。太陽能聽起來對我來說太難嘗試了。

露　露：實際上，太陽能烹飪已經存在一段時間了。太陽能烹飪很簡單，所以任何人都可以在家嘗試。

艾　倫：妳可以用那個來加熱電視餐嗎？

露　露：很有可能喔。

Unit 9

主題閱讀

像賀喜這樣的公司是如何生產出他們的巧克力呢？一切全是從可可樹開始的。可可樹會孕育出果實，每一顆果實裡會有二十到四十粒種子。這些種子就是可可豆，也是巧克力風味的來源。這些可可豆在採收完畢後就會被分成一堆一堆地放著，進行為期一週左右的發酵過程。這些豆子的顏色會變得更深，而且會培育出濃郁的風味。接下來，可可豆會經過乾燥，然後被運送到巧克力工廠，再以高溫來進行烘焙。少了烘焙這個步驟的話，可可豆就沒辦法散發出百分之百的巧克力風味。

可可豆在去殼後就會被搗碎成濃稠的糊狀。要變成我們愛吃的巧克力，還要再添加糖分，也許還要加入一些牛奶。巧克力的種類及配方繁多。其中最為出名也被視為世界之最的當屬比利時巧克力。世界上其它許多地方也有當地特殊的巧克力。有些口感綿密，有些較為苦口，當中或許還會加入各種不同的食材。

有些人會誤以為松露巧克力裡面含有用於美食烹飪的昂貴稀有真菌。事實上，這些美味的甜食內含濃滑的巧克力內餡，外頭則裹以巧克力或可可粉，這使得它們狀似松露這種菌類。另一個常見的誤解就是認為白巧克力是巧克力。事實上，它的主要成分是牛奶、糖還有香草。不論是以何種形式呈現，世人都愛巧克力！

打開話匣子

威　力：我想我對某樣東西上癮了。我可能
　　　　需要尋求專業的協助！

安　妮：真的嗎？是什麼東西讓你上癮了？

威　力：是巧克力！我是個『巧克力狂』。
　　　　那種東西我就是怎樣都吃不夠。

安　妮：我明白你的意思。我也喜歡吃巧克
　　　　力。

威　力：去年我去了布魯塞爾旅行，品嚐了
　　　　一些全世界最棒的巧克力。那次的
　　　　經驗棒到其實連我都在考慮要搬到
　　　　比利時了呢！

安　妮：你比較喜歡吃黑巧克力或牛奶巧克
　　　　力呢？

威　力：黑巧克力！越黑越好！

安　妮：真的嗎？我似乎比較喜歡像是牛奶
　　　　巧克力或甚至是白巧克力那樣甜一
　　　　點的東西耶。

威　力：對我來說，他們添加過多糖和牛奶
　　　　時，那就有損可可豆的原味了。

安　妮：你知道嗎，我從未真正品嚐過很多
　　　　種類的黑巧克力。

威　力：好的，明天我會帶一些黑巧克力給
　　　　妳，那黑巧克力的味道幾乎是苦
　　　　的，但味道還是超讚的！

安　妮：好棒喔！我會很想試試看。

Unit 10

 主題閱讀

你上一次到麥當勞或肯德基用餐是什麼
時候？隨著生活變得更忙碌，愈來愈
多人固定會吃速食。雖然我們知道這不是最
健康的選擇，但自己做飯似乎又太過麻煩。
一九八六年，在羅馬有一群人齊聚集起來抗
議義大利的第一家麥當勞開幕。他們想要鼓

勵人們對食物產生更大的興趣，並使飲食變
成更有意義的體驗。到了一九八九年，慢食
運動及其組織就誕生了。

　　慢食組織的成員相信，我們對速食的依
賴會造成地方飲食傳統消失。他們相信食物
代表人類的文化及歷史，而這都是該被珍惜
的。他們也擔心僅用土地來種植某些蔬果，
或是伺養特定動物品種，只用來送給像速食
餐廳這樣的事業體，將會造成許多原生食物
來源地消失殆盡。這也意謂著消費者能買到
的食物種類將大幅減少。

　　慢食組織如今遍及一百二十二個國家，
超過了八萬三千名成員及八百個辦事處，這
些國家包括法國、英國、瑞士、德國、日本
及台灣。

　　其基本指導原則是：『美味、乾淨、公
平。』美味指的是食物的味道是優先考慮事
項。乾淨則表示食物既健康又富營養。此
外，動物權益和環境保護也須列入考量。公
平是要每個人都有權利吃到健康美味的食
物。這也代表那些食物生產者應該得到合理
的報酬，如此他們的後代就能傳承他們的工
作。他們希望一旦人們重新發現慢食之道，
有害健康的速食生活方式將會是過往雲煙
了。

 打開話匣子

寶　琳：史都華，你對於麥當勞及肯德基這
　　　　類速食餐廳所提供的食物有何意見
　　　　呢？

史都華：我很喜歡——它很方便，而且它吃
　　　　起來味道很棒。

寶　琳：你會擔心吃速食所帶來的負面影響
　　　　嗎？

史都華：不會。我知道速食會讓人變胖。

寶　琳：是啊，而且速食就某種意義上也很
　　　　不健康。

史都華：我總是忙得沒辦法在家裡做飯。

寶　琳：沒錯，自己做飯往往似乎又太過於

麻煩。但那不表示我們需要一直吃垃圾食物。你有沒有聽過慢食運動？

史都華：沒有，我沒聽過。

寶　琳：慢食組織的成員相信，我們對速食的依賴會造成地方飲食傳統的消失。他們想要鼓勵人們對食物產生更大的興趣，並使飲食變成更有意義的體驗。

史都華：喂，妳中餐想吃肯德基嗎？

寶　琳：你認為呢？

史都華：嗯……我猜不想。

Unit 11

 主題閱讀

當你想到高風險的食物時，你會因為狂牛症而首先在腦海中浮現美國進口的牛肉，或是日本含有劇毒的河豚。然而，一項新的研究顯示最危險的食物離家更近。最近由美國消費者權益保護機構『科學公益中心』發表了一份報告，報告中列舉出在美國引發最多食物中毒案件的十大食物。這些『毒』食品幾乎全都在美國人飲食中扮演重要的角色，有些食物還讓人大感意外。

像萵苣這類綠葉蔬菜位居榜首。根據這份報告，在一九九〇至二〇〇八年間，綠葉蔬菜與三百五十多起爆發的食物中毒案例有關，影響了一萬三千多人。問題在於這些蔬菜的葉子會受到感染，通常是染上危險的大腸桿菌，而且會交叉污染其他食品。其他一些具有風險的食物就比較不足為奇了。像是眾所皆知可能含有沙門氏菌的蛋便位居第二。儘管大多數人的飲食習慣中很少吃牡蠣，牡蠣還是一路超越其他食物，位居第四。不過其他榜上有名的還包括像是馬鈴薯等主食，引起了將近四千起食物中毒的病例。

完整的名單也包括鮪魚、冰淇淋、乳酪、蕃茄、豆芽以及漿果類。雖然真正引發問題的原因通常是衛生不佳和缺乏清潔，而非食物本身，但這些數據資料還是令人擔憂。美國的食物鏈既龐大又複雜，像沙門氏菌和大腸桿菌等病菌很容易就進入這個循環中。雖然透過立法能解決部分問題，但根本解決之道是仔細清理及烹煮送進口中的每樣東西。

 打開話匣子

邁克斯：嘿，妳可以在台北哪裡找到賣沙拉的餐廳嗎？妳可以推薦什麼好的餐廳嗎？

安　妮：其實，你可以在很多地方找到賣沙拉的餐廳。你常吃沙拉嗎？

邁克斯：對啊，我愛死了。沙拉很健康。

安　妮：一般說來，是的，但我看了一篇美國的研究，研究中顯示吃萵苣可能會有風險。

邁克斯：這我可不知道。

安　妮：根據報導指出，綠葉蔬菜和三百五十多起食物中毒有關。

邁克斯：真是那樣嗎？我想知道吃沙拉為什麼會那麼危險。

安　妮：問題在於蔬菜葉子可能會被感染。衛生條件差以及缺乏清洗通常會是問題的根源。

邁克斯：吃沙拉會有風險，這還真是有點諷刺啊。

安　妮：我同意。真正的解決之道在於仔細清洗和準備你要吃的每樣東西。

邁克斯：那聽起來是個不賴的建議。謝謝妳的秘訣喔。

安　妮：不客氣。這是我的榮幸。

Unit 12

 主題閱讀

現代化工業農牧使用的方式是以最低廉的成本製造最大的產量。也就是說，農夫能在面積較小的土地上生產更多的糧食，讓大眾能買到更便宜的食物。

工業化農牧提供食物給全球七十億的人口。人們應用許多技術來生產這些農作物。舉例來說，農夫大量使用化學藥物幫助植物生長，並保護這些植物免受蟲害。此外，人們也創造出基因改良種子，使這些種子能比一般種子生產更多作物。

除了農作物之外，工業化農牧的範圍也包含了動物的工廠化畜牧。在一九二〇年代，科學家發現了維生素、疫苗及抗生素的好處。讓動物攝取維生素，農夫便能在室內飼養牠們。疫苗和抗生素則有助於預防疾病的蔓延，這種疾病的蔓延會發生在擁擠的居住環境中。此外，讓動物服用別種藥物能幫助牠們長得更大更快。

雖然工業化農牧提供給人們充分的糧食，但是這些技術當中有許多都帶有風險。例如，密集使用水、能源和化學物質會造成更多的環境污染。在若干地方，像是日本和歐洲，基因改造食品也被認為有食用上的安全疑慮，甚至被禁止食用。工廠化畜牧對環境和人體健康也有嚴重的影響。全球溫室氣體排放總量的百分之十八是由這些工廠化畜牧動物的排泄物所製造出的。

另一個問題在於動物服用抗生素，這可能會導致細菌變得有抗藥性。如此可能會造成人類的感染。動物服用的一些藥物和諸如癌症等的重大疾病有關。因此，身為消費者，人們應該要更能意識到自己所購買的食物。如此一來，農牧業才會步上正軌。

 打開話匣子

保　羅：我好餓。咱們去買熱狗吧。

凱　莉：好噁喔！保羅，你會重視所購買的食品成份嗎？

保　羅：當然囉，如果嚐起來味道不錯，我就會吃啊。

凱　莉：我的意思不是那樣。我有時候會擔心我們所吃食品內所含的藥物和化學物質。

保　羅：喔，我認為我們所吃的東西大部份都是安全的啦。科技一直在進步，使食物變得更好。

凱　莉：那我可不敢保證。你認為食用基因改良的食物安全嗎？

保　羅：我從沒認真想過那件事。我猜很安全吧。

凱　莉：你知道若干地方禁用基因改良的食品嗎，像是日本和歐洲？一些動物服用的藥物和癌症有關。

保　羅：不，我不知道那件事。也許我應該開始購買有機食品，即便那比較貴。

凱　莉：那很有可能是個好主意。

Unit 13

 主題閱讀

有些人認為沒什麼比大口咬下鮮嫩多汁的漢堡，或是撕咬美味雞翅感覺來得更棒的了。不幸的是，人類對肉類的消費卻造成了環境負面的影響。根據研究指出，肉牛的生產是製造碳污染的最大元兇。簡單來說，為肉類而飼養牲畜所製造的污染比車輛、冷氣機或工廠所製造的還多。

要處理這樣嚴重的問題當中一個方式就是要循序漸進。有人建議大家在一個星期中找一天的時間吃素。如果大家通力合作實施這個簡單的步驟，就意味著能減少百分之十五的肉類總消耗量。這樣的結果顯示為供給食物需求而飼養的動物就會變少，進而有助於減少碳污染。只要一週一天不吃肉，就能讓地球的肺呼吸得較為順暢。

台灣有兩位作家對於週一無肉日這個想法非常雀躍。蘇小歡和徐仁修正發起一項活動，旨在將週一無肉日的概念引進台灣。他們主張環保團體應該推廣週一無肉日，所有餐廳也應該開始提供素食菜單。他們期望政府最終能立法規定週一不吃肉。蘇小歡和徐仁修在這件事上並不孤單。在比利時等其他國家也在討論週一無肉日。一週一天只是解決這嚴重問題的一小步，但卻有所幫助。何不今天就開始考慮改變自己的飲食呢？

打開話匣子

蘇　西：賴瑞，你或是有什麼朋友是吃素的嗎？

賴　瑞：我不是吃素的，但是我的確有一些朋友是吃素的。妳為何會這麼問？

蘇　西：呃，我看過報導稱，肉牛生產是碳污染的最大元兇。

賴　瑞：妳不會是想要我戒掉吃肉而改吃素吧，是不是？

蘇　西：為何不呢？為了吃肉而飼養動物製造的污染比車輛、冷氣機或工廠還多。

賴　瑞：聽起來挺嚴重的，但我還沒準備好要戒掉吃漢堡和牛排的習慣。

蘇　西：只要一星期吃一次素怎樣？你對無肉星期一有什麼看法？

賴　瑞：我想我聽過那件事。我想我可以嘗試一星期少吃一天肉。

蘇　西：這就對了。如果大家都能配合此一簡單的步驟，這表示能減少百分之十五的肉類總消耗量。

賴　瑞：我可以想像這麼做能真正解決問題，但大家會同意這個做法嗎？

蘇　西：也許一開始不行，但我想那最後可能會發生喔。

Unit 14

 ### 主題閱讀

東京一名十八歲的少女表示：『這東西那麼方便，但願我自己房裡也有一台。』她說的是販賣機，而且有這種想法的不只她一人。販賣機在日本非常普及，約每五十人就可以分配到一台，而且光是專賣飲料的販賣機就有兩百五十萬台。這個數據甚至不包括販售其他像是香菸、玩具、鮮花、冷藏香蕉、熟食，以及任何你想得到的物品的販賣機。

有這麼多販賣機種類，販賣機公司勢必得發揮想像力，才能讓自家的機器脫穎而出。可口可樂公司為了表示關心大眾，特別推出一些販賣機，這些販賣機會在發生地震時免費供應飲料。然而，自動販賣機最新的技術發展則是出現在東京火車站內的一台機器內。這台販賣機配備有攝影機和軟體，能辨別消費者的年齡和性別。利用那些資訊，機器能猜出消費者想買什麼東西，就彷彿能看出他們心裡在想什麼似的。

舉例來說，一位消費者表示這台販賣機提供她三種選購建議，其中一個恰好是她最喜歡的。她還說當自己無法決定要買什麼時，這項服務就非常好用。根據經營該販賣機的公司表示，消費者的照片會被立即刪除，但是關於是誰在這台販賣機買東西的一般性資料則會被收集起來，供該公司使用。然而，消費者對這點似乎不以為意，因為他們對這台新奇的機器非常興奮。有了這種科技，販賣機簡直無所不能。

打開話匣子

貝　瑞：妳是否會介意我從這台自動販賣機裡買些東西？

拉　娜：不會，去吧。你要買什麼東西？

貝　瑞：只是要買杯可樂。

拉　娜：你通常都從自動販賣機買些什麼東西呢？

貝　瑞：喔，妳也知道的啊——汽水、巧克力棒、洋芋片。

拉　娜：自動販賣機在你們國家流行嗎？

貝　瑞：當然囉；我想就像每個地方一樣。

拉　娜：不過提到自動販賣機，我想日本才是最突出的吧。

貝　瑞：妳這話是什麼意思？

拉　娜：你幾乎能從日本的自動販賣機裡買到任何東西。

貝　瑞：那太棒了。我想用這種方式買東西真是方便啊。

拉　娜：科技是不是很令人驚嘆呢？

貝　瑞：我很同意妳的說法。

拉　娜：你知道嗎？可口可樂產了一些機器，這些機器能在地震發生時供應免費的飲料。

貝　瑞：那對於像日本這樣會發生多次地震的國家來說是個好構想。

拉　娜：有了這種技術，要從自動販賣機購買任何東西似乎都不是不可能了。但我有時候會想生活中是否充斥太多科技了。

Unit 15

 主題閱讀

雖然很多人對辣椒為舌頭帶來的麻辣感敬謝不敏，但在美洲發現的考古證據顯示，人類在史前時代就開始種植這種植物了。這證明辣椒在近一萬年前就是人類飲食的一部分。十五世紀哥倫布首先在西印度群島發現辣椒。不久後，它們迅速傳遍全歐亞，成為許多傳統料理手法的主要食材。

辣椒在不同國家的料理上有各式的用法。在印度，從炸物到複雜的咖哩料理都使用到辣椒，而在義大利料理中，則會在披薩和其他菜餚上撒上壓碎的辣椒末。在土耳其和墨西哥，辣椒則做成辣油或紅椒醬。北非的料理中，辣椒是作為烹煮或上桌後的調味料之用。在亞洲的料理中，辣椒則用來製作韓國泡菜或是其他醃漬佳餚，而辣椒葉有時也作為綠色蔬菜食用。

辣椒之所以有辛辣的味道，是因為它含有一種名叫辣椒素的化合物，這種成分大多存在於辣椒子中。研究發現辣椒素不只能增添風味，對健康還有許多益處，像是減輕頭痛和對付鼻塞。辣椒素也能有效降低血壓，甚至對抗前列腺癌。除了辣椒素外，辣椒含有大量的維他命 B 和 C，以及胡蘿蔔素、鉀、鎂和鐵，這些對人體都相當有益。優格及小黃瓜等能減低辣椒的辣度，和辣椒搭配一起吃可以讓人較能承受味覺上的刺激。這樣你或許可以學會享受辣椒的滋味。

 打開話匣子

辛　蒂：嗨，特雷弗。你喜歡吃辣的食物嗎？這個週末我要在家裡舉辦晚餐會，但我可要警告你：這些食物可不是給膽小的人吃的！

特雷弗：太棒了，我超喜歡吃辣的食物。實際上，我最喜歡的食物之一就是四川菜餚。

辛　蒂：哈！和我們即將要烹飪的東西比起來，那根本就是嬰兒食物吧！我母親的家族來自韓國，而我父親那邊來自墨西哥。我們吃的食物嚐起來都像要噴火似的！你能承受得住嗎？

特雷弗：那聽起來會是個很棒的挑戰！好啊，我想要接受挑戰。你們主要是用辣椒嗎？

辛　蒂：你說對了！我們要用的是紅辣椒！我們使用的辣椒富含大量的辣椒素；我們即將端上的菜餚當中許多都有哈瓦那辣椒。

特雷弗：那我聽過！那是地球上最辣的辣椒！喔喔，我現在要開始擔心了！

辛　蒂：你沒問題啦！此外，辣椒對你的身體也有好處。辣椒中的化合物有助於舒緩鼻塞、富含維他命，而且甚至能幫助降低血壓！

特雷弗：妳把辣椒描述得聽起來像藥似的。

辛　蒂：它們的確是天然藥物啊！不用擔心，如果辣椒太辣，你都還是可以用一些優格或小黃瓜來讓嘴巴和喉嚨冷卻下來。

特雷弗：好吧，算我一份！我準備好要接受這個週末的辣椒冒險了！

Unit 16

 主題閱讀

漫步台北街頭，即便隨意停下腳步四處張望，你都一定會看到幾間便利商店就在幾步之遙。在台灣便利商店數量之龐大，不僅對國外的遊客來說是驚嘆的來源，也是出國在外的台灣人最想念家鄉的事物之一。

以平均每人所擁有便利商店的比例而論，台灣排名世界第一，這反應出台灣人因為討厭等待而對『即時性』產生的癡迷。由於時間是稀有資源，因此便利商店可以被視為時間上的革命──無論你何時光顧，店內都是貨品滿架、燈火通明。你可以收送包裹、從自動提款機內領取現金、支付帳單、影印文件，還能很快買個預先包裝好的飯團當早餐或睡前小點來吃，或乾脆買杯拿鐵，坐在店內翻閱雜誌。在便利商店裡沒有白天黑夜的區別。不知不覺中，你一天的幅度變長了，也掙脫了時間的束縛。

此外，相較於朝九晚五社會所加諸『早睡早起』的限制，現今工作和玩樂之間的界線已然模糊，後現代社會中對夜生活的需求

強烈。台灣人已經普遍將『7-Eleven』這個語彙用來比喻日不落的工作模式。當夜晚時分一切盡歸沉靜，你仍可以在便利商店內目睹城市生活繼續上演，讓這一切成為不夜城的標準化形象。

打開話匣子

查　克：哇，我今天真的會很忙耶！我得去郵局寄包裹、去銀行支付一些帳單、去找提款機領錢、去影印店影印一些文件。接著我最後還得去採買雜貨！

潔思敏：嗯，那些事你在對街的便利商店內都能辦得到。

查　克：什麼？妳是在開玩笑，對吧？

潔思敏：不。在台灣，便利商店真的很方便。你提到的那些事在城裡任何一家主要的連鎖便利商店內都能輕鬆完成。

查　克：但我還是得去郵局領取我在網路上訂購的東西啊。

潔思敏：不用。你可以把包裹寄到便利商店，然後也去那兒領取！我甚至從便利商店裡的機器買到了演唱會的票呢。

查　克：哇！那真是令人難以置信！但我想我還是得去到火車站購買前往高雄的高鐵票吧。

潔思敏：還是不用！我能幫你在網路上訂票，接著你同樣只要去便利商店領取即可。

查　克：那真是太令人驚訝了！在台灣大家似乎能在便利商店裡辦到一切的事。

潔思敏：沒錯！我能在那兒繳納停車費甚至是超速罰單呢。

Unit 17

 主題閱讀

地中海飲食是健康飲食的黃金守則。

因應全球肥胖的盛行,新的節食方法和減重計劃不斷被提出。哪些應該要被認真看待?又有哪些只是一時的風潮呢?對大部分人來說,節食只是另一種在應該要享受食物的時刻、卻剝奪他們用餐樂趣的方法罷了。

然而,地中海飲食法卻在眾多飲食法中脫穎而出。這種飲食法非但不會讓你覺得被剝奪吃東西的樂趣,反而還鼓勵你去享受均衡的各類高品質食物。這並非是個有著嚴屬規定的特殊節食計劃,而是包括像希臘、南義、南法及西班牙等與地中海接壤的國家所共有的一套飲食習慣及偏好。科學家發現這些國家的人民比其他西方國家的大多數人有較長的平均壽命和較佳的生活品質。

地中海飲食有三項關鍵的特色。第一,人們應該要攝取大量的水果、豆類、未精製化的穀類食品和蔬菜以獲取纖維質和養份。第二,乳製品、魚類及紅酒的適度攝取可以提供健康的脂肪和抗氧化劑。這項飲食的最後一個特色就是攝取少量的肉製品。

橄欖油是地中海飲食烹飪中油脂的主要來源,幾乎應用在所有食物的烹調中,從義大利麵、麵包或是沙拉和燉品都包括在內。橄欖油不只增添食物風味,也有助於調節膽固醇,以及減少心臟疾病和高血壓的風險。

由於諸多健康益處和預防疾病的特質,地中海飲食經常被視為健康飲食的黃金守則。也難怪現在地中海飲食會被世界各地的人採用。

 打開話匣子

蘿伯塔:我已經受夠且厭倦了按照飲食方式進食了。我努力留意我吃了什麼,但是我似乎還是變胖了。

麥　特:妳聽過地中海飲食法了嗎?這種方式變得相當受歡迎。

蘿伯塔:聽過了,我知道那種飲食法就是要吃很多蔬果,並以橄欖油來烹調食物。

麥　特:對我來說,遵循地中海飲食似乎很有道理。

蘿伯塔:你採用哪一種特定的飲食習慣呢?

麥　特:並沒有特定耶,但是我的確會設法經常吃水果及蔬菜。垃圾食物雖然如此美味且誘人,但我儘量不要吃太多。

蘿伯塔:我想我真的應該在我的飲食中多加一點水果及蔬菜了。

麥　特:別忘了運動──這一點也是很重要的。

蘿伯塔:要找到足夠的時間來運動還真難。

麥　特:蘿伯塔,那種不去運動的藉口聽起來真憋腳。不論妳多忙,總是能找到些時間的。

蘿伯塔:是啊,我想你說得對。

Unit 18

 主題閱讀

外國遊客來台灣時,他們最想去哪兒?當你得知夜市的排行已經超越故宮博物院及台北一零一大樓,成為了觀光客的首選景點,這個消息可能會令你大吃一驚。

台灣夜市至少有兩百年的歷史,時間可追溯至那段攤販群聚創建市集的日子。如今,夜市促進地方經濟、協助保存傳統小吃文化,但無可否認地,這些夜市同時也佔據空間、阻礙交通、製造大量髒亂,且對市容產生了負面的影響。

自從一九九○年代起,台灣的百貨公司

及大型超市甚至試圖複製夜市的優勢，將夜市小吃搬到地下室美食街。雖然這些有著冷氣空調的地方既現代又舒適，百貨公司美食街並未對那些露天市集的生意造成任何影響，知名夜市依然生意興隆。

夜市消費者文化的特徵是什麼？為何難以被美食街取代？『民眾逛夜市的動機絕不只是為了吃小吃和購物，而是為了讓自己縱身於那種特殊的消費樂趣和感受中，這些感覺都是來自於人群中的喧嘩和混亂。』中研院民族所副研究員余舜德說。

台灣美食已經汲取了許多外國的影響，但台灣也創新並創造出許多自身的「點心」，也就是中文說的小吃。雖然你無須到夜市才能吃到這些小吃，但夜市的氛圍卻讓在那兒吃小吃這件事變得格外有意義。

 打開話匣子

佛瑞達：葛蘭，你喜歡去台灣的夜市嗎？

葛　蘭：喜歡啊，那是我住這兒真正喜歡做的事情之一。

佛瑞達：你知道夜市已經超越故宮博物院及台北一零一成為島上最熱門的景點了嗎？

葛　蘭：我不知道那件事。那還挺有意思的。

佛瑞達：你曾經去過哪一個夜市呢？

葛　蘭：我特別喜歡饒河街夜市和士林夜市，士林夜市很大。

佛瑞達：你去夜市都在做什麼呢？

葛　蘭：我大部分會吃些街頭小販賣的點心。

佛瑞達：你對台灣食物有什麼看法呢？

葛　蘭：我很喜歡台灣食物──種類很多。

佛瑞達：你曾嘗試過什麼台灣食物是你不喜歡的嗎？

葛　蘭：呃，我不太喜歡臭豆腐或豬腸，那是肯定的。

佛瑞達：除了吃之外，你在夜市還會做些別的事吧？

葛　蘭：確實是的；我以很便宜的價格買了一個背包。我認為那個背包品質並不是很好，但至少價格很棒。

Unit 19

主題閱讀

在台灣，以西式或亞洲料理為特色的餐廳比比皆是，但你是否聽過專門賣泡麵的餐廳？經營專門賣泡麵的餐廳聽來滿荒謬的，特別是泡麵這麼便宜又方便在家烹煮。那麼，去餐廳吃泡麵有什麼意義嗎？在泡麵裡加進熱水是一回事，但要用泡麵煮出一道美味料理可又是另一回事了。

對那些不以為然的人，字面上意思正是『泡麵達人館』的 Pao Mian Da Ren Guan 準備好要用他們的招牌料理，也就是泡麵，來顛覆你的想法。這家餐廳提供各式各樣的泡麵，從台灣本地到日本、韓國、新加坡和印尼所進口的牌子都有。顧客可挑選自己喜愛的牌子，然後告知廚師他們想在泡麵裡加入的食材。可選擇的食材包括蛋、蔬菜、豬肉、牛肉、金針菇和其他常見的火鍋料。每種食材各有不同的價格，但餐廳也提供各式套餐。

事實上，把泡麵加入菜單並非新鮮事。南韓的小吃攤和香港及澳門的飲茶餐廳多年來一直把泡麵供為主要餐點。儘管大家都會擔心泡麵可能會對健康帶來的風險，但價格便宜、口味眾多及烹煮方便的特性使泡麵在亞洲蔚為流行。

打開話匣子

蓋　瑞：嗨，傑絲敏。妳在吃什麼？

傑絲敏：喔，只是泡麵啦。在西方有很多人吃泡麵嗎？

蓋　瑞：有些人會吃，但泡麵在西方不比在亞洲風行。我之前吃過，但我覺得泡麵有點平淡乏味。

傑絲敏：在台灣，有家餐廳名為『泡麵達人館』，那家餐廳專售美食泡麵。

蓋　瑞：去餐廳吃泡麵有什麼意義呢？妳在家就可以加熱水吃泡麵啦。

傑絲敏：嘿，你沒試過就不要批評。我的一些朋友去那兒吃過，他們說那些食物還挺不賴的。

蓋　瑞：我在想那會不會只是一時的風潮，又或者會是流行很久的事物。

傑絲敏：這很難說耶。我想時間會證明一切吧。你在台灣有沒有哪家最喜愛的餐廳是你常去的？

蓋　瑞：有啊，那就是麥當勞。

傑絲敏：蓋瑞！你在台灣時應該要體驗更多台灣食物才對。

蓋　瑞：我想妳說得沒錯。

Unit 20

 主題閱讀

夏日炎炎，沒有東西比得上一杯加了小小粉圓的奶茶一樣那麼清涼有勁。這個絕妙的點子到底是怎麼想出來的？一九八〇年代初期，一名台中春水堂的員工開始做實驗，在茶裡加上不同種類的水果、糖漿及蕃薯等。最後，她在奶茶的杯底加入粉圓，並給它取了一個『珍珠奶茶』的暱稱。大約在同時期，台南翰林茶館的老闆正在研發自己的配方，並且開發出他也稱為珍珠奶茶的產品。

南台灣許多民眾都對珍珠奶茶愛不釋手，但直到一個日本節目簡介了春水堂後，珍珠奶茶才真正在各地風行起來。不久，老老少少都在排隊購買這個『有料的』奇特混和飲品。其它茶飲店模仿春水堂的點子，在茶裡加入小顆的糖果或果凍。近來，還有茶飲店老闆為吸引顧客，有別於其他同業，在奶茶中加入彩色粉圓。

珍珠奶茶是台灣最知名的珍寶之一，全世界有許多人每當能購買到珍珠奶茶時，就一定會喝上一杯。泡沫紅茶店在擁有眾多亞裔人口的地方開張，像是加州、多倫多和紐約等地，就連歐洲一些國家也能看見這些店的蹤跡。

打開話匣子

唐　尼：我渴了。咱們喝點東西吧。

瑪　麗：唐尼，你有什麼建議呢。

唐　尼：妳喝過珍珠奶茶嗎？

瑪　麗：如果那是和泡沫紅茶一樣的東西，那麼是的，我喝過。我覺得那很棒

唐　尼：我也這麼認為。在炎熱的夏日裡，沒有什麼比奶茶的味道更讓人感到清新了。

瑪　麗：珍珠奶茶已經在台灣流行很久了嗎？

唐　尼：珍珠奶茶一開始沒有真正到處流行。直到日本電視節目特別介紹泡沫紅茶，它才真正變得受歡迎。

瑪　麗：是這樣嗎？我猜這顯示了媒體的力量。

唐　尼：今日，珍珠奶茶是台灣最有名的寶藏之一。而它的流行也蔓延到了其他地方。泡沫紅茶店已在有眾多亞洲居民的地方如加州，多倫多，紐約，甚至是歐洲的一些國家開張營業了。

瑪　麗：是的，我想我也有在加拿大的溫哥華看過一家泡沫紅茶店。

唐　尼：好的，那麼，咱們去喝點珍珠奶茶吧。

Unit 1

 暖身練習

1. Yes, I am. I usually drink one or two cups of coffee every day.

2. I like to drink coffee without cream or sugar in it. The type of coffee I like best is from Brazil.

 閱讀隨堂考

1. __B__   2. __D__

 隨堂小測驗

Part A

1. __B__   2. __B__   3. __A__
4. __C__   5. __D__

Part B

1. This meal is the tastiest I've ever had.

2. I think that swimming is the most refreshing exercise.

3. Not only is coffee delicious, but it is stimulating, too.

4. Some people really drink a large quantity of coffee.

5. Jim was shocked by the expensive price of the coffee.

Unit 2

 暖身練習

1. I like eating strawberries the most. My least favorite fruit is guava.

2. I once got sick after eating ice cream. I think the ice cream was spoiled.

 閱讀隨堂考

1. __C__   2. __A__

 隨堂小測驗

Part A

1. __B__   2. __B__   3. __A__
4. __D__   5. __A__

Part B

1. rich in   2. allergic
3. break out   4. Occasionally
5. spreads   6. cases
7. partial   8. end up

Unit 3

 暖身練習

1. When I drink alcohol, I usually have beer, but sometimes I prefer wine. I only drink alcohol occasionally.

2. I enjoy watching the races during Dragon Boat Festival.

 閱讀隨堂考

1. __D__   2. __B__

 隨堂小測驗

Part A

1. __A__   2. __B__   3. __C__
4. __A__   5. __A__

Part B

1. __a__   2. __f__   3. __e__
4. __c__   5. __d__   6. __b__
7. __g__   8. __h__

Unit 4

 暖身練習

1. Yes, I really like eating sushi. I like salmon the best in sushi.

2. I think having robots make my food is a little bit strange. I hope they don't make mistakes.

 閱讀隨堂考

1. __C__   2. __A__

 隨堂小測驗

Part A

1. __A__   2. __C__   3. __C__
4. __D__   5. __B__

Part B

1. chain   2. automated
3. take   4. linked
5. operation   6. satisfying
7. cut down   8. affect

Unit 5

 暖身練習

1. I don't usually eat healthy snacks. When it comes to snacks, I prefer chocolate bars or potato chips.

2. I can name roasted peanuts, cashews and walnuts.

 閱讀隨堂考

1. __B__   2. __A__

 隨堂小測驗

Part A

1. __A__   2. __C__   3. __B__
4. __B__   5. __A__

Part B

1. lately   2. cut down
3. diet   4. procrastinating
5. prevent   6. cancer
7. stress   8. almonds

Unit 6

 暖身練習

1. I know that hot pot has been around for a long time in Taiwan, probably for decades.

2. I like spicy hot pot with chicken, corn and many other ingredients the best.

 閱讀隨堂考

1. __D__   2. __B__

 隨堂小測驗

Part A

1. __A__   2. __D__   3. __A__
4. __B__   5. __C__

Part B

1. The **popularity** of that company's products is very high right now.
2. In the **beginning**, Kelly didn't like Ben, but later they became friends.
3. Spending on electronic products is at an **all-time** high.
4. The theater **is** full of people today.
5. My job **involves** a lot of hard work.

Unit 07

 暖身練習

1. People use honey in tea and

other drinks, on toast and waffles, and in desserts.

2. Honey can help a person feel better when he or she has a sore throat.

 閱讀隨堂考

1. __B__   2. __D__

 隨堂小測驗

Part A

1. __C__   2. __A__   3. __C__
4. __B__   5. __A__

Part B

1. natural   2. treat
3. process   4. wound
5. stick   6. heal
7. sore   8. infections

Unit 08

 暖身練習

1. The cooking methods I can name are frying, roasting, boiling and baking.

2. Of those methods, I think I like food that has been fried or roasted the most.

 閱讀隨堂考

1. __A__   2. __B__

 隨堂小測驗

Part A

1. __D__   2. __B__   3. __A__
4. __C__   5. __A__

Part B

1. __e__   2. __g__   3. __c__

4. __f__   5. __b__   6. __a__
7. __h__   8. __d__

Unit 9

 暖身練習

1. I am one of those people who really, really love to eat chocolate.

2. My favorite chocolate dessert is a hot fudge brownie. My favorite non-chocolate dessert is a cherry pie with ice cream.

 閱讀隨堂考

1. __A__   2. __B__

 隨堂小測驗

Part A

1. __D__   2. __A__   3. __D__
4. __B__   5. __D__

Part B

1. My brother is addicted to chocolate.

2. Did you know that chocolate is made from seeds?

3. I've never really liked the taste of bitter chocolate.

4. Chocolate truffles look similar to real truffles.

5. There is still one chocolate left in the box.

Unit 10

 暖身練習

1. I like to eat hamburgers, fried chicken and fries.

2. I probably go to fast food restaurants about twice a week.

閱讀隨堂考

1. A   2. A

 隨堂小測驗

Part A

1. B   2. A   3. D

4. A   5. B

Part B

1. Over time, some animals have completely **disappeared**.

2. What do you think **of** the Slow Food Movement?

3. I'm not sure whether or not most people care **about** environmental protection.

4. Have you **taken** into consideration that traffic might be heavy?

5. **Eating** healthy means consuming lots of fruit and vegetables.

Unit 11

 暖身練習

1. Yes, I have been sick a few times after eating food. Once, I ate some chicken that I think wasn't cooked properly. I was really sick for the whole night and even the next day.

2. Regarding raw food that I eat, I like sashimi a lot. However, I only eat it at good restaurants. Therefore, I don't worry about the quality of the food.

 閱讀隨堂考

1. A   2. C

 隨堂小測驗

Part A

1. C   2. B   3. A

4. C   5. B

Part B

1. Ron is the **healthiest** person I know.

2. Olive oil is central **to** cooking in Mediterranean countries.

3. Eating certain foods may **carry** some health risks.

4. Judy got **infected** with the same illness her friend had.

5. Of all the foods he liked, pizza topped his **list**.

6. Let me give you a piece of **advice**.

7. The more you learn, the more you **know**.

8. I'm sorry; nothing **comes** to mind right now.

9. Be careful; those wild berries are **poisonous**.

10. These **statistics** are really something to worry about.

Unit 12

 暖身練習

1. I don't really think about the chemicals in the food I eat too much because I don't know much about them. However, sometimes I read news stories about dangerous ingredients.

2. I have been to a few farms in my life. I remember seeing a lot of

chickens grouped together in a small space. They didn't look very comfortable.

 閱讀隨堂考

1. <u>C</u>　　2. <u>B</u>

 隨堂小測驗

Part A

1. <u>A</u>　　2. <u>D</u>　　3. <u>B</u>
4. <u>D</u>　　5. <u>C</u>

Part B

1. <u>d</u>　　2. <u>g</u>　　3. <u>h</u>
4. <u>e</u>　　5. <u>b</u>　　6. <u>c</u>
7. <u>f</u>　　8. <u>a</u>

Unit 13

 暖身練習

1. Yes, I think being a vegetarian is a good idea because it's a healthy lifestyle. I think eating too much meat can be bad for a person.

2. I think some people don't eat meat because they don't want to hurt animals. Also, meat can be very fattening.

 閱讀隨堂考

1. <u>A</u>　　2. <u>A</u>

 隨堂小測驗

Part A

1. <u>D</u>　　2. <u>C</u>　　3. <u>C</u>
4. <u>D</u>　　5. <u>C</u>

Part B

1. <u>f</u>　　2. <u>b</u>　　3. <u>d</u>
4. <u>h</u>　　5. <u>c</u>　　6. <u>g</u>
7. <u>e</u>　　8. <u>a</u>

Unit 14

 暖身練習

1. I believe vending machines are popular around the world because they are so convenient. You can buy many things from them 24 hours a day.

2. The last item I bought from a vending machine was a bottle of water last week.

 閱讀隨堂考

1. <u>A</u>　　2. <u>C</u>

 隨堂小測驗

Part A

1. <u>C</u>　　2. <u>B</u>　　3. <u>D</u>
4. <u>B</u>　　5. <u>B</u>

Part B

1. As the best student in the class, Pam really stands **out**.

2. The flashlight on my key chain often comes in **handy**.

3. Artists need to be very **imaginative**.

4. Being in an earthquake is a **terrifying** experience.

5. **Have** you deleted the file already?

6. **Waking** up late, Carl had to run to catch the bus.

7. Bill didn't know where to find more **information** on the topic.

8. I don't know what you are **referring** to.

9. The store gave **out** free chocolates to customers.

10. Jim was **hugely** embarrassed when his pants fell down.

Unit 15

暖身練習

1. I like to eat kung pao chicken, Thai food and curry.
2. I think it's because spices like chili give the food an interesting, delicious taste.

閱讀隨堂考

1. __C__   2. __A__

隨堂小測驗

Part A

1. __D__   2. __A__   3. __C__
4. __D__   5. __D__

Part B

1. After eating a huge meal, my stomach started feeling a bit **painful**.
2. Sometimes at night, I feel a **pain** in my leg for some reason.
3. My favorite restaurant has a good **variety** of food.
4. There are **various** reasons why I like spicy food.
5. Can I interest you in another **pickle**, Theresa?
6. Do you like to eat **pickled** onions?
7. Is this medicine very **effective**?
8. What will the **effect** be of eating too many chili peppers?
9. Do you ever put **crushed** nuts on ice cream?
10. Ben wanted to **crush** the can, but he couldn't.

Unit 16

暖身練習

1. I often go to 7-Eleven to pick up items I need. I would say that I typically shop at 7-Eleven three or four times a week.
2. When I go to a convenience store, I usually buy food or a drink. For example, I often buy chocolate bars and coffee.

閱讀隨堂考

1. __C__   2. __C__

隨堂小測驗

Part A

1. __A__   2. __D__   3. __C__
4. __C__   5. __A__

Part B

1. __c__   2. __f__   3. __g__
4. __h__   5. __d__   6. __a__
7. __b__   8. __e__

Unit 17

暖身練習

1. Yes, I was on a diet once. I lost a few kilograms, but I gained the weight back soon afterwards.
2. I usually eat chicken or pork with rice or noodles for lunch and dinner.

閱讀隨堂考

1. __C__   2. __D__

Part A

1. <u>D</u> 2. <u>A</u> 3. <u>B</u>
4. <u>C</u> 5. <u>A</u>

Part B

1. <u>g</u> 2. <u>e</u> 3. <u>c</u>
4. <u>h</u> 5. <u>b</u> 6. <u>d</u>
7. <u>a</u> 8. <u>f</u>

Unit 18

 暖身練習

1. I like the Shilin Night Market the most because it is huge. There are a lot of good things to eat and buy there.

2. I like to eat a variety of snacks when I go to night markets, such as fried chicken, stinky tofu and squid. I've bought clothing, jewelry and purses at night markets.

 閱讀隨堂考

1. <u>B</u> 2. <u>D</u>

 隨堂小測驗

Part A

1. <u>D</u> 2. <u>A</u> 3. <u>B</u>
4. <u>B</u> 5. <u>B</u>

Part B

1. Night markets have many interesting **characteristics** that people enjoy.

2. Night markets are great places to visit, **with** many cheap prices available.

3. The decision will have a big impact **on** many people.

4. During the past few decades, night markets **have become** very popular.

5. Do you enjoy **going** to night markets in Taiwan?

Unit 19

 暖身練習

1. Yes, I like eating instant noodles because they are easy to make and delicious to eat.

2. I'm not sure. It depends on how delicious and expensive the instant noodles are.

 閱讀隨堂考

1. <u>A</u> 2. <u>A</u>

 隨堂小測驗

Part A

1. <u>B</u> 2. <u>A</u> 3. <u>B</u>
4. <u>B</u> 5. <u>B</u>

Part B

1. **What's** the point of eating ice cream on a cold day?

2. Prices range **from** $180 to $920.

3. I haven't **heard** of that restaurant before.

4. Tim often eats at the Golden Crown Restaurant, **which** is near his home.

5. I think more onions need to be **added** to the chili.

6. These noodles are too **plain**.

7. Running a business is one thing; running a successful one is **another** other.

8. Make sure to separate the documents **into** different piles.

9. There are **various** ways to cook eggs.

10. Are these candies **imported**?

Unit 20

 暖身練習

1. I think people like pearl milk tea so much because it tastes wonderful. The flavor is great, and so are the balls at the bottom.

2. I like coffee, pearl milk tea, Chinese tea, orange juice and milkshakes the most.

 閱讀隨堂考

1. <u>C</u>   2. <u>A</u>

 隨堂小測驗

Part A

1. <u>A</u>   2. <u>B</u>   3. <u>B</u>
4. <u>C</u>   5. <u>D</u>

Part B

1. I'm not sure if this new flavor will catch on.

2. A lot of people like pearl milk tea.

3. Do you find this drink very refreshing?

4. Are there any stores that sell bubble tea in your country?

5. This drink is quite famous on the island of Taiwan.

國家圖書館出版品預行編目(CIP)資料

和老外打開話匣子－談飲食 / 賴世雄總編輯--初版
臺北市：智藤，2012.02
面： 公分--(活化閱讀口說系列；EV01)

ISBN 978-986-7380-68-5（平裝附光碟片）

1. 英語 2. 會話

805.188 101003040

活化閱讀口說系列 **EV01**

和老外打開話匣子－談飲食

總 編 審：賴世雄
執行編審：吳崇維
編輯小組：吳崇維・王昱翔・陳世弘・林宏謀
Sharon Laird・Brian Foden・Eryk Smith
Li Chen・Marcus Maurice・Matthew Brown
封面設計：姚映先
電腦排版：王玥琦・王雅莉
照片提供：達志圖庫
顧　　問：賴陳愉嫻
法律顧問：王存淦律師・蕭雄淋律師

出 版 者：智藤出版有限公司
台北市忠孝西路一段33號5樓
行政院新聞局出版事業登記證
局版臺業字第 16024 號 L000031-5028

服務電話：(02)2331-7600
服務傳真：(02)2381-0918
定　　價：**500**元（書＋MP3）

＊如有缺頁、裝訂錯誤或破損　請寄回本社更換

郵票黏貼處

10041 台北市忠孝西路一段 33 號 5 樓

常春藤有聲出版有限公司　行政組　收

常春藤　www.ivy.com.tw
愛上英語的第一站

【EV01 和老外打開話匣子－談飲食】讀者回函卡

感謝您購買本書！為使我們對讀者的服務能夠更加完善，請您詳細填寫本卡各欄，寄回本公司或傳真至（02）2381-0918，我們將於收到後寄發回饋小贈品「常春藤網路書城優惠折價券（面額 50 元 1 張）」給您（每書每人限贈一次），也懇請您繼續支持。若有任何疑問，請儘速與客服人員聯絡，客服電話：（02）2331-7600 分機 10～13，謝謝您！

姓　　名：＿＿＿＿＿＿＿　性別：＿＿＿＿　生日：＿＿＿年＿＿月＿＿日

聯絡電話：＿＿＿＿＿＿＿　E-mail：＿＿＿＿＿＿＿＿＿＿＿＿＿＿＿

聯絡地址：□□□□□＿＿＿＿＿＿＿＿＿＿＿＿＿＿＿＿＿＿＿＿＿＿

教育程度：□國小　□國中　□高中　□大專／大學　□研究所含以上

職　　業：①　□學生

　　　　　②　教　　職：□教師　□教務人員　□班主任　□經營者　□其他＿＿＿＿＿

　　　　　　　任教單位：□學校　□補教機構　□其他＿＿＿＿＿＿＿＿＿＿

　　　　　　　教學經歷：□幼兒英語　□兒童英語　□國小英語　□國中英語　□高中英語
　　　　　　　　　　　　□成人英語　□其他＿＿＿＿＿＿＿＿＿＿＿＿＿＿＿＿

　　　　　③　社會人士：□工　□商　□服務業　□軍警公職　□其他＿＿＿＿＿＿＿

①　您購買本書的原因：□老師、同學推薦　□家人推薦　□學校購買
　　□書店閱讀後感到喜歡　□其他＿＿＿＿＿＿＿＿＿＿＿＿＿＿＿＿＿

②　您購得本書的管道：□書店　□網站　□廣播電視　□他人推薦　□其他＿＿＿＿＿

③　您最滿意本書的三點依序是：□內容　□編排方式　□印刷　□試題演練　□封面
　　□字詞解析　□售價　□信任品牌　□廣告　□其他＿＿＿＿＿＿＿＿＿＿＿

④　您最不滿意本書的三點依序是：□內容　□編排方式　□印刷　□試題演練　□封面
　　□字詞解析　□售價　□信任品牌　□廣告　□其他＿＿＿＿＿＿＿＿＿＿＿
　　原因：＿＿＿＿＿＿＿＿＿＿＿＿＿＿＿＿＿＿＿＿＿＿＿＿＿＿＿＿＿＿
　　對本書的其他建議：＿＿＿＿＿＿＿＿＿＿＿＿＿＿＿＿＿＿＿＿＿＿＿＿

⑤　您發現本書誤植的部份：書籍第＿＿＿＿＿＿頁，第＿＿＿＿＿＿行
　　有錯誤的部份是：＿＿＿＿＿＿＿＿＿＿＿＿＿＿＿＿＿＿＿＿＿＿＿

⑥　如果有常春藤手機版購物專頁，您的看法是？
　　□不錯！隨時都可以上網學習　□介面一定不好用，不使用
　　□還是習慣用電腦上常春藤網路書城！□其他＿＿＿＿＿＿＿＿＿＿＿

⑦　現在智慧型手機慢慢普及化，為了響應綠化地球，書本漸漸走向數位電子書，
　　請問您對常春藤出電子書的看法是？
　　□很好！常春藤出電子書，我一定買！　□還不錯！但是還是比較習慣紙本書
　　□沒意見！但有兩種選擇也很好　□不好！已經養成看紙本書的習慣　□其他＿＿＿

⑧　您對我們的其他建議：＿＿＿＿＿＿＿＿＿＿＿＿＿＿＿＿＿＿＿＿＿＿

感謝您寶貴的意見，您的支持是我們的動力！　常春藤網路書城 www.ivy.com.tw